SCHEMING WOMEN SEEK REVENGE

TALES OF THE UNDEAD & DEPRAVED

ADRIAN J. SMITH

SCHEMING WOMEN SEEK REVENGE

CHAPTER 1

Jerry stood on her rock, pushing the tips of her toes into the cold surface. A ship approached on the horizon. Her heart raced. She almost couldn't believe it. A few ships had flown by, but none had stopped. This one wouldn't either. Her heart sank. She stood calmly, sure she was right.

It came closer, the blurry lines forming into something solid. Dropping her hand from her forehead, she saw the sleek white lines of a medical vessel come into view. Well, if they were going to be picked up from being marooned, that would be the ship to do it. Still, it didn't come directly toward them, skirting to the north before veering south.

Are they coming back around?

A blast from the beach shook her in surprise. Jerry clenched her fist and glanced away from the oncoming vessel toward the edge of their little island, trying to see what the noise was. The foliage and trees were too thick to make anything out. Another blast reached her ears.

The ship turned again. Jerry twisted on her toes and followed the flight path as it circled. Every nerve in her body told her this was it. This was their rescue. But they'd been fooled before. And five weeks on an island with no one but her crewmates and a rotting corpse she kept eating to survive, Jerry didn't want to hope.

"Did you see it?" Sacha panted as she raced up to the rock.

Jerry frowned and faced the young girl. She had aged drastically in their time on the island, her clothes hanging off her form as they struggled to find food enough to survive. Her pale skin was now a leathered tan, and her eyes baggy from lack of proper sleep and care. But they had all perked up when Jerry had killed Damon.

Instead of answering verbally, Jerry just stared at her. Jerry had been oddly cold and calm since she'd killed Damon. Sacha had been the one to form that connection with him in Potelia, and Jerry had struggled not to blame Sacha for Damon's betrayal that landed them marooned, shipless, and without the drugs that would allow them to survive.

But if this vessel didn't stop and rescue them, it was very likely Sacha would be next on the menu. Jerry clenched her jaw and raised her chin up again to see the vessel pull hard to starboard. They were still at least a thousand meters off from the island, if not more, but they did seem to be circling.

Skeptical as always, Jerry waited it out. Sacha stepped in close, moving her hand to shield her eyes from the sun as Jerry did. Weren't they the pair? Jerry stayed still, nearly motionless, as she waited to see what would happen next. The ship maneuvered, circling the island one more time. There wasn't a third blast, and Jerry was sure Azar had managed to rig something and had run out of materials. It was as good a sign for help as they could manage with zero resources.

The ship slowed. Jerry pursed her lips and rolled her shoulders, attempting to figure out what they were doing. They were certainly acting oddly. She'd never seen a ship circle around like this and not either stop or just move on. Eventually, Yafe climbed her way up to the rock.

"Do you think they'll stop?" Yafe asked, a tremor in her

voice, but those dark eyes that matched her skin didn't turn on their leader.

Again, Jerry didn't want to answer. She was tired of being the person who had to dash hopes, the person who had to make decisions, and the person everyone relied on. She needed a break. Five weeks stuck on an island because of a decision she made based on information she was given was enough punishment. Wasn't it?

She could only hope this vessel rescuing them didn't contain members of the authorities, who would only wrap their arms in ropes and march them straight to Joab. Swallowing hard, Jerry looked on as the ship slowed and moved straight toward them.

"They're coming," Yafe whispered.

Sacha let out a whoop before she jumped off the top part of the rock and climbed her way down as fast as possible. Yafe threw her arms around Jerry's shoulders and pulled her in tight for a hug. Except Jerry didn't want to be hugged. She didn't want anyone to touch her. She remained stiff, but Yafe didn't seem to notice.

Stepping back, Yafe skittered down the side of the rock, too. Jerry stayed put, watching the sleek curved lines of the ship as it flew in closer to their little island, the one Jerry had known she wouldn't get off. And hope fluttered in the center of her chest. She had to stop it. Even with a ship coming directly for them, it could still mean certain death.

She stayed there until the ship settled, hovering over the waters with her port side pulled up to the beach. Below, the others shouted their excitement. Still, she couldn't make herself move. Frozen to her spot, Jerry waited to see who would die first, which one of her team she would have to eat next.

Time became lost to her, and the voice behind her was startling.

"Yafe said I could find you here."

That voice—it was so pure, so perfect. But usually it was something in Jerry's imagination. She wasn't sure she wanted to turn around and find once again that the voice was an apparition instead of the woman.

"Jer." She breathed Jerry's name as though it were a prayer. "Are you all right?"

Jerry still didn't want to turn around. She didn't want to face what had happened, who she was now, what she had done—not just what she'd done in Potelia, that was nothing—but what she'd done to Damon.

The hand on her shoulder was gentle but also persistent. Unlike when Yafe had hugged her, this touch was hesitant. They weren't supposed to touch without express permission. That was one of the rules of their planet, something created by the aristocrats to protect women. Jerry's lips twitched at the thought. Yafe rarely asked for permission anymore and certainly not since they'd been stranded there. But this woman, she wasn't like the others.

Finally, Jerry turned slowly. Her gaze started at the rock, at the pointed black boots peeking out from the bustle of skirts Jerry abhorred to wear but loved on this woman. A lump caught in her throat as she followed the lines of the fabric, the rustles, the embroidery that formed stories in gold thread of mermaids and women that Jerry had never taken the time to notice before.

The corset was tight, and no doubt suffocating in the heat of the day on their little island. If she'd known this woman were real and not her imagination, Jerry would strip it from her in seconds, ease that discomfort, all the while touching every inch of skin reverently. She would press kisses so delicately that she wouldn't leave a mark except raised goosebumps.

"Jer," her voice was lower, firmer this time. "You're worrying me."

She should be worried. Jerry had been without her for far too long, and the last five weeks had been so trying that she was imagining ships and her standing right in front of her. Hands on Jerry's cheeks raised her gaze to the face staring intently at her, to the plump lower lip and thin upper lip, to the age lines around her eyes and mouth, those steel-blue eyes that were typically full of passion and energy. Now all Jerry found in them was deep concern. Well, she should be concerned. Jerry was hallucinating.

Her curls trailed over her shoulders, the wild mass of them unconfined for the first time ever since Jerry had met her. Lifting her hand, Jerry pushed them over her shoulder and followed the move with her gaze.

"Jeraldine Adelric."

That snapped Jerry to attention. She looked directly into those eyes.

"What's wrong?"

"Why are you here?" Jerry asked, letting her hand fall onto her shoulder. "You shouldn't be here."

"I'm here to bring you home."

"Impossible."

"No, Jerry. I've been looking for you for weeks."

A hand cupped Jerry's cheek, bringing them closer. In one breath, their lips touched. Clenching her eyes shut tight, Jerry held on to the sensation of being pressed so close together. She gripped the woman's hands, breathed her scent, and finally her brain caught up with her heart.

"Arloa," she breathed out, closing her eyes and bending to press their foreheads together. "You shouldn't be here."

"This is exactly where I'm meant to be."

Arloa carefully led Jerry off the rock. Jerry stepped around the far side, following the more traveled path toward the beach where she'd seen the ship set down. By walking that way, they avoided what was left of Damon's body, shoved against the part of the island that was shaded the most throughout the day, the part where his flesh wouldn't rot as quickly.

Their fingers were curled together as they walked out of the brush and onto the sandy beach—a beach that Jerry wasn't sure she'd ever be able to forget. The ship hovered off the island, the door open to allow them in. A rope ladder hung from the edge of the cargo door, the only way to climb up since there was no dock or place for the ship to set down.

"I've got a healer on board," Arloa murmured as she grasped the end of the rope ladder.

"Maisie?"

Arloa smiled, as though she were happy that Jerry remembered the healer she'd paid to fix Jerry up one night. "Yes. I'm surprised you remember her."

"She's hard to forget." Jerry was still distant, despondent, not connecting that this was her reality—that she might actually see Raegina's harbor again. "Where's *Yarrow?*"

That had been the burning question on her mind for five weeks. She had wondered and dreamed of her vessel, wanting to know how mistreated she was at the hands of Captain Blaise Lotchski.

"We'll figure that out as soon as we can. First we need to get you well."

"Well?" Frowning, Jerry helped Arloa up the first two rungs of the rope ladder, making sure it was steady as she climbed by putting her boot over the bottom rung so it sat firmly in the sand. "I'm not unwell, Arloa."

"We'll let Maisie determine that."

"I'm not," Jerry argued.

Arloa stopped her ascent and glanced over her shoulder and down at Jerry. "Like I said, we'll let Maisie decide."

Frowning, Jerry held the ladder firmly as Arloa climbed to the ship. She put her foot on the second rung, about to climb, when the stupid thought occurred to her that she didn't have to leave if she didn't want to. She could very well choose to remain there. But when she looked up into Arloa's steel-blue eyes, Jerry knew exactly which decision she would make. Because truthfully, she didn't have one. Anything Arloa wanted her to do, she would.

They were already flying away by the time Jerry managed to get belowdecks. The ice-cold air from the ventilation system hit her skin like a knife. It hurt her to stay there, but she gritted her teeth through it because she knew she had to. Arloa led her down three decks to a large room filled with what were clearly Arloa's things.

"Sit on the bed," Arloa commanded her.

Jerry did as she was told. Arloa got onto her knees and pulled at the leather laces to Jerry's boots. Jerry wasn't sure she wanted Arloa to see her naked, not in this form, but she also wasn't sure she was going to have a choice. Sand fell from everywhere, landing on the floor, the bed, Arloa's perfectly embroidered dress.

"You should let me do that," Jerry interrupted, her voice low. "Why do I have to change anyway?"

"You stink," Arloa stated simply. "You need a bath."

The way she said it was so insulting. But Jerry couldn't fault her. It wasn't like they had a proper washroom on the island.

"I'll have Maisie come in here first."

Jerry undid the ties on her tunic so the fabric was loose at her chest. She didn't miss the second glance Arloa gave her, but she couldn't tell if it was out of concern or curiosity or arousal. Pushing the pieces to the side, Jerry stripped naked. Arloa handed over a nightdress and Jerry donned it, albeit reluctantly. She stayed seated on the edge of the cot while Arloa took Jerry's clothes and left the room, the door shutting with a quiet snick.

She hadn't seen anyone from her crew since she'd come aboard, but she expected they were getting the same treatment she was, stripping down and being cared for by the healer, not that there was much to heal. They hadn't been harmed when they were left on the island, and it wasn't like they'd been injured much during their exile. Jerry was probably the worst, since she'd gotten into a scuffle with Damon.

The cold air hadn't eased up yet. Jerry's nipples were hard little points, and she bent forward slightly to get the fabric of the nightdress off them so it would hurt less—hopefully.

Arloa returned, sitting next to Jerry and not quite touching her. "What happened?"

"You mean how were we marooned on an island without my ship?" Jerry's tone was sharp, an air of sarcasm in it.

"Well, yes," Arloa murmured softly. "I wasn't sure I'd ever find you, not to mention find you alive."

Jerry sighed. "The pirate was pirated. My heist was heisted. Someone turned on me—I'm not entirely sure who or if there was more than one person, but when we left Potelia, we were tracked and boarded and left here to die."

Arloa frowned. "Why wouldn't he just kill you?"

"Because he's a sadistic fucker," Jerry flippantly answered. "I don't know. I don't understand him. I'd never met him before he boarded us."

"You don't think there's something else going on?"

"Pirates live and breathe these seas, Arloa. I know you don't experience that from your hilltop, but I do. It's not uncommon to be boarded and to have your livelihood stolen from you. I will get *Yarrow* back. I promise you that."

Sighing, Arloa reached out and touched Jerry's hand. She nearly jumped at the contact, but managed to hold it in so Arloa didn't notice.

"I do appreciate your coming to find us, and I will repay you."

"I sent you out there," Arloa hissed. "I sent you on this quest."

"And we found what we were looking for." Jerry's eyes widened as she made eye contact. "We found it. We had it. It wasn't as good as vestigen, but it was there, and I will find it again because the alternative..." Jerry trailed off.

Arloa sent her a confused look.

"Forget it. Where's that healer?"

"Jer, what were you going to say?"

"It doesn't matter." Jerry pressed her lips hard together, not wanting to confess what they had all done to survive while they were stranded. Arloa would think of her differently, and there would be no rectifying that.

Arloa's palm on her thigh stilled her. When Jerry faced her, those steel-blue eyes were full of compassion. Jerry was about to confess everything when there was a knock on the door to the cabin. Releasing a breath of tension, Jerry kept her gaze on Arloa as she stood to answer.

"That'll be Maisie," Arloa stated firmly as she walked swiftly.

Jerry wasn't sure she'd ever been on a vessel as rich as this one. The linens under her were clean and pressed, tucked neatly into the cot. In *Yarrow* they didn't even have linens. They slept on wooden cots. Her heart raced as Maisie stepped into the cabin, the door shutting behind her. Maisie had healed Jerry once before, taking a heavy sum of credits from Arloa to do it. She couldn't imagine what Arloa was paying her this time around.

"Do you mind?" Maisie asked, indicating the cot.

Jerry shook her head as her only answer. Having lived in relative silence for the last five weeks, being surrounded by so many people was overwhelming. All she wanted was to curl up on the cot and listen to the wind as they moved across the sea.

"You have a bite wound that's infected."

Snapping her gaze to Arloa's eyes, Jerry ground her molars. She had forgotten about that. Damon had bit her before she'd killed him, ripping her skin in his blood-crazed state. Maisie put one hand delicately on Jerry's neck, warmth seeping from the touch and into Jerry's body as her magic worked. Healers were rare on Penum, and rarer still was finding a healer who was willing to work on unsightly creatures like Jerry.

Maisie went through the rest of Jerry's body, healing small scratches here and there, the broken ribs that weren't fully mended yet, the strain on her muscles. The healing was precise, quick, and more than Jerry had ever expected when being rescued.

As Maisie left, Arloa shut the cabin door and leaned against it. "Would you like me to stay?"

"No," Jerry muttered, staring at the deck just in front of Arloa's feet. "Leave me."

"I'll have clothes brought to you and your crew so you have something to wear."

"Thank you." Jerry appreciated the gesture even if it seemed slightly empty. She said nothing else as she let silence fill the cabin and Arloa finally left. Cast into the quiet, Jerry did the only thing she could think of. She stumbled to the washroom to clean herself.

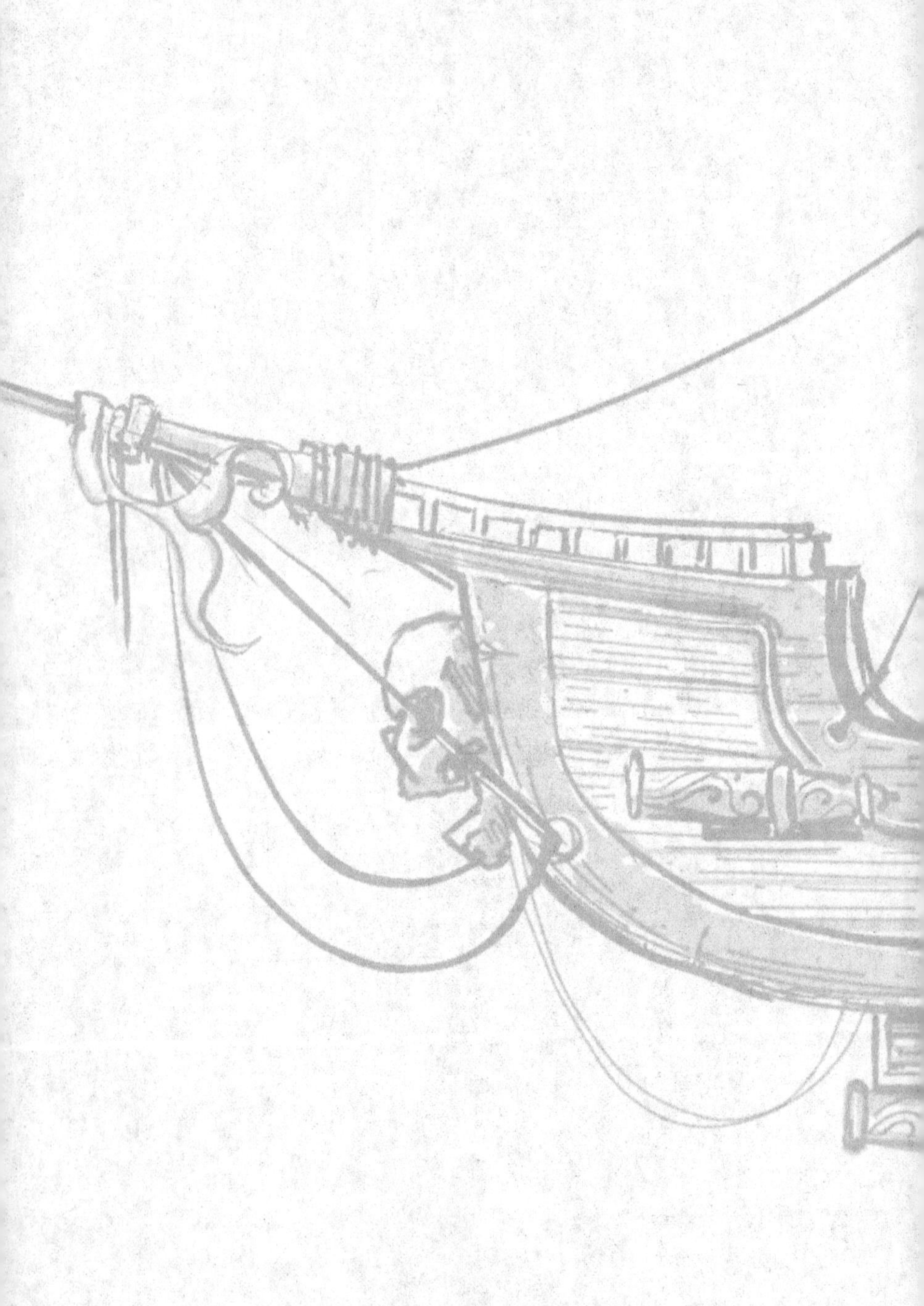

CHAPTER 2

At midday Jerry made her way topside. The medical vessel didn't move as swiftly as *Yarrow*, which was unsurprising considering it wasn't built for speed. She leaned over the railing with her hands folded in front of her and closed her eyes as her chin dipped down.

Arloa hadn't come to find her again. Even though it had been an entire day since their rescue, Jerry still struggled to believe that they were no longer on the island, that they weren't going to die there. Yafe stepped up next to her, mimicking her position and letting out a long sigh.

"I see Maisie healed you up." Yafe was so calm, and Jerry relished it.

Jerry pursed her lips. She wasn't usually the silent one in the room, but for some reason, since she'd killed Damon, she hadn't found a way to adequately express anything.

"Do you think they'll start wondering why we're not crazy yet?"

Jerry hadn't thought about that one. She'd been so distracted with the fact that she'd killed Damon and they'd all done the unmentionable in order to survive. She hadn't banked on anyone finding them. She hadn't thought of an excuse as to why in five weeks without vestigen they weren't all ripped to shreds.

"Fuck," Jerry muttered. Arloa wasn't stupid enough to fall for any easy lie she could come up with of the top of her head. Not to mention, with their checkered history, she wasn't sure she could even manage to lie to Arloa anymore and have it accepted as the truth, not that blatantly. Jerry could avoid with the best of them but not about this.

"We're not even a little insane."

"I mean…" Jerry frowned as she thought. "That's an accurate statement."

Yafe's lips pulled into a wide smile. "I was thinking we just lie and say we had a stash still."

"Except I told Arloa before we left Potelia we'd run out of vestigen."

"But she doesn't know how much of the reverse engineered drug we managed to steal and stash away before we were marooned."

Raising an eyebrow, Jerry faced her. "Enough cirax for five weeks with four people?"

Yafe raised a shoulder and dropped it. "It's a possibility. I did manage to grab some before we left."

"Not enough," Jerry mumbled and went back to staring across the waters. She hated that they were having this discussion. But the alternative was they kill to continue to live, and Jerry wasn't sure they were all going to make it a week back to Raegina without something to tide them over. Unless Arloa had a stash of vestigen on the ship, they were doomed to live out the same fate as on the island.

"What are you two talking about?" Azar's voice boomed as he came toward them.

Jerry sighed. "Let's go inside."

And away from onlookers, she didn't say. The two of them followed her down to Sacha's room, where they all crowded into the small cabin, sitting on the hard floor and staring at each other. Jerry finally broke the silence, knowing she'd have to be the one to lead them through this conversation.

"They can't find out about Damon."

"Why not?" Sacha asked. "I mean, if it's an alternative—"

Jerry cut her off. "Yes, let's kill one person for each person infected so we can eat their brains to survive a little longer in our mostly non-crazed state. That'll work great until there's no one left to kill."

"Right." Sacha was thoroughly chastised.

"This is for our own protection. If they find out we killed him, we'll be on the first ship to Joab."

"You mean that you killed him." Sacha's blue eyes locked on Jerry's face.

"Who do you think they'll believe if I tell them otherwise?"

Sacha looked at each of them, as if expecting someone to step in and support her, but Jerry knew Azar and Yafe would have her back no matter what. They were her family, and family stuck together. Though she did expect they would break at some point. Jerry stretched her legs out in front of her and pressed the back of her head into the cabin wall.

"Yafe's idea was sound, though I don't think Arloa will buy it."

"Which was?" Azar pushed.

"Lie and say we had a stash of cirax and that kept us sane throughout our tenure on the island."

Azar frowned and so did Sacha. He's the one who voiced the same concern Jerry had, however. "But we're far from being on the edge, and we would have been rationing it out, like we did. Also, we just magically ran out of the drug right before they rescued us?"

"I don't have a better idea," Jerry answered. "It's not like we can go back to the island and be rescued four weeks ago before we ran out."

"We could tell the truth." Yafe pulled her lower lip between her teeth, her beautiful black curls haloing her face for the first time in a month.

"Not an option," Jerry fired back. "We need to come up with a plan that we're all going to stick to."

Sacha rubbed her hands over her face. "I think saying we had more drugs is the only answer, but we'll have to keep the amount small enough because we wouldn't have been left there on purpose with life-saving medications."

"Right," Azar added. "So enough to get us through a month."

"But we haven't had any since being here, and we're all currently sane," Yafe added.

"So maybe we start acting a little crazy." The glint in Jerry's eye was not a welcome sight amongst her crew. Anytime she gave them that look, it usually ended up in trouble.

"We won't make it to port without something," Yafe added.

They all knew she was right. Jerry pressed her thumb into the center of her palm, easing the tension she had there. The callouses on her hands were thick and had grown thicker in their time on the island. She hadn't meant for this to be so difficult a conversation, but they had rationed out Damon's body as long as they could, and they would need something to make it the week back.

"Then our story might just hold."

"Oh, we ran out right when they arrived?" Sacha snorted. "I still think we should tell them the truth."

"No." Jerry was firm in her position. "No, it'll put us all at too much risk."

"What if…" Yafe started and then stopped. She started again, "What if you just tell Arloa? Can you trust her?"

Jerry pursed her lips, closing her eyes halfway as she thought through the last year and a half she'd known Arloa. They had met in her favorite bar on the edge of town, Arloa's having been called away immediately. They'd met up several times in between then and when Jerry contracted the virus, and then they hadn't seen or talked to each other for an entire year. In the short span of the last few months, they'd fucked, they'd exchanged information, they'd trusted the other one to pull their weight to help Raegina.

And yet, she still didn't have an answer to Yafe's question.

"Do I trust her?" Jerry shook her head and eyed each of them. "I don't know."

"You're going to have to make that decision, Cap," Azar stated, and Jerry tensed at the nickname.

She wasn't a captain anymore, not in the normal sense. Her ship had been stolen out from under her boots, without much preamble or fight either. She'd been drunk, celebrating, and not prepared to be overrun by another vessel. Sure, she owned one more ship that was currently in harbor in Raegina and captained by her good friend, but she had no ship to claim as her own.

Yafe must have sensed her sadness, because she reached out and touched Jerry's arm lightly. "Cap?"

Jerry shook her head. "We had extra drugs. That's our story."

Standing sharply, Jerry left Sacha's cabin and her crew behind. She couldn't stand to be with them anymore. She wasn't any kind of leader they should follow. She'd nearly gotten them killed a dozen times over. Walking through the halls, Jerry let herself get lost in the ship. She wandered aimlessly, not knowing where she was going until she stopped sharply right in front of Arloa. *Perfect, the one fucking person I didn't want to see.*

"How are you feeling?" Arloa's voice was sweet, concern littering every word.

Jerry's heart thumped hard, and she knew she needed to answer even though she didn't want to. "Well."

"Maisie said your injuries were extensive."

"There was a scuffle," Jerry started and trailed off. She didn't want to explain any more beyond that. She didn't want to have to admit anything more than what was necessary.

Arloa reached out, her fingers curling around Jerry's wrist. "Are you all right?"

The question was stupid. Jerry knew that, but she also knew there was more to it than was she physically fine. Arloa meant mentally because she had no understanding that getting into scuffles was almost a routine occurrence for her.

"I'm fine, Arloa." Jerry twisted her arm and jerked it to break the contact. Arloa could undo her with a look and a touch, and she needed to protect herself and her crew.

Arloa's lips parted, her high cheekbones flushing. Jerry wanted nothing more than to reach out and smooth away the worry lines, the embarrassment, the hurt she had caused, but she held herself still. She could do this. She could protect herself and her crew.

"Come here," Arloa ordered. She dragged Jerry into the nearest cabin, and as soon as they were inside, Jerry knew they had landed in Arloa's cabin.

The scent hit her first, and it was nothing but the woman in front of her, the short spunky woman who controlled the world Jerry lived in. Clenching her jaw, Jerry straightened her shoulders and told herself she could do this. She could answer questions and avoid giving truths. Dashing her tongue against her lips, the way Arloa used to press against her came unbidden into her mind.

"What is going on with you?" Arloa questioned, her voice low and demanding.

"Nothing. I'm fine." Jerry plastered herself against the wall. Everything in this room screamed Arloa. The chests of clothes and items, the scent, the decoration. They'd clearly been on the vessel for some time. "How long were you looking for us?"

"Weeks."

Jerry stepped up to the small window and ran her fingers over the windowsill. "How many weeks?"

"Since you didn't return at the designated time."

Jerry shot her a look. "Four weeks?"

"I joined the enterprise two weeks ago."

"And how long would you have continued?"

"Until I had no other choice but to leave."

They stayed standing meters apart, not saying anything, but

only looking at each other. Jerry wanted to wrap her arms around Arloa, thank her for coming to the rescue, but at the same time she wanted to tell Arloa how stupid the venture had been. Jerry was a pirate, an unsightly creature not deserving of any attention.

Finally, Arloa broke the tension. She stepped forward, taking Jerry's hand in hers again. "How are you feeling?"

"Why do you keep asking me that?"

"Because I imagine it's been some time without vestigen."

Jerry held her breath. She knew this would come up sooner rather than later, and she knew she'd have to have an answer. "It has."

"You said you ran out before you left Potelia."

Jerry frowned. "And we did."

"Jer, how did you survive?"

Jerry wanted to tell her. When she'd answered the question about trust, she had wanted to say yes, to let Arloa in on the secret they all held, but the reality was, she didn't trust Arloa. She couldn't trust someone who was born an aristocrat, who didn't understand what it was like to go through life as the daughter of a whore.

"We just did."

Arloa shook her head sharply. "No, don't do that. Don't push me out."

Jerry's lips parted, but she pressed them shut tightly. She wouldn't say anything she shouldn't.

"What happened on the island?"

"Nothing. Nothing happened. We sat around and waited to see if we'd be rescued. We waited to die."

"And how did you survive?"

Jerry dragged her gaze up to Arloa's eyes. "I'm not sure we did."

"Oh, yes. Yes, you did." Arloa stepped in closer, their clothes rustling as they touched.

Staring down into Arloa's eyes, Jerry knew she was lost to her. She couldn't flat-out lie to this woman.

"I don't know when we can get you vestigen," Arloa continued. "It's so difficult to find right now."

"I suppose the world is dying off in droves," Jerry commented, staring into those steel-blue eyes.

Arloa gave a slight nod. "We have to do something about it. What did you find out about the alternative?"

Her heart raced until she realized Arloa wasn't talking about Damon. "It doesn't work as well as vestigen, and we suspect that was Potelia's intention. They give out medication to their citizens freely."

"I had wondered how they were managing to fare so well. Even with the laws of the great unification, they wouldn't share that one with us."

Jerry suspected it was because they knew the other countries wouldn't listen to a voice of reason, especially Raegina. She had spent enough of her life traveling around Penum in a ship with her mother that she learned a little bit about a lot, something she'd always admired in herself. Giving in to the urge, Jerry curled her fingers around Arloa's cheek. She dropped her hand when she remembered how much life she had taken.

"There is another alternative." Jerry swallowed hard. She couldn't be guilty letting others die because she didn't share. One brain could feed a multitude of people. It might be just the stop gap they were looking for.

"What do you mean?" Arloa tilted her chin up, her brow creasing in the center.

Jerry held her breath for a moment before answering, dropping her voice to just above a whisper as if others were listening in. "The alternative to the drugs isn't something that will be acceptable. People will die, more than we already have been."

"What's the alternative?" Arloa's eyes widened, and that air of innocence she always managed to carry with her came flooding back.

Reaching forward, Jerry cupped Arloa's cheek as if it was going to be the last time because it likely was. "There were five of us marooned on that ship. Four from my crew, including me, and one from *Wench's Dream*. He was seen as a traitor and left with us to fend for himself."

"What happened to him?"

"I killed him," Jerry whispered. "After the virus took hold of him, I promise you that. It wasn't out of cold blood."

"I would expect nothing else."

Jerry wasn't sure she wanted to tell Arloa of the other men she had killed in her past, but that was neither here nor there. They didn't need to have that discussion now. Choosing her words carefully, Jerry said, "When the virus runs in your system, you have an unquenchable thirst for blood."

"Blood?"

Nodding, Jerry continued. "It's always there. Like right now, I can smell it on you. I want it. But when I'm in control, it's easy to ignore."

"Jer..." Arloa paused, as if gathering her courage to speak. "How are you in control if you were left with no medication?"

"Because what not many know is there is an alternative that we all carry with us." This was going to break Jerry's heart.

"What is it?" Arloa's attention was rapt, completely on her.

"Our brain."

Arloa's breathing stuttered.

"We won't make it to Raegina without something."

"We're all out of vestigen."

"I know." Jerry frowned. "So the alternative is something neither of us wants to talk about, and the other alternative—death—is really something we don't want to think about."

Arloa stayed quiet. Jerry stepped away from her and took to pacing the room. Energy sizzled under the surface of her skin, which was a sure sign that Damon was wearing off. Clenching and unclenching her fingers dozens of times, Jerry spun around and faced Arloa with a wild look in her eye.

"Say something."

"I don't know what to say." Arloa raised her chin up in defiance.

"Then say nothing. I know where you stand on it." Jerry wrenched open the door to the cabin and stalked out.

So much for telling no one about what happened, and the reaction she got was less than thrilling. Still, they only had a few days before the four of them wouldn't be able to hold back much longer, and unless Arloa managed to staff an entire vessel that large without anyone infected with the virus—which Jerry doubted—they were all doomed before their trip began.

Jerry walked into her cabin, clenched her fist and punched it right into the wall. Her knuckles cracked from the pressure, and she knew she'd broken at least two or three of her fingers in the process. Giving in to the impulse, Jerry did it again. And again. And again.

By the time she stopped, tears trailed down her cheeks. She lay huddled against the wall, her eyes clenched shut as she couldn't control any part of her reactions. Damn, it was already too late for her. Cursing under her breath, Jerry shook her head.

"So much for being rescued."

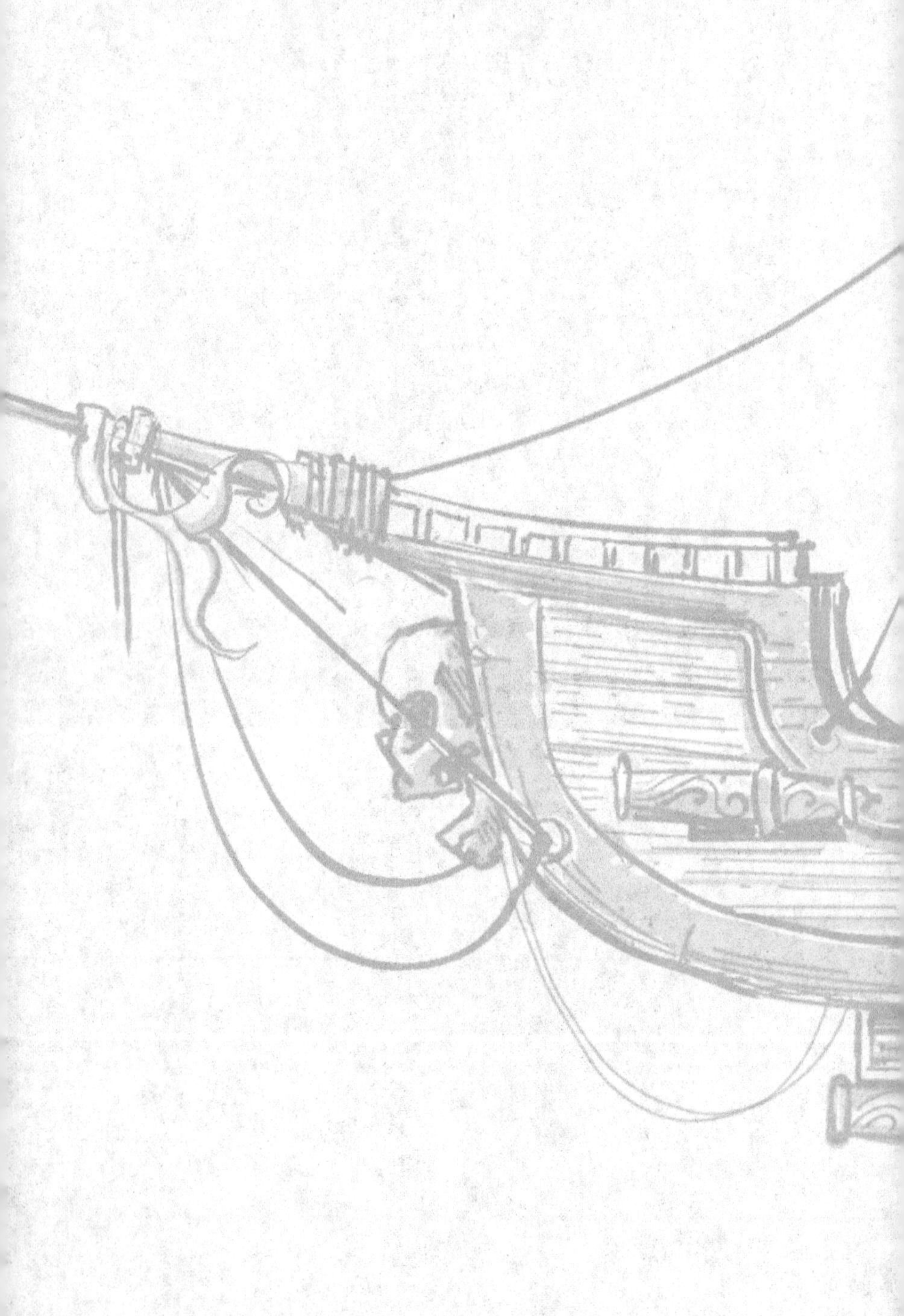

CHAPTER 3

The jitters in Jerry's veins were getting stronger by the second, and after a full day alone in her cabin, she realized that the crash from brains was far more devastating than the crash from vestigen. She didn't dare step outside the door to her cabin.

The others must be feeling the same crash she was, and as much as she wanted to go to them, she didn't dare let herself loose on the poor crew. Jerry quickly moved from the window to the door and back again. Every nerve in her body was vibrating with energy, telling her to go do something—something she definitely didn't want to do. She was about to be crazed.

Fuck, this crash. It was the worst one she had experienced yet, and if she was going to have to continue to consume brains in order to survive, she would have to remember this. The amount of Damon she had eaten hadn't been much, but the withdrawal was drastically different.

Frowning at the knock on the door, Jerry cocked her head to the side. Clenching and unclenching her fists, she took deep steadying breaths to find the calm center that was quickly slipping from her grasp. As soon as she felt able to control herself for a little bit, Jerry called, "Who is it?"

"It's me." Arloa's voice was so sweet, tempting. Jerry would love to eat her. Shaking that thought, Jerry found her calm again, but it was slippery.

"What do you want?"

"Let me in, Jer. Trust me."

Curse that damn word again. She didn't want to trust Arloa, any time or any place. What she wanted was to be free from this woman to live out her demise the way she wanted to. But fuck, Arloa was everything to her. Striding to the door, Jerry opened the hatch to let her in.

Arloa stepped inside, then shut and locked the door. Jerry raised an eyebrow at her. "I wouldn't do that if I were you."

"Why?"

"You said to trust you. Trust me. You don't want to be in here with me."

"Is it that bad already?"

Clenching her jaw, Jerry stared down at Arloa. "What the hell are you talking about?"

Arloa's lips twitched as if she knew already. "You're already feeling the effects of the virus. You're struggling to control it."

Jerry growled. The sound leaving her throat was a surprise to both of them, but where Jerry hated it, Arloa seemed spurred on by it. Arloa touched Jerry's hand, but Jerry ripped it away. "Don't touch me."

Arloa frowned. "I have something for you."

Nothing would make this better. None of them would survive the week without vestigen, and Arloa had already told her she didn't have any. Stepping away from Arloa, Jerry put space between them, afraid she might do something stupid if Arloa were too close to her.

"Here." Arloa reached for the small pouch attached to her waist.

Jerry hadn't even noticed it. She eyed Arloa's small dexterous fingers as she pulled at the string and then took out a white cloth. When she unwrapped the cloth, red covered it. The scent hit Jerry first. She jerked her head to the side, her entire body tensing as the smell filled her completely. She knew exactly what that was.

"How did you get that?"

"It doesn't matter."

"It does." Jerry frowned. "Trust me, it does."

"On the way here, a crew member had an accident. He didn't make it."

Jerry wasn't sure if she believed Arloa or not. Accidents happened all the time on ships, but not usually ships as pristine as this one. Whenever they lost a crew member, they always tossed them overboard to let the sea do its work. Why wouldn't Arloa do the same?

"What happened?"

"We hit turbulence, and he was in the galley cooking. The knife slipped. It was a slow death."

"Why couldn't Maisie heal him?"

"She wasn't paid for them."

Jerry locked her gaze on Arloa's face. "She was paid for us?"

"No one else knows she's on board."

"It's her duty as a healer."

Arloa shook her head sharply. "No. We pay only for those we want healed."

"And you didn't want your crew healed?" Jerry didn't know whether to be offended or impressed by Arloa's clear ethical miss. Stepping closer, Jerry pulled away the cloth to see exactly what she was looking at. Her stomach churned at the thought, not just of what she knew she was ultimately going to do, but that Arloa had done it as well. She may not have consumed whoever this was, but she had carved him up for her.

"I didn't agree to heal them in their contract."

"You are ruthless." Jerry couldn't tear her gaze away from the brain matter. It was only a small sliver, enough that it would sustain her but not give her a high.

"Take it," Arloa whispered, pushing it toward Jerry.

With a deep breath, Jerry plucked the red mass from Arloa's

palm and shoved it between her lips. She didn't chew. She didn't try to taste it. All she wanted to do was swallow and move on. Arloa handed her a packet of water, something Jerry hadn't seen her bring in. She downed it to wash the flavor from her tongue.

"Thank you." Jerry wasn't sure she could look Arloa in the eye after that. She wanted to hide away at the embarrassment that raged through her. It was enough that she was completely infected with a virus, but to have to stoop so low as to eat another person in front of the one person she—Jerry stopped that thought in her tracks.

Arloa moved in, her skirts brushing Jerry's boots. "Talk to me, Jer. You've hardly spoken since we found you."

"There isn't anything to say."

"There has to be. The way we left off—"

"We didn't leave off anything, Arloa. We're not together. We fuck, sometimes, when it's convenient. You gave me information that would benefit both of us, and so I took it and ran with it, and look where it landed me."

"But I came to find you."

"Yes, and you have wasted your precious time because there is nothing that can save me." Jerry hardened her gaze, glaring. "I can't be saved."

"I don't want to save you." Arloa's lips parted as if she was offended, which had been exactly what Jerry was hoping for. She wanted to push her away, make her stop being so damn nice.

"You've always wanted to save me. Why the fuck else would you go into that bar?"

Arloa gripped Jerry's hands hard, holding her in place as if she was going to bolt, which perhaps she had been about to do. Staying put, Jerry stared down into Arloa's eyes. "Don't talk to me like I don't know you."

"You *don't* know me."

Arloa blinked slowly. "You are stunning in your ability to be so obtuse sometimes."

Jerry's heart raced. She ground her teeth together, bending

lower so her lips were right against Arloa's ear when she spoke next. "And you are stunning in your ability not to recognize reality."

"And what reality is it that you see? Hmm?" Arloa raised an eyebrow and turned into Jerry. "Because all I see is a lost woman searching for something, and I'm not even sure you know what that is yet."

"Fuck you," Jerry cursed.

"I want you to thrive, Jer. I want Raegina to thrive. That's why I ran for Senate. We need new voices who care about the people."

"You don't even know the people."

"Don't try me." Arloa glared. "I know far more than you think I do, and I understand Raegina's politics better than you could imagine. I grew up in that world, and I have lived it far longer than you have. I will make change."

"Nothing will change." Jerry's upper lip curled in a sneer. "Nothing has ever changed, and it's only gotten worse. We're dying and no one gives a flying fuck."

Arloa pursed her lips, anger lighting in her eyes. They had never argued like this. They'd had verbal battles, but never a true argument. Jerry knew it was because she still couldn't control herself, because she was embarrassed, and because she didn't want Arloa to see her like this. Ever. She barely wanted Yafe and Azar to see her like this and she lived with them. They were her family.

"Tell me, Jeraldine Adelric, do you truly want change in Raegina? In Penum? Or are you just going to throw your weight around when that change is made?"

"Fuck you and your politics. Until you live like I have, you'll never know what it truly means to be a citizen of our grand world." Jerry went to move away, but Arloa's hands on her arms were firm and held her in place.

Arloa leaned up on her toes. "I know you've had a rough start to life, but before this virus, you were making a name for yourself. You were an owner of a ship doing legal work. Don't think I know you chose that line of work without a purpose. You could have continued pirating as soon as you got out of Joab."

Jerry tensed. "How did you know I was in Joab?"

"I am Joab," Arloa whispered. "Well, my family is. I didn't miss when we met last year that you recognized my name from that. We hadn't been in the news during that time. I drew that connection on my own, and it seems as though I was right."

Jerry growled again, hating how Arloa kept backing her into a corner.

"And you know what? I don't care. I don't care that you were in Joab. I don't care that you run illegal jobs and pirate things. I don't care that you aren't from a rich family."

Her heart thundered. What the hell was Arloa getting at? Her mouth went dry, and Jerry wished she had another packet of water, but she knew they were likely in as short supply on this ship as they were everywhere else. "What do you care about?"

"You," Arloa murmured. "I care about you. Why do you think I spent weeks of my time searching these waters for you? Hmm?"

Jerry stared down at her, still not sure what to say or how to break the moment. Instantly, the high from the hormones she had been lacking hit her. Within a second, she crashed their mouths together, turning Arloa to push her against the wall and cover her entirely. Jerry skimmed hands down Arloa's body and back up, cupping her breasts through the corset. She kept it rough, knowing Arloa liked it with *passion* as she would say.

Arloa moaned, the sound Jerry had dreamed of for months echoing in her ears. She'd longed for that sound, to be the cause of it, and here she was standing with Arloa against her. She nipped at Arloa's lip, pulling it hard enough that Arloa squeaked, but Jerry didn't let up. If Arloa wanted her, like she had implied so many times, then Jerry would give her want she wanted.

Arloa dug her nails into Jerry's sides, the thin material of her newly cleaned tunic doing nothing to protect her. Shoving one leg between Arloa's, Jerry cursed the skirts she wore and readjusted herself.

"You brought some to the others, right?" She breathed heavily as she pressed kisses with bites in between her words down Arloa's neck to the tops of her breasts. "You helped them, right?"

"Yes," Arloa groaned, her fingers dug deep into Jerry's hair. "Yes, I gave them some."

Jerry scraped her teeth along the tops of Arloa's breasts, marveling at the red welts she left when she pulled away. Jerking back, she twisted Arloa around and pressed her front into the cold wall of the vessel. She tugged sharply at the ties to the corset, needing to have Arloa's skin against her hands immediately. She didn't want to wait. She couldn't wait.

Arloa stayed perfectly still while Jerry worked her clothes, getting the damn overskirt off first, then the under one, then the undergarments. Leaving the corset half undone, Jerry pushed her fingers between Arloa's legs. She dripped.

Biting the top of Arloa's shoulder, Jerry shoved two fingers inside her. Arloa cried out, her eyes clenched against the intrusion, but in two seconds, she pushed back against Jerry. Smiling, Jerry trailed her tongue against Arloa's unblemished skin, tracing lines from freckle to freckle along her back and connecting them.

She took the slow route, knowing it would torture Arloa until she was begging for release, which Jerry would eventually give her. Arloa pressed the side of her face against the metal wall of the vessel. Jerry wished it was wood. It would feel so much better than the cold. She reached around Arloa's front and cupped her breast, massaging as much as she could through the bones of the corset.

Arloa let out heavy breaths, and Jerry knew she was getting closer. She rocked her hips in time with her hand until she added her thumb to the back tightly puckered opening they had never played with before. Arloa cried out, but she moved in time with Jerry.

"Do you like that?" Jerry muttered harshly in Arloa's ear. "Do you like being fucked like a whore?"

Arloa whimpered. Jerry had no idea if what she'd said was something Arloa liked or not, but she wasn't complaining so far. Her heart hammered in her chest, not just from the moment of sexual energy but from the hormones as they shifted back to normal and her body moved into balance again. As soon as it was in place, she wouldn't be the person who was doing this.

"Tell me," Jerry ordered.

Arloa normally gave commands as they fucked, telling Jerry exactly what to do, where to touch, how to please her, but she remained absolutely silent this time. As Jerry's brain clicked slowly back into the place it should be, she stayed her pleasurable torment and did nothing new until Arloa caught her breath.

"Clit," Arloa murmured.

"There's my girl," Jerry whispered before lowering her hand from Arloa's breasts to between her legs.

"Rub it. Pinch it."

Chuckling lowly, Jerry did exactly as she was told. This was why she loved fucking Arloa. They were on even footing, Jerry wanting to please in whatever way Arloa wanted, and Arloa telling her exactly what she needed. Both were absolutely open to the other, no barriers in place.

"Oh, fuck." Arloa's voice was so quiet that Jerry almost missed it as she cried out her release. The tight pull against Jerry's fingers was exactly what she had been hoping for, and as Arloa stayed put, Jerry thought about putting her through the rounds again. "I need to breathe."

"What?" Jerry slid away slightly, looking over Arloa's face. Her cheeks were red, but her lips—they were not looking the right color.

"My corset."

"Fuck." Jerry ripped her hands from Arloa's body and pulled

the ties on the corset. She thought she'd undone it enough, but once she looked, she realized she'd tangled the ties and it had been pulling tighter with each breath Arloa had taken. She was about to grab for her knife to cut them when finally she got the knot loose.

Arloa dragged in a deep breath of air, holding herself against the wall of the cabin with her palms on the metal. "Thank you."

Jerry snorted "For what? Fucking you or nearly killing you?"

"That..." Arloa paused a minute, then finally opened her eyes to lock her gaze on Jerry. "That was the best damn orgasm I've ever had."

"Really?" Jerry raised an eyebrow at her.

"Yes." Arloa slowly turned around, putting her shoulders on the wall. She pulled the corset and dropped it down her body to kick it away. She stood completely naked in front of Jerry except for the heeled brown leather boots she wore, ones that were so pristine Jerry would know from a mile away that she was rich. "Fuck me again."

Jerry canted her head to the side as Arloa pushed her fingers between her legs, dragging her wetness on her stomach, the trail clear in the light of the room.

"With your mouth this time."

Doing as commanded, Jerry got onto her knees. She gathered Arloa's juices on her tongue, swallowing, and then latched her mouth onto her already-swollen clit.

"Yes," Arloa whispered. "I have missed you, Jer."

The feeling was mutual, not that Jerry could say that with her mouth on Arloa—and not that she would ever admit that to anyone but herself. Dreams of this woman had been what kept her going when she thought she was going to die—not dreams that they would see each other, but just the distraction from her reality.

She would give Arloa whatever she wanted. When Arloa finally came again, she screamed. Jerry knew anyone in the vicinity of her cabin would know what they were doing in there, and she quite honestly didn't care. Her crew knew she had sex, and they'd all done it a time or two where the others heard. The tight confines of ships were like that.

Arloa slipped down the wall, Jerry catching her as they went. They kissed, this time messy and uncoordinated. Arloa's limbs looked weak, as though she couldn't hold herself up even if she wanted to. Jerry cradled her gently as they sat on the floor together.

"I'm so glad I found you," Arloa said, her voice barely loud enough for Jerry to hear her.

Jerry didn't know what to say in return. Was she glad? Yes. But she would have been glad even if Captain Blaise Lotchski himself had come back for her. She was just glad to be off the damn island of death. Arloa pressed a gentle kiss to Jerry's neck.

"I promise you that I'll find a new drug. I'll find something that will help you."

Jerry wanted to believe her. She really did. But there was that pesky word again, and Jerry didn't know if she could trust Arloa.

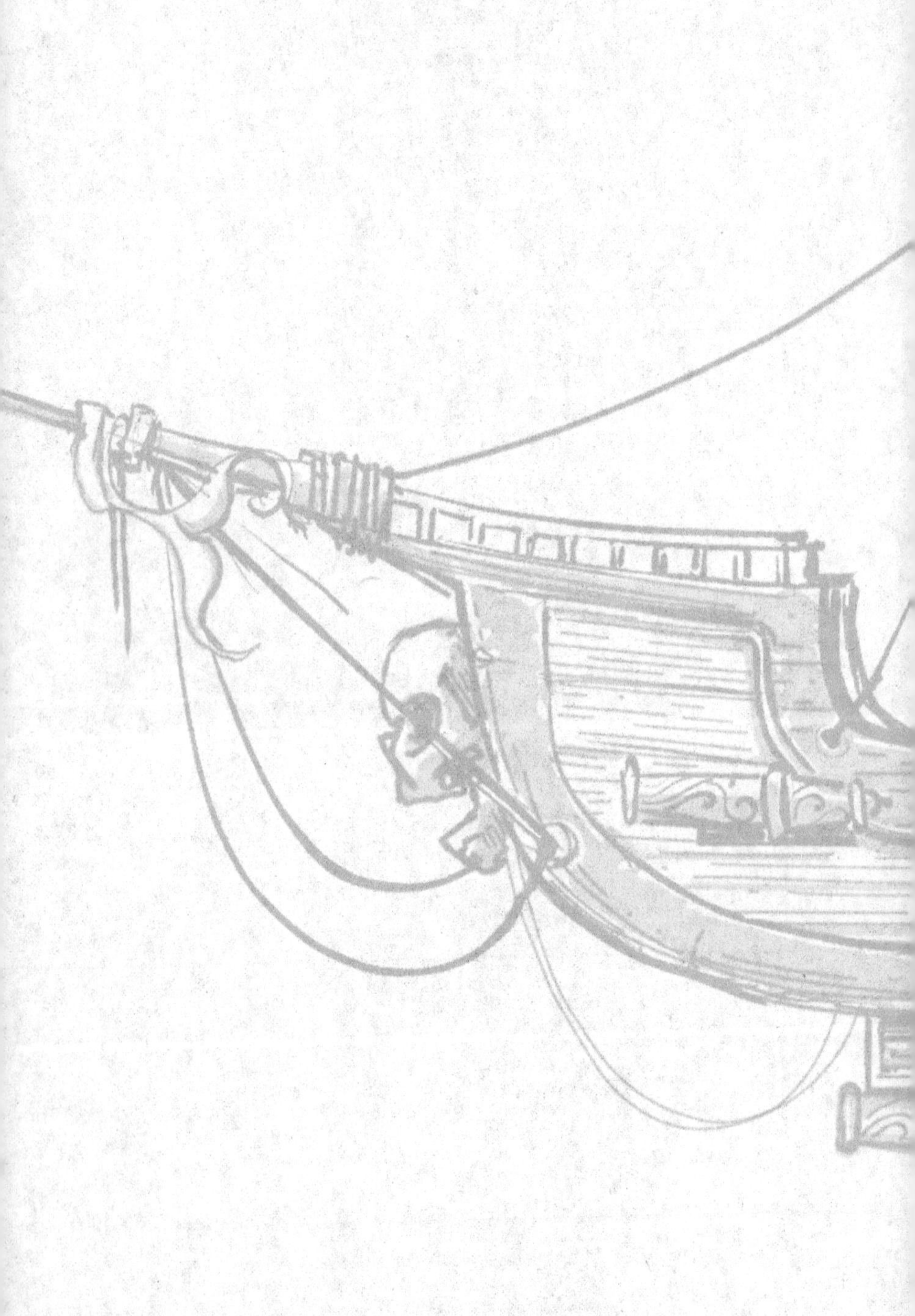

CHAPTER 4

Jerry had all but moved into Arloa's cabin. Not that she had much to move other than herself and the clothes on her back. They lay naked one morning, Arloa tracing patterns on Jerry's chest and around her breasts and nipples. Arloa wasn't meaning to incite anything, rather just absentmindedly thinking.

This was the most time the two of them had spent together in an entire year. Jerry frowned at the thought. She couldn't get this woman off her mind most days, and yet they had never spent more than a handful of hours together in the same room. That week, the journey back to Raegina had been an oasis in the middle of a storm.

"What are you thinking?" Arloa asked so innocently.

Jerry was *not* going to answer that question honestly. She stared at the ceiling and tracked another thread to follow. "The others aren't doing as well as I am, Sacha particularly."

Arloa sighed. "I know. And they have inspections now."

"What?" Jerry furrowed her brow and faced Arloa. "What do you mean inspections?"

"When a medical vessel comes into harbor, it's inspected— including all of the crew and travelers."

"What for?" Jerry tangled her fingers in Arloa's mass of

blonde curls. She'd taken great pleasure in undoing the pins that held Arloa's hair up a few hours ago, finding out just how much of it there was.

Arloa took her time answering, flicking Jerry's nipple before she spoke. "To avoid bringing the virus into port."

"It's already there."

"I know, but they don't want any variations of it."

"Has it mutated?"

Arloa nodded slowly. "It has. I forget you've been gone so long."

Jerry swallowed hard. She wondered if Ursula had thought she was dead and begun the process to transfer her other ship into her hands. Frowning at the thought, Jerry knew she'd have to rectify that. "What's the new mutation?"

"It's affecting more people."

"You mean the upper classes."

"Yes." Arloa flicked Jerry's nipple again before settling her hand on Jerry's hip. She buried her face into Jerry's chest and breathed deeply. "They're working on a vaccination, but these things take time."

"Nice that they're just now working on one," Jerry muttered, even though she knew Arloa could hear her. The scientists and the government didn't seem to care so long as it was only the unsightly creatures who were infected.

"I pushed for it before this happened. Please believe me."

Jerry did believe her. She'd followed the news as much as she could, and Arloa's name had popped up several times as putting forward a bill to increase funding, but she'd been shot down every time. The excuse had been that viruses like this swept through the lower class often because of how *dirty* they were.

The perfect world that Penum claimed to be was far from it. Advanced in so many ways and behind in so many others—a dystopian utopia. Frowning, Jerry tightened her grasp around Arloa's back. The air was still cold against her skin, but after a week on the vessel, she was far more used to it than the others.

"How are they inspecting?"

"What do you mean?" Arloa questioned.

"How are they deciding if we're infected or not?"

"Visual inspection only. They're afraid to come into contact with anyone in case they might also become infected."

"Well, I guess that's a bonus." Jerry turned onto her side, pushing Arloa onto her back. Pressing their lips together, Jerry cupped Arloa's breast and squeezed before she moved off the bed to dress.

"Where are you going?" Arloa stretched her arms above her head, the thin sheet falling to her waist, her perfect perky breasts on full display. Jerry had to force herself to keep moving and to pull her pants over her legs.

"I need to speak with my crew, and I likely need to increase Sacha's dosing."

"She won't pass."

"There are alternate places you can leave us that I can find." Jerry swept her gaze over the beauty in front of her. If she were weaker, she'd take Arloa again. But her crew came first, and if they were to return home so she could leave again and find Captain Blaise and *Wench's Dream*, they were going to have to pass inspection.

As soon as Jerry was dressed, she sat on the edge of the cot to tie up her boots. Arloa lifted the edge of her tunic, splaying her fingers across Jerry's back and toying with the skin right at her side. Jerry shot her a few silent looks, telling her to stop, but Arloa kept touching.

"When we return, I must return to the Senate."

"Understood," Jerry grunted out as she pulled the laces on her boots tight. "I never expected otherwise."

Arloa sighed. "I have a confession."

"What?" Jerry's tone was sharper than she intended it to be, but when she looked over her shoulder into Arloa's soft eyes and high cheekbones, she relaxed. She hated and loved how Arloa could do that with one simple look.

"When I'm with you, Jer, when we're here like this or in my apartment like this or anytime I'm with you…" Arloa sat up, naked in all her glory as she turned Jerry's cheek to face her fully. "…I don't want to return to the Senate."

"Then don't."

"It's not that simple. I fought to be elected."

"And your term ends when?"

Arloa raised her gaze, not answering. "When I'm in the Senate, I want nothing other than to stand up for our people."

"*Our people?*" Jerry pushed.

She still didn't think Arloa understood what it was like to be from the poor parts of Raegina, to be regulated to the harbor and never able to leave. The quarantine hadn't been the reason she couldn't travel elsewhere in the city. The few times she'd gone to Arloa's apartment or even the Senate to find her at the government building, she had been far from welcome. She'd been gawked at, no matter how well she'd dressed to fit in.

"Let's get one thing clear, Arloa. We're not *your* people. No one wants us." Jerry stood up sharply and walked straight to the cabin door. "You might have found a good fuck in me, but beyond that, there is nothing between us."

Jerry shut the door behind her without giving Arloa an opportunity to respond. Immediately she walked down to the lower levels of the vessel and found her crew. She knocked on each of their doors and dragged them half-asleep from their cabins to hers.

As they sat around the small cabin, Jerry with one knee up and her arm resting on it, she waited for the mood to shift. "I talked with Arloa. There is a new variation on the virus."

"The fuck?" Sacha said, her voice booming.

Jerry cut her a sharp look. She didn't need the rest of the ship to know they were convening. "There is another variation, and the authorities have instituted an inspection for all medical vessels coming in."

"Only medical?" Azar questioned, raising an eyebrow at them. "We've been marooned for weeks, so we don't have it."

"Who knows if you can even be infected with it and the previous variation at the same time." Jerry lifted a shoulder in a shrug. "She was not heavy on details, and I didn't answer. The result of the conversation is we must pass an inspection in order to enter port."

"What about Ursula?"

"That's a backup plan, assuming she hasn't squandered the contract with Mortimer Blair and is still going to Beren Island for salt. However, I have my doubts she would keep the contract if she thought we were dead."

Azar gave her a look that said he quite agreed with that assessment. Jerry had met Ursula before the last time she'd gone to Joab. Still, they had managed to keep a friendship throughout the years, but Ursula never seemed to be one for listening to Jerry in the end, and Jerry suspected it would be to her own detriment that she had given Ursula a ship.

"We need to make sure that we are all functioning in order to pass." Jerry cut a look directly to Sacha. "So, no outbursts."

Sacha and Yafe frowned. Yafe, however, was the one to speak. "I can feel myself slipping. The...alternative to vestigen comes with a swift end to when it stops working."

"I've noticed that." Jerry shifted and put both her legs straight in front of her on the floor. They'd been sitting this way every time they had a meeting of minds. "I don't believe there is much left, however, and we'll need to make it last two more days until we can return to harbor."

"Two days?" Sacha's blue eyes grew large in her surprise. "I can't last two more days in this ship."

"We don't have a choice, and you need to start pretending to act right, otherwise, we'll never pass."

Sacha harrumphed and crossed her arms over her chest.

"I'm serious." Jerry glared. "I won't be forced from Raegina because you can't keep your tongue. I'll kill you first."

"And then eat my brains for your satisfaction."

Jerry snorted lightly. "Nothing goes to waste in Penum. You know that."

Sacha rolled her eyes and hit her head lightly on the wall behind her.

Jerry had successfully tamed that one. "We need to find a better balance of how we're taking this alternative."

It was as if they had all agreed without even speaking never to say the word *brains*, never to say they were eating people, the same people they spurned. The thought must disgust all of them, but it was their only way to survive.

"What are we going to do when we arrive in Raegina?" Azar, always the voice of reason, questioned.

Jerry pressed her lips together hard as she eyed each one of her crew. "We'll meet up with Ursula, and I'll take possession of my vessel again."

"Then what?" Yafe asked.

"You are all free to make the decision any time we begin a new mission. You can either join and stay or you are free to leave without any hard feelings."

"What's the mission?" Azar this time.

Jerry sent him a firm look. "I want my ship back."

"So we're going after Captain Lotchski?" Sacha stared directly at Jerry, that air of innocence she usually had about her back in place.

Jerry held the tension in the room. She wasn't sure how they could think she wouldn't go back and get her ship. The drugs they'd stolen would be a happy bonus if they were able to get them, but she wanted *Yarrow* back. *Yarrow* had been the only home Jerry had felt completely comfortable in, and she wanted it back. She wanted her life back, and she was going to make damn sure she got it.

"I am. You all are free to make the choice whether you're coming or not."

"But where is he?" Sacha questioned.

"No clue, but I imagine somewhere between here and Potelia. Those are his waters, and he wouldn't stray too far from them if he could help it."

"I'll be happy to join you," Yafe said, smiling.

Jerry looked to Azar. "And you?"

"Even if *Yarrow* is in parts," he sent a sidelong glance to his sister, "I will help you put her back together piece by piece."

Yafe shook her head at him but touched his arm at the same time. They hadn't been the ones Jerry was worried about losing. While Sacha was the newest member of her crew, she'd been the most volatile and hardest to control, yet she was the only one who could pass for innocent, so her skills had come in useful in Potelia. Either way, Jerry knew she was going to have to hire more crew, probably double the size of hers, just so she could take *Yarrow* and whatever ship she needed to commandeer in order to track Blaise down.

"I'll go," Sacha murmured. "I have nowhere else."

"We can always see if Ursula needs another crew member."

Sacha shook her head. "No offense, Cap, but I don't like that woman."

"Nor do I, for the record," Yafe chimed in.

That was more telling than Sacha's declaration, and it made Jerry pause and think about her decision to hire Ursula on in the first place. She was a rude and rough captain, the power having gone to her head. Jerry had hoped that it would even out eventually, but in the months she'd owned *Calluna*, Ursula hadn't seemed to even out at all. Yet Ursula was also vastly different with Jerry than the others.

"Duly noted," Jerry answered. "As for inspection, we need to find a way to pass."

"We'll have to keep our mood even and perhaps take a small extra dose a few hours before we arrive." Jerry could tell Yafe was already doing the calculations in her head. She was a wonder with numbers in a way Jerry had never managed to be. Then again, Yafe had at least some formal education where Jerry had grown up hiding under the cots her mother fucked sailors on.

"Do we have enough?" Jerry raised an eyebrow in Yafe's direction before sliding her gaze to Sacha. The young girl was flicking her fingers against her thumb in a nervous tic, one Jerry had seen her do so many times when she needed more vestigen. Her body chemistry—according to Yafe—was different enough that she needed more drugs. They lasted her less time than they did the rest of the crew. She'd seen it before. Jerry had her doubts but listened to her friend.

"It will be close."

"Right." Jerry relaxed into the wall. "As for chasing *Wench's Dream*, we need to find two things."

"What's that?" Sacha asked.

Jerry shook her head slowly. "We need to find Captain Blaise Lotchski, and we need to find *Yarrow*. The two might not be in the same place."

"And if they're not, which one will we go after?" Azar's dark eyes were wide with curiosity.

Jerry had seen that look in his gaze before. He wanted to know exactly what he was getting himself into, and considering the last mission Jerry had convinced him to go on had been an absolute failure that nearly killed them, she understood his hesitation and fear.

Swallowing hard, Jerry looked at him directly. "First we find *Yarrow*."

"And then *Wench's Dream*?"

"Yes. I want vengeance for what he did to us, and I have no problems taking what is rightfully mine."

Azar nodded slowly. "I'm in. It's a monster who would leave us stranded on an island like that. He probably thinks we're as dead as Ursula does."

Right. Jerry was going to have to figure that one out, especially if Ursula had already started the process to transfer ownership. Hopefully she hadn't completed it yet, because showing up alive when she was supposed to be dead was another story entirely, and she had no doubt that she would easily gain her ship back.

They had to find access to their cards first, however. Jerry knew they were filed away on some system, and Arloa would come in handy for that with her access to government systems. Jerry was debating whether to get up and leave when Yafe's voice reached her ears.

"What about *her*?"

Jerry raised an eyebrow at Yafe. They all knew exactly who Yafe was talking about. Jerry hadn't hidden what was going on between her and Arloa. The others had known it the first time Arloa had brought her back to *Yarrow* the year before. Jerry shook her head slowly.

"Nothing has changed."

"What do you mean by that?" Yafe pressed for an answer, one that Jerry was hoping to avoid at all costs.

"I mean nothing has changed. We are not together."

"Cap," Yafe implored.

"Nothing has changed," Jerry reiterated. "We will use her to get what we need, to return to Raegina, and then we will be done with her."

Yafe gave Jerry a look as though she didn't quite believe her, but that was fine. Jerry didn't need to be believed, she just had to believe it herself, which was going to be a much harder feat.

"Let's make plans for Blaise. I'm tired of only thinking of ways to kill him in my mind."

Azar chuckled. "I won't lie and say I haven't had some creative ideas on that front."

"Good. I want blood. I want to make him pay for what he did to us. Damon already paid for his betrayal."

Sacha frowned. "When are we going to get our next dose?"

"I'll get it now," Yafe said, pushing herself to stand.

As she left the cabin, Jerry stayed put. This was her family, these three people she'd been marooned with. Yes, even Sacha.

She had to keep reminding herself of that when she became distracted with Arloa. She was good for nothing other than sex and information. The two of them would never work beyond that. Frowning, Jerry picked at her freshly laundered clothes, not remembering the last time they had been laundered so thoroughly. They were still clean against her skin even though she'd worn them all week.

"Let's get through inspection and go from there as far as plans. We'll need to likely find lodging when we arrive in Raegina if *Calluna* isn't in port."

They had the basic steps figured out for what they were going to do next, and that was all Jerry could have hoped for. She'd have her crew with her every step of the way for the next little while.

CHAPTER 5

Jerry bent her head down as she spoke quietly in hushed tones to Yafe. "Once we're permitted to leave the vessel, let's find *Calluna*."

"On it, Cap."

Yafe stepped away, heading toward the cabins. They had passed inspection earlier that morning, and Jerry knew their time was in limited supply. They needed to get somewhere where they could keep themselves contained until they found another supply of *medicine* that would keep them sane. The slide into insanity was something Jerry didn't want to experience again.

Arloa had been scarce since their last argument, and Jerry had all but moved back into her own cabin. Unlike everyone else on the vessel, Jerry and her crew had nothing to pack, so they were ready to leave. However, they couldn't until the captain gave explicit permission.

As Jerry opened the door to her cabin to wait for the captain, she was surprised to find Arloa sitting on the cot, her legs crossed, one hand behind her, just simply waiting for Jerry to show up. Anger surged in her chest, indignation over who she couldn't be. "What do you want?"

Arloa sighed. "I feel as though we're leaving on a bad foot."

Jerry agreed with her on that, but it was a chosen way to leave—at least on her part. They weren't a couple. They didn't have to make nice. Jerry put her hands on her hips and scowled. "I would like to leave this ship."

"And then what?"

Jerry snorted lightly. "Get back to the *legal* work that I do."

"Without *Yarrow*?" Arloa raised a thin eyebrow, as if she was testing Jerry's answer.

She didn't know why she was trying to hide it from Arloa. She'd all but said it already, but she'd hoped Arloa would have forgotten by then. She should have known better—this woman forgot nothing. Frowning, Jerry squared her shoulders and looked down her nose. Two could play at this power game.

"That's what I thought," Arloa interrupted. She stood and moved directly in front of Jerry.

Arloa must have figured out what Jerry was attempting. And stupidly, any time she moved within touching distance, Jerry's brain would go haywire and become absolutely distracted by her body. Deciding she would hold her own this time, Jerry clenched her jaw and didn't budge. She wouldn't let Arloa get the best of her this time.

"I think you should leave Captain Blaise Lotchski alone and focus on what you do have. Here."

"I have nothing here," Jerry muttered, her voice low as a warning she was pretty sure Arloa was going to ignore.

"You do have something here." Arloa reached up and tenderly brushed fingers across Jerry's lips.

Jerry opened her mouth, her tongue itching to dash out and taste, to see if Arloa was salty or if she still had Jerry's flavor lingering on her skin. Pulling her tongue back in sharply, Jerry chided herself for the thought. *Oh, this woman and her wiles.* "I need to get my crew in order."

"On your other ship?"

"Yes." Jerry was surprised Arloa knew about *Calluna*, but she couldn't remember if she shared that information or not. Perhaps she had in some misguided conversation before she'd left for Potelia.

"What will you do on that ship?"

"The same as I was doing before," Jerry answered, still staying as motionless as possible. She didn't want to be the one who gave in, the one who finally took a step back because she couldn't handle the tension any longer. "All I need is permission to leave this vessel, and I'll get my life back in order."

"What if I find another drug, a third alternative?" Arloa implored her, that gaze deafening in the silence of the room.

Jerry shook her head slowly. "You'll have to find someone else to do your dirty work. I'm not volunteering anymore."

"Pity." Arloa's tone dropped on the word, and she skimmed her finger along the column of Jerry's neck to the loose leather ties of her tunic. "I quite enjoy working with you."

"You nearly got me killed," Jerry answered, her voice firm. "If I hadn't taken that intel from you, we wouldn't have been stranded—"

Arloa tsked, but her voice remained calm and cool when she spoke. "I never forced you to go."

"No, you didn't." Jerry leaned down, moving so she was hairsbreadth away. "But you are the cause of it."

"You asked for my help, and I provided what you asked for."

Jerry frowned. "Do you always twist things to be to your advantage?"

"Usually only when I'm in the Senate."

"Right." Jerry stepped away then, backing up from Arloa and heading toward the door. "I'm going to find the captain."

She cocked her head to the side and left the room. Arloa could be as manipulative as Jerry some days, but this was the first time Jerry truly felt at the center of it. They had talked about her going on the mission, and yes, it had been her choice. But Arloa should have known that the prospect of another drug, something other than vestigen, would be the perfect lure for it. Not to mention, especially with the current circumstances, if

Arloa were to offer a similar choice again, Jerry knew exactly what decision she would make.

She would still go.

Finding the captain, Jerry obtained permission for her and her crew to leave the vessel. They stepped out of the ship and onto the dock in Raegina, finally home. Warmth and pleasure and satisfaction filled her chest. She was ecstatic to be home again.

They were all on *Calluna* within the hour—thankfully, she had been in port. Ursula, thoroughly shocked, hadn't even started the paperwork yet, and Jerry suspected that had been a tactic to get away with some of her illegal business without getting caught.

Either way, she'd taken the ship back as hers. They'd each been assigned cabins. Yafe and Azar, sharing, and Sacha shacked up with a newer hire, Vivian. Jerry had been given her own cabin on the second level. Ursula sat with her in the room, eyeing her carefully.

"What happened, Cap?"

"It's a long story. First, what really matters. Vestigen?"

Ursula shook her head slowly. "We've got a few pills left, but we've been rationing as low as we can go."

"Have you been finding any on the seas?" Jerry crossed her arms and leaned against the wooden chest she sat against. Ursula had taken over the small cot, her fingers curling around the edge of it.

"No, we haven't. We've tried, but *Calluna*, bless her soul, doesn't maneuver swiftly. It's hard to catch those damn speedy ships."

Jerry gave a small smile, remembering that had been one of the main reasons she'd kept *Yarrow* to begin with. That, and *Yarrow* was her first. Jerry rolled her shoulders, easing the kinks out of her muscles. "So, you've been purchasing from Miriam?"

"And a few other places, but we haven't found any to buy in over three weeks."

Jerry hissed. "Sacha is going to need something."

"I'll make sure she gets a half pill, but that's all I can offer."

"It'll have to do. Any discussions on alternatives?"

"No."

Jerry pressed her lips together hard. She knew what alternative they could use, but she still wasn't sure she wanted to tell anyone about it. They were going to have to create a market for it, but she didn't want it to become a mass killing spree either. At the edge of her mind, Jerry shivered at the fact that *this* would be the corner of the underground that she ended up in. The most gross and negligent side of things.

"What are you thinking, Cap?"

"Nothing," Jerry muttered. "Just worried we won't survive this long enough to even bother with living."

"You used to say there was no living with this virus. What changed?"

Jerry knew exactly what had changed. It was seeing Arloa in the underground for the first time in over a year, reconnecting with her when she least expected but never wanted it. Shaking her head, Jerry changed the topic of conversation. "I'm going to get *Yarrow* back."

"Cap." Ursula gave her a look of pity.

Jerry sat still, eyeing her.

"She's not worth it."

"She's mine, and I want her back."

"Will you take *Calluna*?"

"I thought about it, since she's my only other ship at the moment, but I'm not entirely sure that'd be wise. She's not steady or maneuverable in a chase. *Wench's Dream* will be ready for her."

"So what are you going to do, then?"

"I don't know yet. But I do know I'm going to get *Yarrow* back, and I'm going to kill Captain Blaise Lotchski."

"Shh, don't say that too loudly. These walls have ears, you know."

Ursula had always been slightly paranoid, but since the virus had taken her it seemed to get worse, especially when she didn't have enough vestigen in her system, and Jerry suspected they all were in the same boat when it came to that.

"I'm going to come up with a plan. Until then, we'll stay here and help out with daily operations. I assume you're still working for Morty?" Jerry leaned on her knees, ready to talk business.

"No, we're not."

Jerry was about to question her when there was a knock on the door. They shared a quick look before Jerry called, "Come in."

"Hey, Cap," Yafe stated, a flash of worry etching into the corners of her eyes that she failed to mask. "There's someone here to see you."

"No one knows I'm fucking alive."

"Yeah, well, if you don't answer this one, everyone might know that."

Cursing, Jerry stood up and stalked out of her cabin and toward *Calluna's* main door. She hit the imaging system and saw Arloa standing on the other side at the sensor. Hitting the button to allow two-way communication, Jerry started, "Don't you know when to leave well enough alone, woman?"

"No. Let me in."

"No."

"Jer, this is not a conversation up for debate. Let me in."

Cursing under her breath, Jerry put in the code for the door. It descended, lowering down to connect with the dock so Arloa could walk right across it, which she did with fire in her steps. Arloa poked her finger into Jerry's chest, her small form full of energy.

"You don't walk away from me like that."

Jerry snorted. "Talk to me like that again and you'll never be allowed on one of my ships."

Arloa seemed to catch where she was and squared her shoulders. "Where can we talk?"

Jerry jerked her head to the side and stepped into the narrow hallway. She closed and locked *Calluna's* door, not wanting any other stragglers to come find her. She led the way up to her cabin, even though she knew the walls were thin. There was no good place to talk in a ship like this. It was built for capacity, not privacy.

Yafe met them in the hall, stepping back into her cabin with a glint in her eye. She was nearly laughing. Jerry sent her a scowl and shut the door to her cabin after Arloa stepped inside. Taking a step into Arloa's space, Jerry pinned her against the wall, hands against Arloa's wrists and keeping them above her head.

"Don't talk to me like that in front of my crew. Ever again." Leaning in, Jerry made sure Arloa understood perfectly.

She wouldn't be able to escape from Jerry's grasp, unable to move or twist and turn. Jerry needed her to understand who was in charge when they were on her ship. Jerry pushed in more, bending Arloa's wrists to the point she knew they would be hurting.

"So you're allowed to talk to me like a servant?"

Jerry's lips twitched, but she managed to keep the smile from showing on her face. "In here, you aren't one of them. In here, on this ship, and on any ship that I own, you are what I say you are."

Arloa shivered. She downright shuddered, and her breathing increased, her pupils dilated. Brazen, Jerry shifted her stance to shove one thigh between Arloa's legs, pushing against her to see exactly what she would do.

Arloa stayed still. Well, as much as she could. Her breasts pushed against her corset, the fine blue of the dress bringing out the blues of her eyes, the silver embroidery this time displaying women in salacious scenes, which Jerry never would have noticed had she not been so close and staring directly at it.

"Then who am I?" Arloa asked, her tone firm and demanding.

Jerry opened her mouth and then shut it. She hadn't quite

anticipated that Arloa would make her come up with an answer. Cocking her head to the side, Jerry bent down and scraped her teeth—hard—down the line of Arloa's neck. "You're no one."

Arloa dragged in a gasp, trying to cover it up. "How can I be no one and be in the captain's cabin?"

"I'm not captain of *Calluna*. Here I'm simply a passenger." Jerry bit the top of her breast, leaving teeth marks in her wake. The call to dig her teeth in deeper, to force blood, to taste it was strong, but she managed to resist it at the last moment.

"You *own* this vessel."

The way Arloa said it, so precise in her words, as if it was what elevated Jerry to the standard she needed in order to fuck, put Jerry off. Frowning, Jerry debated whether or not to just walk away and leave. That tone of voice was so uppity, so classist.

"Do you think I'm lesser than you are?"

"No," Arloa stated, any trace of her previous tone gone. This time there was an underlying moment of compassion and understanding in it. "No, I don't. I think I grew up with privilege you had no chance of having. That makes us different. It doesn't make me better than you."

"Right, but in here, this is my ship—"

"You just said you weren't captain."

"I'm not captain of *Calluna*, but I do own her." *Like I'm going to own you*, Jerry didn't say but wanted to. She pushed her thigh harder, and Arloa had to hold back the squeak.

"Jer," she begged.

"Yes, Arloa?"

"Don't use that tone with me."

"What tone? The one where I know I'm right and you're wrong."

Arloa wrinkled her nose. "You're not right."

Jerry bellowed a laugh. "Of course, I am, just like I know right now your biggest debate is whether or not you can ride my leg and get away with still being in control as you do it."

"You're allowed to fuck me." Arloa's lips pressed together tight, the only sign she was struggling.

Jerry loved to see it. This wasn't they first time they had verbally battled like this, but it was the first they were so explicit about it. "Fuck you? Like you're some whore?"

Arloa's cheeks reddened, the blush following lightly down her chest.

"Do you like that thought?" Jerry reached up, her hand still gloved from when she arrived. She circled Arloa's neck and pressed in slightly. "Do you want to be treated like one of us? Is that what turns you on?"

"What turns me on is a woman who knows her own mind."

Jerry cupped lip curled into a sneer. "But don't you know, dear Arloa, that since the virus has struck me, I have no mind to know."

"You are a perfect mind." Arloa moved her free hand up to encapsulate Jerry's wrist. Her hand around Arloa's neck faltered slightly, and she dropped it. "And I want you to fuck me already."

"How?" Jerry breathed sharply.

"Like this." Arloa pulled her skirts up, and Jerry slid back enough so that Arloa's heat reached her thigh through only her undergarments. They weren't even going to undress for this. Damn it, that was sexy.

Bolstering herself, Jerry grabbed Arloa's wrists again and held them high above her head, stretching out her body against the wall. Jerry pushed in harder, and Arloa grunted. As Jerry moved, Arloa ground down on her, no doubt increasing the pressure between her legs exactly how she wanted it.

"You shouldn't do it," Arloa stated, but she didn't stop moving.

Confused, Jerry jerked her gaze from Arloa's heaving breasts to her eyes. "Do what?"

"Go after him." Arloa moaned and threw her head back,

abandoning the restraint she had earlier and grinding freely against Jerry's leg. "You should forget him."

"He has my ship."

"He has *a* ship. You have one here."

"It's not *Yarrow*." Jerry moved in and sucked against the hollow of Arloa's neck, hoping to distract her to the point that she couldn't formulate conversation, but she was equally sure that would never happen.

"*Yarrow* is just a ship."

"You don't understand." Jerry halted her movements, but Arloa didn't stop hers. She continued, meaning she must be close to orgasming. Placing one hand over Arloa's breast while the other continued to hold her arms above her head, Jerry bent down and kissed her hard. She stole Arloa's breath, her concentration, everything that was holding her back from falling over that edge.

In seconds, she jerked and lost her rhythm. Jerry held her still, keeping her upright as she continued to move against her, slowly. Jerry pressed her forehead to Arloa's shoulder and steadied her breathing.

"You don't understand, Arloa. I don't think you ever will."

"Understand what?" Arloa still didn't move as Jerry held her against the wall, her body stretched out as she calmed.

Jerry sighed, finally moving to look directly into Arloa's eyes. "*Yarrow* is my home. Unless you've ever had your home taken away from you, never had a home to go to, you won't understand."

"I think I do now." Arloa pursed her lips. "I'll help you find her. If you want me to, that is. I'll help you."

"This is something I have to do on my own. I lost her, now it's time I find her."

"Like I found you?" Arloa lifted her chin to meet Jerry's gaze.

"No," Jerry answered firmly. "You didn't have to come find me. I need to go find *Yarrow*."

Arloa looked as though she was going to disagree, but she

didn't say anything. Nodding, she pulled her lower lip between her teeth. "Let me go."

Jerry did as she was told and stepped away. Arloa rubbed her wrists to ease the ache in them. They stared at each other awkwardly before Arloa fixed her skirts and straightened her back, drawing in a breath and making herself seem taller.

"Come find me when you're ready."

This time, Arloa left without another word. Jerry watched her go. She heard the door slowly lower so she could leave and raise back up when she was gone. Swallowing hard, she made her way topside to watch Arloa as she walked to the pier and vanished from sight. In her heart, she knew it wouldn't be the last time they saw each other, nowhere close to it.

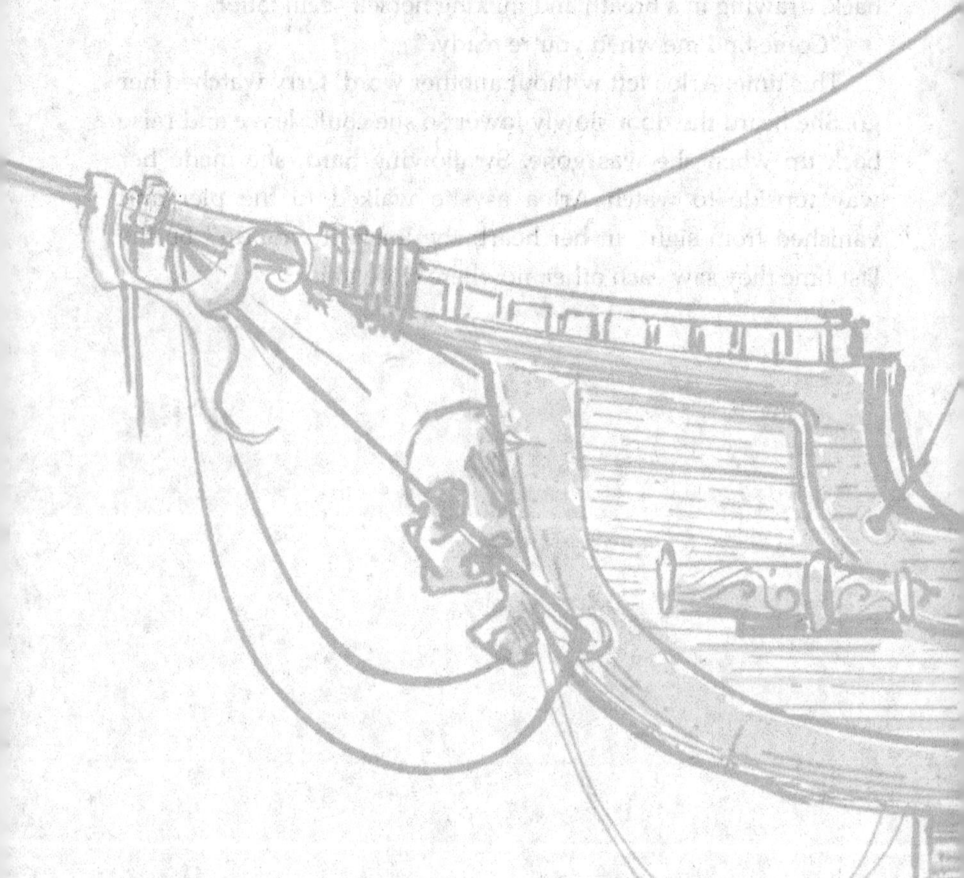

CHAPTER 6

We never finished our conversation from earlier." Finally with time and no interruptions, Jerry cornered Ursula in the wheelhouse.

Ursula looked up at Jerry, those bright eyes and the red mass of curly hair around her shoulders. Ursula raised an eyebrow at Jerry and pursed her lips. "Is your new woman gone?"

"New woman?" Raising an eyebrow, Jerry sneered. "She's not my new woman."

"When did you meet her?"

Jerry's heart rocked when she recognized that tone. She'd forgotten it was there in the upheaval of the last year. Ursula was envious. She'd propositioned Jerry for a relationship multiple times throughout the years, but the last time had been right when Jerry bought *Yarrow,* and she had turned Ursula down. Now they were both captains, but Jerry was owner, and Ursula worked for her. It would be inappropriate—not that Jerry usually cared about such things, but she did need to find an excuse as to why she had zero desire to fuck Ursula again—one that Ursula might accept.

"I met her over a year ago." Jerry crossed her arms, the chill in the air not just from the weather outside. She'd have to go buy a new leather jacket and top hat, since all of her belongings were likely in the sea. "She gave us the rumor, or rather confirmed Sacha's rumor, that there was an alternative drug being manufactured in Potelia."

"So you left because of her?"

That tone was dangerous, and not in a good way. Jerry clenched her jaw hard. "Yes, ultimately. And the information was correct, by the way. Potelia has manufactured a new drug, but it's in no way as powerful as vestigen."

Ursula's eyes lit up. "When will it hit the market?"

"I'm not sure it will. Add in, I'm not sure Raegina will purchase it from them." Jerry leaned against the wall, eyeing Ursula over. At least it seemed as though she'd managed to sidestep the tension that had built rather quickly. She was going to have to watch that if they were going to be living on the same ship for a while.

"Why wouldn't they?"

Jerry gave Ursula a hard look. "Because Raegina doesn't care about its lower-class citizens, which isn't news to you."

Ursula frowned. "So what do we do?"

"There is an alternative. I'm going to speak with Miriam to see if there's a market for it yet. I'm hoping there is already."

"And your lady friend?"

Jerry scrunched her nose. "What about her?"

"What's her role in all this?"

"Nothing." Jerry eyed Ursula firmly. "If you resigned from working for Morty, what have you been doing for credits? You're still feeding the crew, I hope."

Ursula at least had the audacity to flush. "Nothing you want to know about."

"It's my ship. You can damn well assume I want to know about it." Jerry straightened her shoulders, ready to fight to the end for her vessel if she had to. She wouldn't let Ursula run it into the ground, which she was now reminded was the hesitation she'd had when she allowed Ursula to be captain of *Calluna*.

Well, now it seemed Jerry might be taking over that role again for a while.

"We've been doing runs for Miriam."

"With my name, I assume."

"Yes."

Jerry sighed. She'd never wanted to use the underground in quite that way, but if it was the only way to make sure her crew was fed, then she could understand it. Still, she had been picky about which runs she would do for the mistress of the underground. She doubted Ursula would be so scrupulous.

Jerry started, "I'll let you continue to run this ship as you were, under my supervision now that I've returned. But I am making plans to find *Yarrow*. I want her back."

"Cap, you sure that's a good idea?"

Jerry frowned. Did she think it was a good idea? No. She should just give up the quest, but never would she allow someone to best her so well without a rematch. And *Yarrow* was hers. She wanted her ship back.

"Can't you wait and let the heat die down?"

"No." Jerry looked Ursula directly in the eye. "Blaise thinks I'm dead no doubt. I can't keep a low profile and manage to survive for long, and my name is well enough known in these parts that if Blaise comes near Raegina, one question or comment will tip him off. I can't wait him out to make it a better surprise in the end."

Ursula leaned against the dash where the controls for *Calluna*'s systems were. "So what are you going to do?"

"We'll stay here until we can figure out a detailed plan, but I know I have to find another ship. I can't take *Calluna* into that battle and win."

"Where will you get another ship?"

"Surely there's some abandoned somewhere I can confiscate."

Ursula raised an eyebrow. "The authorities have been

burning and sinking any vessel they come across that's infected with this new strain of the virus. They're so scared of it."

"I wouldn't be surprised if the authorities are already infected and just not telling anyone." Jerry rolled her shoulders. "So they're getting rid of not only history but our livelihoods. Perfect."

"There are still ships out there. We could steal one."

Jerry snapped her gaze up to Ursula. *We?* She hadn't quite anticipated that one. Jerry needed to get a better plan in place, and that was what they were doing, but she still had to decide what Ursula's role was going to be.

"I think stealing—or borrowing—is going to be my only option for now. Any leads on good ships?"

"There's a few we can check out. Some of the new crew members were on other ships before they came here."

"Yes, how many new crew do you have?" Jerry narrowed her gaze. She had noticed in the short time she'd been on *Calluna* that she didn't recognize a lot of the faces. Vivian, yes, and a few of the others, but that was about it.

Ursula ran a nervous hand through her hair. "We were hit hard by this new strain."

"And?"

"And we had to let some crew go."

Jerry understood the implication in that statement. She understood what Ursula wasn't saying. They'd been killed by other members of the crew, and then dumped in the seas never to be seen again. Suddenly the toll of people who were gone and never reported hit her stomach. She'd contributed to that surely, but the mass quantity of lives lost would be devastating to the world. She'd need to find current numbers on how many were dead from this thing—well, reported dead. They could probably easily double it to find a baseline number.

"Right. I'll introduce myself later. Right now, I'm going to visit Miriam."

"She had to move."

Raising an eyebrow, Jerry waited for Ursula to continue.

"I can take you there."

"Fine."

They locked up the controls on *Calluna's* dash quickly enough after adding Jerry's command codes back into the system. She was a little miffed they'd been taken out in the first place, but Jerry wasn't going to comment on it just yet. Ursula led the way as they left *Calluna* and walked down the dock, the very same path that Arloa had taken.

Jerry stayed in step with Ursula, even though she wished Ursula would walk faster. She'd never been one to take her time when moving from one place to the next, always going at a jaunt, but Ursula was slow. She took her time. She let the men leer at her. Jerry frowned and ducked her chin, really wishing she had a top hat, which would help to cover some of her face. She wasn't sure she was ready for the world to know she was alive yet.

Which reminded her… "Ursula, where is Miriam?"

"The little hotel off the main drag."

Jerry swallowed hard. "I'll stick around the corner. You go in and tell her she has a visitor who wishes to remain hidden."

"Cap?"

"Trust me. The world doesn't need to know I'm back yet. Miriam can keep that secret."

"All right."

They walked swiftly, but Jerry made sure to keep her head down. She was sure she still looked a mess. A week recovering on Arloa's ship had been good, but she was still skin and bones compared to when she'd left. Her hair was a knotted tangle that she had yet to even begin to think about taming it. Honestly, the thought of chopping it off had occurred to her more than once. She could more easily pass for a man then.

As they reached the small hotel, Jerry stepped between the brick buildings and waited for Ursula to come back out. Not many people passed them. If Jerry had thought that the streets were empty before she'd left, they were deserted now. No one walked anymore, it seemed. She'd barely seen people when she'd gone to find *Calluna*. She wondered if that was because they were dead or because they were scared.

The knock of wood against cobblestone caught her attention. Jerry jerked her head up to find a muscular black man standing in the mouth of the alley. Her stomach clenched tightly. Would she have to fight her way out of this? She was about to say something when Ursula's voice reached her.

"Cap, this way." Ursula pushed by the man and grabbed Jerry's arm. "He's intimidating, but he won't hurt a fly."

"Right." Jerry frowned, but the man led them deeper into the small alley between the buildings. As the shadows elongated, he ducked down and stepped into a cellar. Jerry went against every warning in her head as she followed him. Ursula stayed put.

"I'll see you at *Calluna*, Cap."

"You're not coming?"

"No."

Cautiously, Jerry continued to follow the man. Ursula better not be setting her up. Jerry stepped down the cement staircase trepidatiously. Her heart was in her throat the entire time. The dark and dank cellar didn't offer anything to tell her where she was going, but soon they found another door. The man unlocked it, and they took a thin stairwell straight upward, back and forth as they moved up floor by floor.

By the time Jerry reached the landing, she was struggling for breath. Being stuck on that island hadn't given her much for exercise aside from pacing, and this was more than she'd done in over a month. The man eyed her cautiously before he rapped three times, then two, then three on the door.

"Send her in," Miriam's voice carried through to them.

Jerry had no idea how Miriam knew it was her unless Ursula had spilled the secret, but she should have guessed that there'd be some sort of recording on the way there.

"Miriam," Jerry said by way of greeting as she stepped into the small room in the attic of the hotel.

"Jeraldine, I thought you were dead."

"So did I." Jerry grinned as Miriam stepped around the desk and opened her arms. Jerry collapsed into them. If there was one person on all of Penum who would miss her, it would have been this woman. Jerry sighed into her, feeling as much at home in Miriam's arms as she did on *Yarrow*.

"Where were you?"

"Stranded on an island. It's a long story, but I'm here now."

"That you are. I suppose you're here for vestigen."

Jerry frowned and straightened her shoulders as Miriam sat on the edge of the desk, one foot on a chair and her skirts shifting to reveal she wore nothing underneath them. "I've heard you don't have any."

"I may have a couple lying around."

"Didn't want to sell them to Ursula?"

"I don't like that woman." Miriam wrinkled her nose as if Ursula was a nuisance.

Jerry chuckled at the thought. Ursula always tried to come off better than she was, and that often led to a lot of people not liking her. "I'll take what you're willing to sell."

"Still have credits? That woman didn't steal them?"

Jerry had checked when she first got access to Arloa's systems to make sure, and it was all there still—her personal stash of credits, anyway. Ursula had run through what she'd kept aside for the ships. Which honestly hadn't surprised her since there hadn't been much in those accounts. "She didn't. I was in Potelia for a while. Have you heard anything about a large shipment of drugs from there? Sometime in the last month or so, or coming up?"

Miriam shook her head, her fingers playing with the sheer fabric of the top skirt she wore. "I haven't. What kind of drug?"

Jerry had hoped Miriam would accept that as an answer, but

she wasn't surprised when she'd asked for clarification. "A drug that rivals vestigen."

"Oh, I would have heard about that." Miram's lips curled upward. "There is no alternative."

Well, that helped Jerry at least know Miriam had nothing to do with their capture and subsequent marooning. That made the list of people who knew where she was very short. Although Miriam hadn't known exactly where Jerry had been, she'd known she was gone from Raegina. The woman seemed to know everything that happened there and even many things that happened elsewhere.

"I was hoping since I'd been gone there was."

Miriam shook her head slowly. "That would be progress, and Raegina isn't exactly known for progress."

"No, they just like to have others think they are. Well, Penum is, anyway." It was true. They had so many advances that one would think they were for the world, but when it came down to it, they were as misogynistic and patriarchal as ever, and the economics dictated there would be a large gap between classes. Jerry had lived in that reality her entire life, never able to raise herself above her current station.

They stared at each other silently agreeing. Jerry had known Miriam since she was born, having grown up under her watchful eye as Jerry's mother worked for her. At one point, Jerry would have told Miriam anything, done anything, to be in her good graces. But years had hardened her. She may not be twenty-four yet, but she had lived dozens of lifetimes in those short years.

"What about this new virus? Tell me, because I haven't heard anything with being gone."

Miriam blew out a breath and slumped. She looked defeated. This strong woman who ran the entire underground looked as though she was never going to win or perhaps even survive. Jerry wanted to say something to comfort her, but instead, she kept to herself.

"It's bad, love. There's nothing that works with this new strain. The only solution is death."

"How bad is it?"

"Bad. I've lost over half my workers. We had to move." Miriam spread her arms out to indicate the new digs. "Killing your best whore with your bare fingers because it's the only saving mercy there is…that's not something I'd wish on anyone."

Jerry whistled. "Can you get the new strain if you have the first one?"

"No, that seems to be the bright spot for now. Except now we're learning how many people were never infected to begin with."

"Just angry assholes using it as an excuse."

Miriam's raised eyebrow was enough to show her agreement.

Jerry clenched her jaw. "So what do we do now?"

"Nothing. We keep finding the cracks and that's where we live."

Jerry sighed and rubbed a hand at the back of her head before remembering how tangled her hair was and dropped it. "Do you know anything about a ship called *Wench's Dream*?"

Miriam shook her head swiftly and then slowed the movement. "I worked with a ship once. Sent a few girls there. When they returned them, my girls said they were mistreated, so I never allowed them to take girls again. That was twenty years ago."

Jerry hummed. For Miriam to listen to girls being mistreated, it must have been bad. She'd never seen Miriam to get in a huff if someone hit her girls once, but for her to take that stand, either there was more to the story or it was an awful place. She could only imagine what they were putting *Yarrow* through in the meantime.

"If you hear anything about that ship, or *Yarrow*, will you let me know?"

"Anything for you, my sweet Jeraldine. Just tell me one thing."

"What?"

"Did Senator Kauket rescue you herself?"

Shock rang through Jerry, cold washing through her to the point that she knew she hadn't been able to hide it. Miriam suddenly waved her off, telling her it was no big deal silently. Jerry cocked her head, waiting for the explanation.

"She came asking for information on your disappearance."

"Well, she is a resourceful woman, that's for sure."

"You haven't answered my question."

Jerry grinned broadly and bowed as she backed toward the door. "And I don't plan on it."

"That is an answer in and of itself."

Laughing, Jerry stepped out of the small room and tried not to stumble her way down the stairs. She did trip on the last floor but caught herself on the railing. The man who had shown her where to go was nowhere in sight, but Jerry didn't believe for one second that Miriam was left unprotected. As she emerged into the daylight again, she straightened her back. The next order of business was to buy herself some new clothes. Finding her way to the tailor, Jerry went on a small shopping spree.

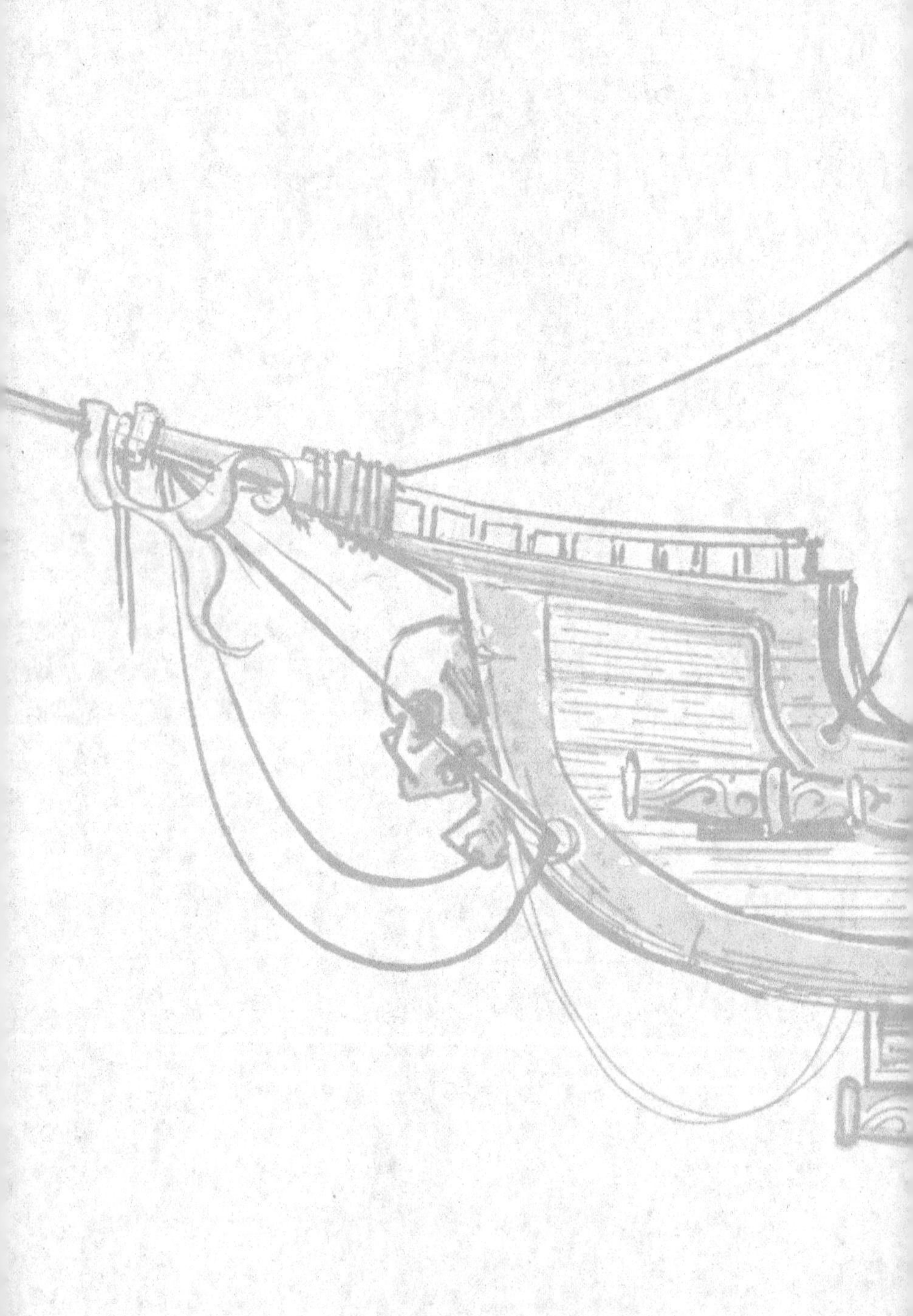

CHAPTER 7

Jerry had no other option. She hated that she was going to have to eat crow, but she had exhausted her other sources without revealing to too many that she was alive. She wanted to catch Blaise as unaware as possible. Rolling her neck, Jerry dressed in her new clothes, the long jacket stopping just below her knees, dark leather this time instead of her preferred brown. She was going to the dark side in more ways than one.

With her top hat sitting perfectly on her head, Jerry squared her shoulders. She could do this. Dawn was just hitting Raegina, the sun coming over the horizon of the city. Jerry had always wished the harbor faced east like in some of the other towns she'd been to, but she would have to do with the eerie glow of the sun against the stone buildings in town.

She trotted along the cobblestone streets, walking through alleys and along streets to get to Arloa's apartment. The building was several floors high, and Jerry tipped her chin to look up to the floor she knew was Arloa's. She hadn't told her that she was coming. Tightening her jaw, Jerry pushed her button on the sensor and waited for the artificial intelligence to talk to her. "State the name of the resident."

Lowering her tone, Jerry spoke into the small microphone near the sensor. "Arloa Kauket."

She hated that name. She hated what the Kaukets held over her, that she couldn't escape them. They had held her captive in their so-called rehabilitation center for two years, a prison of torture, and she refused to go back there, and yet she couldn't sever her relationship with *this* Kauket. No matter how much she may want to or how many times she had tried.

The door clicked, and Jerry grabbed it, not willing to let the one lifeline she had be cut again. "Fourth floor, second door on the left."

Somehow, Jerry still had permission to enter. Surprised by that revelation, Jerry slid her way into the building. She took the stairs two at a time until she reached the fourth floor, managing much better this time around than she had when visiting Miriam. She remembered this building like it was yesterday. The white-washed shiplap walls, the glass doorknobs, the extravagance it boasted.

Standing in front of Arloa's door, Jerry steadied herself for the conversation they were about to have. Pressing her hand to the sensor, Jerry waited for Arloa to answer. She folded her hands behind her back, pushing up on her toes and rocking back onto her heels. She had never had to wait this long for Arloa to answer, but she supposed after the way they left off, it shouldn't surprise her the woman would make her wait.

"Arloa, I know you're in there," Jerry said into the door, biting her tongue when she knew it was the lack of drugs in her system causing her patience to wear thinner than she wanted. When the door clicked, Jerry sighed in relief. "Thank you."

"What do you want?" Arloa raised a perfectly plucked eyebrow, her face gaunt compared to how it had been when they'd met. Jerry was reminded of the age difference between them, and how Arloa probably struggled with traveling around to find her. Guilt ate away at her briefly before Jerry managed to shut it down.

Arloa looked perfectly pinned up, surely ready to go to the

government building that morning. Jerry's fingers itched to touch her, but she schooled them into behaving.

"Oh," Arloa laughed a little. "Run out of other options that quickly? Need to use me some more?"

Jerry frowned, her voice quiet as she answered, "I don't want to *use* you."

"Then why are you here?"

"I need help."

"I gave you help." Arloa stepped back from the door, moving to shut it.

Jerry wasn't quick enough, and when it clicked, her heart sank. She leaned against the door and closed her eyes, trying to decide if she should try again or just leave. She stayed there for another thirty seconds before she straightened up and turned in her boots. She was halfway down the hall when Arloa's voice reached her.

"Get in here, Jer."

Jerry's lips curled upward, but she managed to hide her smile before she turned around. Staring at Arloa from down the hall, Jerry moved her jacket aside as she put her hands on her hips. She held her ground, saying nothing as Arloa stalked her down. When Arloa reached her, she shimmied her palms up to Jerry's shoulders and curled around her.

"Come inside."

Before she knew what she was doing, Jerry bent her head and pressed their lips together in a gentle kiss. No matter how hard she tried, she could not get enough of this woman. Arloa hummed but broke the embrace as if she didn't want Jerry to touch her, and Jerry supposed she should have asked for permission like she normally did. She was becoming far too familiar with Arloa if that was happening.

"I need help."

"So you said. Come inside, please."

Jerry frowned but followed Arloa inside. Perhaps her change of tune hadn't been emotional but rather due to the fact they were standing in the hall where all the rich aristocrats could see them and could see how Jerry absolutely didn't fit in their world.

"I like your new jacket."

"Thanks." Jerry's voice was low as she pulled off her top hat, hanging it on the rack by the door. She opted to leave her jacket on, not wanting this to be a long visit.

Arloa moved to the stiff couch and sat down, pouring a cup of tea for herself. Jerry noted there was no second cup, so she was not invited to that party. Walking to the short sofa, Jerry lowered herself onto it, trying to act as normal as possible.

"What do you need help with, Jeraldine?"

Arloa's tone stung slightly, but Jerry had been quite closed off with her in general, not wanting to deepen their relationship beyond what it was already. Bypassing a deeper conversation, Jerry focused on why she was there. "I need help finding my ship."

Arloa gave her a wry smile right before she sipped her steaming tea. "You'll have to remind me why I should help you."

This was likely the most they had talked in Arloa's small apartment. Usually, when Jerry had been here before, it was for other reasons, minus the one time Arloa had brought her in for healing. Jerry straightened her shoulders. "In full honestly, you probably shouldn't know."

That must have gotten Arloa's attention, because her shoulders stiffened and she sent Jerry a curious look, imploring her to say more. They fell into a silence, Arloa setting her cup down before she straightened her back again and clearly waited for Jerry to continue.

"I'm a pirate, Arloa. The things I do aren't exactly legal, and you're with the government. Set out to find me and stop me."

Arloa's lips twitched. "Find you I did."

"But you didn't stop me. In fact, a few months ago, you sent me on a mission."

"Desperate times call for desperate measures." Arloa's voice was gravelly as if she hadn't slept much. "I want you to give up this quest to find *Yarrow*."

"I know you do, but I don't think you understand why I can't."

"Then tell me." Arloa was back to drinking her tea.

Jerry's stomach was a ball of knots. She had practiced so many times in her head how she was going to make this ask, but she wasn't coming up with those words now. Not to mention, the lack of drugs in her system was making it difficult to think. Grinding her teeth, she tried to find words that would convince Arloa to help her.

Instead, she went with her gut and the truth. "*Yarrow* is my only home. I never had a home when I was a kid. We moved— my mom and I—moved often, wherever her work took her."

"Her work of using her body," Arloa supplied.

Surprised Arloa had figured that one out, Jerry nodded. "Yes. We would stay with Miriam sometimes, but more often than not, Mother preferred to be on ships as the only whore on board. It meant she got more of the credits in the long run."

"Sound business thinking. Create a monopoly."

Jerry gave a half smile. Arloa would turn that into a positive and have it make sense. "Yeah, I guess, but when I bought *Yarrow* after being in Joab for two years, I was ready to have a home, a place to be who I wanted to be."

"You can do that anywhere, Jer."

The tender way Arloa said her nickname gave Jerry some hope that this had been the right tack to take. "Sure, but *Yarrow* is where I want to do it."

Arloa eyed her over the rim of her teacup before settling it on the small table off to the side of the small sofa. "I understand this is your stand."

"My stand?" Jerry furrowed her brow.

"Yes. You want to prove to him and perhaps to yourself that you're not weak. It's revenge."

"Sure, in some ways, but—"

Arloa interrupted her. "I don't think it's wise for you to go after him."

"I don't think you get a choice in that matter."

"I don't." Arloa nodded. "You won't give me one, so I'm left with the choice to either help you find him swiftly or let you spin in your boots, so to say."

Jerry was confused. Was Arloa going to help her or not? She wanted to know. "Arloa…"

"I'm not done yet." Arloa cut her hand across the air. "What do you think of when you think of me?"

"What?" Jerry's stomach twisted hard, cold washing through her. She hadn't known this conversation would take this turn, and she wasn't sure she wanted it to either. She'd done her damned best to avoid making any declarations of who they were to each other.

"I understand you're a pirate, Jeraldine Adelric. I even understand you have a checkered past."

"Where are you going with this?"

Arloa let out a little puff of air, her lips thinning as frustration took over her. "Stop speaking and you might hear."

Thoroughly chastised, Jerry waited for Arloa to continue.

"I know who you are, Jer." Arloa leaned in, pressing her small hand to Jerry's thigh. Warmth seeped into her bones, heating her, electrifying her. When Jerry raised her gaze, Arloa stared directly into her, as if she could read every thought and feeling she had, even if she couldn't name it herself. "I know who you are, and I still want you."

"That's a bad idea."

"We need to talk about this."

"I don't want to." Jerry couldn't stop herself from leaning in, their mouths nearly brushing. She would win this battle as much as she would the next. "It doesn't matter in the end. It'll never work out."

"You don't know that." Arloa moved her hand up to Jerry's cheek, caressing her.

Jerry leaned into the soft touch. Arloa did always have a way with gentleness that she'd never managed to attain. Closing her eyes, Jerry listened to the steady thrum of her heart, her stomach twirling in discomfort, and the call for blood in her veins.

"I do know that, Arloa. I'm infected with the virus. I'm nothing in Raegina, and you hold all the power. I'm an unsightly creature, and you are a beautiful woman, someone people look up to, someone who can and will make a difference. It will never work the way you want it to."

"We'll never know if we don't try. You seemed willing to try once, all those months ago."

Tears stung Jerry's eyes, and she hated that she couldn't control herself. She used to be so good at it, but since the virus had taken over her, she'd had to find a new method of managing that, one she'd yet to grasp. "I was willing to fuck you. That's all."

"Are you sure?" Arloa's voice was barely above a whisper, and this time when their lips brushed, Jerry was filled with warmth and not regret. "I don't think you are."

"Arloa…" Jerry trailed off.

"I know we have our battles to face where it concerns a relationship, but I'm willing to take that stand. Are you?"

Jerry didn't have an answer. She wanted to have one. She wanted to be able to say yes, but there were too many barriers holding her back. "I'm going to die, and it's not going to be a pleasant death."

"Then live while you can."

Jerry swallowed the lump in her throat, wanting and needing to be able to take that step, but she couldn't. She couldn't open her heart the way Arloa was asking. Not yet. Instead, Jerry surged forward and pressed their mouths together in a brutal kiss. Arloa sucked in a breath, threading her fingers into Jerry's matted hair and holding her tight. She may be a small woman, but she was strong—not just physically but emotionally, mentally.

She nipped Arloa's lower lip and cupped both sides of her cheeks, keeping her in place. She didn't want to stop. This hadn't been what she'd come looking for—or at least, what she had told herself she was looking for. Arloa moved up, leaning on the sofa with a knee and pulling Jerry down to cover her—their mouths never leaving each other.

Arloa parted the sides of Jerry's jacket, reaching forward to pull at the leather ties to the new tunic Jerry had purchased. She'd purposely chosen not to buy a corset even though it was proper dress for a woman. She wasn't going to waste her money of those things anymore, and when Arloa had free and easy access to her body, Jerry knew she'd made a perfect choice.

Raising her hips up, Jerry shifted and tugged Arloa so she was fully on top of her. "What are we doing?"

"Anything you want," Arloa replied. "And yes, Jer, I will help you find your home."

Her heart skipped a beat. Jerry ran her hands up and down Arloa's back, into her hair and kissed her hard. "How much time do we have?"

"An hour, until the second morning bell."

"Perfect." Jerry reached around Arloa's back and tugged hard at the ties of her corset until she could squeeze her hands in there. She wanted skin against skin this time, she wanted everything to be the way they'd done it the first time—almost. Jerry did as much untying and undressing as possible as Arloa lay prone on top of her, putting small kisses against Jerry's neck and the top of her chest.

Arloa swirled her tongue, finally reaching Jerry's small breast and her nipple. She'd once told Arloa she hated how she looked naked as she awkwardly had stood awkwardly in front of her, and this woman had managed to make her feel beautiful in every moment since they'd met. Jerry had never had a doubt that they were physically attracted to each other.

As soon as they were both undressed, clothes in a pile on the floor next to the sofa, Arloa raised up on her knees, her breasts hanging and swaying as she sent Jerry a saucy grin. She bent down, pressing one kiss and a bite to the top of Jerry's breast before making a pathway down to the tops of Jerry's thighs.

Jerry parted her legs, anticipating Arloa's direction. Sure enough, Arloa's mouth reached her clit. Instantly, Jerry fell into the sensation of Arloa against her, of pleasure soaring through her. She reached over her head to hold onto the arm of the sofa and keep herself in place as Arloa continued to touch her. One finger, and then two, and Jerry's mind warred between Arloa's ministrations and the need for her brain to steady herself into normalcy.

"Arloa, I don't know if I can do this," Jerry murmured. She didn't mean sex. She meant the fact that she was crashing hard from lack of drugs in her system, and she was liable to turn into a raging addict at any moment.

Arloa stopped, moving to look up at Jerry. She must have realized what was going on, because she covered Jerry's body again, sliding against her and whispering, "Hold on. Feel my touch. Hear my voice. Use me to center yourself."

Jerry's heart hammered, thumping too hard for what they were no longer doing. Her brain spun, as if dizzy while lying down. She tried to do what Arloa was telling her, tried to focus on her sweet voice, the commands she was giving, the sensation of skin on skin. Arloa soothed fingers all over Jerry's torso, pulling her mind from the chaos it was slipping toward, right back into the moment.

When Jerry opened her eyes again, she knew she had control. "Thank you."

"Anytime." Arloa's lips quirked into a smile before she shifted down Jerry's body and picked up right where she left off —latched to Jerry's clit.

It took Jerry a minute to find the level of pleasure she was searching for, but when she found it, she was ready to go. She curled her fingers into Arloa's hair, scraping her nails against Arloa's scalp. Raising her knees up, she rocked her hips into

Arloa's mouth and rode each wave of pleasure as it crashed through her. Her entire mind was void of the need for drugs and focused entirely on the woman between her legs and the teasing of her body higher and longer into pleasure.

When Jerry finally relaxed, Arloa covered her again, kissing her way up Jerry's body to her mouth, her lips. Arloa buried her face in Jerry's neck and drew in slow, deep breaths. "Let me comb out your hair."

Jerry snorted. "Sure, if I can fuck you while you do that."

"Challenge accepted."

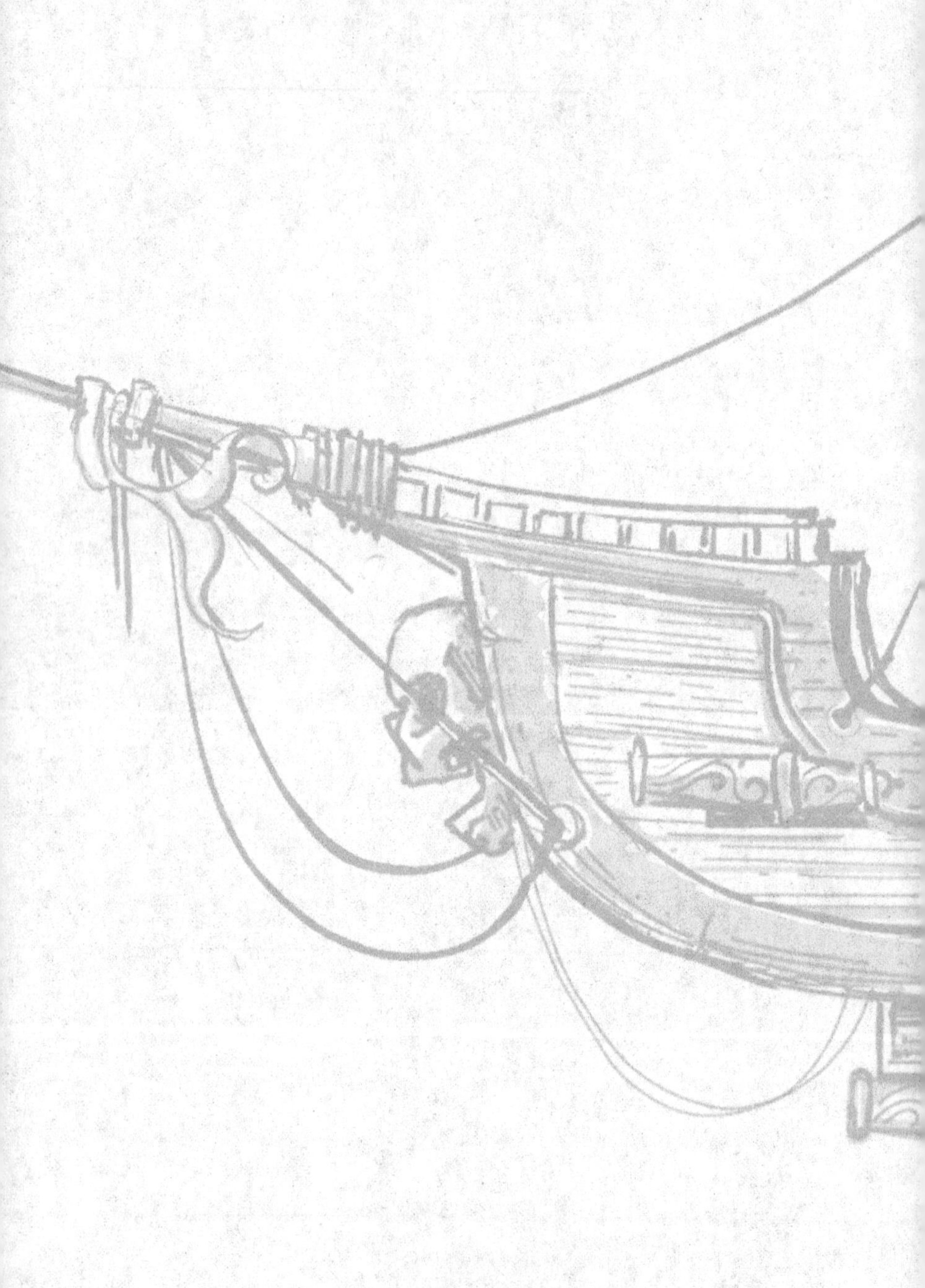

CHAPTER 8

Jerry sat in her small cabin, worrying her bottom lip. She'd managed to find some semblance of control for a few hours, but after she left Arloa's apartment in the innermost part of the city, she'd felt it slipping. They had to find a solution. The crew on board *Calluna* was already going wild, especially her crew.

Out of options, Jerry shoved herself upward, swaying when the lack of hormones in her body hit her harder than she expected. There was limited time to deal with this problem. Jerry didn't stop by Ursula's cabin, not wanting to let her in on what was happening. Instead, she strode straight to Yafe's. Knocking as she pushed open the door, Jerry stepped inside to find the room dark.

Azar snored loudly from the cot along the far wall, and Yafe stared at her with wide eyes from a sitting position from the other. Jerry put her hands on her hips and wrinkled her nose. "We've got a problem."

"I know, Cap. It would have been better to be left on that island."

"Took the damn words right out of my mouth." Jerry's fingers itched. She wanted to hit someone, feel the flesh as it resisted, the snap of bone as she broke it. She had to do something to get the desire out of her.

Yafe stood up, the picture of control so far, but Jerry could tell from her wild eyes how on edge she was. They would make the perfect team for this. Jerking her head toward the cabin door, Jerry stepped outside. As soon as Yafe followed, Jerry pressed her smaller frame against the wall, pinning her.

"We're going to have to do it," Yafe whispered, her pupils fully dilated.

"I know," Jerry sighed. "But it doesn't mean I want to."

"Do the others know?"

"I don't think so." Jerry used the cold temperature of the wall to center herself. She had to keep herself controlled, as much as was humanly possible. "I don't know how it's gotten past them."

"They haven't been in as dire need as we have."

Except Jerry had suspected this was a solution well before they were marooned. It happened the night she'd found Sacha. Hints the universe had dropped in her lap so many times that when they'd been stuck on the damnable island, she hadn't been able to deny it any longer. And she would have gladly killed Sacha and the others if it had meant her survival. The virus had taken her over, and as much as she had contemplated ending it all before, once she'd been fully ensconced with the virus raging through her and nothing combatting it, she'd known exactly how she would die.

Fight.

"The bar?" Jerry questioned.

Yafe bit her lip. "It's the middle of the day."

"I don't know where else to go."

"We need someone who won't be missed."

Jerry cocked her head to the side. "None of us will be missed."

"True," Yafe dragged out the word. "Well, I would miss you, and I have a feeling *she* would miss you."

Jerry snorted loudly. "She has no idea what she's in for with me."

"I think she knows better than you think she does."

"Yafe, this isn't the time—"

"I know," Yafe whispered again. "We should do it under the cover of dark."

Jerry flitted her gaze up and down the small corridor, looking to see if anyone was listening in. When she glanced back at Yafe, she cursed under her breath. Paranoia had already started to set it. "We can't wait. Come on."

Jerry grabbed Yafe by the wrists and dragged her toward the main door of the ship. She supposed it was to her benefit that Ursula had lost her contract with Morty because they hadn't been traveling when it hit them. Jerry checked her knives at her waist and her wrists as she hit her palm against the sensor to lower the door.

"You do have weapons, right?"

"Yeah."

Jerry knew Yafe preferred to avoid weapons if she could, but she did typically carry them on her person. Jerry had sharpened the knife she'd had on the island and slid it back into its place along her ankle, making sure she'd never lose that reminder of what they'd once been.

"Let's get the fuck out of here."

They were on the dock in seconds, then the pier. Yafe wasn't that far behind her, keeping pace. Jerry tilted her head down but kept her gaze up so that she could see anyone who they might come close to. It took until they were one street inland before they found a single soul.

"Too stinky," Jerry muttered, either to herself or Yafe, she wasn't sure. She didn't really care either. She just wanted something to make her sane again.

They walked further into the city. The cobblestones became newer as they approached the center. They would be insane to try and find someone to kill just on the inside of the city, someone who was rich, whose absence would start an uproar if they were to go missing. They walked through the main gate.

Jerry's heart thundered, but not from worry about what might happen if they were caught, from the need she couldn't satiate. Jerry dashed her tongue across her lips, remembering the flavor of Damon. He had been gristly, which she hadn't particularly appreciated, but she knew all brains didn't taste like that.

"What about her?" Yafe's eyes locked on a young woman who stepped through a gate.

Jerry followed her gaze, her heart skipping a beat. She had blonde curls in waves, falling for ages down her back as she let them loose. Her shoulders were squared, but she kept her head held high. They were right on the edge of town. It would be reasonable enough to assume that someone might go missing there.

"She'll be perfect." Jerry hadn't wanted to wait too much longer.

"We need some place to take her." Yafe gripped Jerry's hand.

Jerry cocked her head to the side, not taking her eyes off the young woman as she walked. "Miriam's isn't far from here. She'll want to edge in on this anyway."

Jerry stepped quickly and as quietly as possible. She'd stalked people before. She'd stalked entire ships before. Jerry held her ground, staying far enough behind that she wouldn't seem threatening but close enough that she could take a few long strides and catch up for the snatch.

She was just about to go in for the grab, when the young woman turned and faced her, eyes wide with recognition. Jerry sputtered and froze on the spot. Every gut instinct in her body told her to run the other way while at the same time telling her this was the *only* way.

"Captain?" The woman stuttered.

Jerry shook her head and took two long steps, reaching up and covering Whitney's mouth with her hand to prevent her from screaming. She grabbed the back of her head to hold her still, twisting her around so her back was against Jerry's front as she held on tightly. She wasn't going to let Whitney go.

Yafe wrapped her belt around Whitney's wrists to hold her still as Jerry dragged her backward into an alley. As soon as they were hidden away, Jerry dragged in a deep breath and settled herself. Whitney smelled just as good this time as the last time she saw her—clean, freshly laundered, as if she had some money.

Jerry kept her hand over Whitney's mouth, unable to decide if she really wanted to do this or not, but still not seeing any other option. They had to do something to assuage their hunger, their appetite, their desire for brains. Yafe hissed when she turned and saw the woman.

"Cap?"

"I know," Jerry muttered.

"What do you want—"

"I don't know." Jerry tensed as Whitney whimpered, and Jerry tightened her grip on her mouth. "I'm going to move my hand, but don't yell."

At Whitney's nod, Jerry counted to three before she did as she'd said. She had hoped their previous connection would at least give Whitney some trust so that she would listen.

"W-what are you doing?" Whitney breathed the question.

"I didn't think I'd find *you*." Jerry could have cursed. Of all damn people for her to find to kill, it had to be someone she'd already saved. Her heart hammered, no doubt to the point that Whitney could feel it against her back. "Where were you going?"

"The library to study."

"Fuck," Jerry muttered. "Are you infected yet?"

"No."

"And the orphanage is letting you out?"

Whitney nodded slowly. Yafe's eyes widened, but her gaze didn't move from Whitney's face, probably just as stunned as Jerry herself. They had to do something about this. They had to find some sort of resolution that wouldn't end with Jerry killing the girl she had saved.

Without warning, Whitney stomped her heel onto Jerry's boot and threw her elbow back by turning her body into Jerry's stomach. Grunting and cringing in pain, Jerry didn't give her a chance to get away. Flipping Whitney around and shoving her face into the brick wall, Jerry pressed into her back, her forearm against the Whiney's neck to hold her in place.

"I wouldn't try that again if I were you."

"Why can't you just leave me alone?" Whitney ground out.

Jerry had been wondering the same thing, although the first time and this time, Jerry hadn't sought her out. It was only when she'd wanted answers that she'd gone in search of this young woman, a woman who by no means should still be living at the orphanage. She was old enough to be out on her own, and surely there were enough children—stop. Jerry had to stop that line of thought. If she was going to kill Whitney, she was going to have to stop imaging her as a woman, someone Jerry had kissed.

"Fuck," Jerry muttered but held her ground.

"Cap?" Yafe questioned, her voice wavering as if some sense was coming back into her.

Swallowing hard, Jerry reached forward with her other hand to snap Whitney's neck.

"Jeraldine Adelric!" Miriam's voice boomed through the alley.

Jerry startled but still held Whitney against the wall. She wasn't going to give up this opportunity if she could. Turning her head to face the entry to the alley, Jerry eyed Miriam. She rarely came out into the sunlight. She stalked forward, one foot in front of the other, completely alone—equally something Jerry rarely ever saw.

"What are you doing?" Miriam accused.

"The only thing I can to survive."

"There's vestigen."

"There's none left," Jerry hissed, and this is the only way.

"Look at her, Jeraldine."

She didn't want to. Jerry did *not* want to look at Whitney, didn't want to see her, hear her, be reminded of who she was and what they had done. Finally, in the silence, Jerry raised her chin and looked at Whitney's profile. The girl was so young, barely old enough to be out of the orphanage. She was beautiful, and she reminded Jerry of Arloa in so many ways. Her hair, her attitude, that know-it-all-damn-it-all persona she tried to project.

Jerry slowly shifted away and loosened her grasp on Whitney. She didn't go far enough that she would completely lose her if she still needed her. Glancing over her shoulder at Miriam, Jerry raised an eyebrow at her. "Now what?"

"Come with me."

In a flash, Miriam was gone. Jerry blinked three times trying to figure out where the hell she had gone when Yafe touched her arm and pointed up. When Jerry turned around, Whitney had escaped down the alley and out into the road. If she reported the incident, Jerry would be on the fast track back to Joab. She shouldn't have let her go so easily.

Grabbing the damn rope that had obviously pulled Miriam up, Jerry put her boot against the wall and prepared herself to climb. She was going to regret this. Each pull of her stiff body up the wall was more than Jerry could handle. She was halfway when Yafe followed. Groaning, Jerry reached the last floor and pulled herself over the edge.

Miriam stood with her hands on her hips and two guards flanking her. The look on her face was pure disdain. As Yafe dragged herself over the edge, Miriam finally spoke. "They're here for my protection."

"Like I'd be stupid enough to try and kill you." Jerry sneered at the thought. She needed Miriam far more than she wanted her dead—though the thought had occurred to her on occasion throughout her lifetime.

"Can't tell if you can control yourself or not."

"Can't you?" Jerry pushed back.

Miriam just raised her eyebrow, the disappointed parental glint in her eye, and Jerry knew she was in trouble. "What's going on, Jeraldine?"

"There's no more vestigen, Miriam." Attitude seeped through every word. "What do you expect me to do?"

"Find an alternative."

Jerry raised an eyebrow, waiting for Miriam to understand. When neither said anything, Jerry raised her hand and crooked her finger toward her. Miriam hesitated but finally stepped in closer. Jerry silently told her to move even closer still. As soon as Miriam was inches away, Jerry leaned in. The two guards stepped forward, but Miriam flung out a hand to stop them.

Lowering her voice, Jerry whispered, "I did find an alternative. You interrupted it."

Miriam remained silent as she leaned back to look Jerry in the eye. They held that moment, Miriam judging her to see if she was telling the truth. At the snap of her fingers the guards were told to leave. In another instant, Jerry and Yafe were following Miriam through a maze of rooms inside the building. They squeezed through corridors barely big enough for each of them, darkened hallways, under broken through walls.

When they finally stopped, pushing aside a rug on the wall, Jerry realized they were in Miriam's newest hideaway. *Interesting.* Jerry put her hands on her hips and stared at Miriam. "What are you going to do now?"

"What's the alternative?" Miriam eyed Jerry up and down.

Jerry shook her head sharply. "That's not how this works. I have the information you want, and you tell me how much you're willing to pay. No pussyfooting around either. I want the full amount."

"There's nothing in a credit anymore, Jeraldine."

Walking around the small office, Jerry sent Yafe a look, trying to figure out exactly what she would ask for, then it hit her. "I want a ship."

"I don't have one."

Jerry snorted. "Get me one."

"I can get you information on one, but you know as well as anyone else that the seas are not my territory."

Miriam wasn't lying. She'd stopped farming out women to the ships when Jerry turned sixteen. Frowning, Jerry eyed her. There wasn't anything else that she wanted, but she could play this to her advantage. "I want eighty percent."

"Thirty."

"Sixty."

Miriam's lips quirked. "Fifty. Fair's fair, and you know I deal kindly."

"Deal." Jerry stepped forward and stuck her hand out so they could shake on it. Yafe was their witness.

"What's the alternative?" Miriam asked again.

"Brains."

To her credit, Miriam barely moved a muscle, but Jerry saw the twitch in her nose of disgust. Silence permeated the room, and Jerry wondered just exactly what Miriam was going to do with the information.

Finally Yafe stepped forward. "We need one."

"I understand," Miriam answered. She grabbed a small device on her desk an input a few commands into it. "It's done."

"What's done?" Yafe asked—Jerry thankful she didn't have to, though her stomach already sunk with the understanding.

Miriam didn't answer. "Why do you want a ship?"

"To get my ship back."

Miriam shook her head. "You should give up on that old thing."

"You wouldn't understand." Jerry put her hands on her hips, turning sharply when the door opened. The guards who had been with Miriam earlier brought in a young man, crazed from the look of him. They dropped him onto the floor and stepped out of the room.

"Your alternative has arrived."

Jerry kept her mouth shut. She hadn't realized she was going to have to be the one to kill him. She'd hoped one of Miriam's minions would do it. She ran her hand through her hair and rolled her shoulders as the man stood up. Drool slipped out of his mouth and down his chin. His hands were still tied together.

"Who is he?" Jerry asked.

"Dead."

Jerry closed her eyes. Miriam wasn't wrong. He was dead. They all were if they didn't get some kind of drug into their system, and this was going to be the only way to do it. Not to mention, Miriam would want proof that Jerry's alternative worked.

Without thinking, Jerry stomped right up to him and wrapped her forearm around his neck and tightened her grip. She gritted her teeth, pulling tighter and cutting off his airflow. She held him until he stopped fighting her. Cold washed through her, but also the rush that she was about to get exactly what they all needed.

When he fell to the ground, she bent down and put both hands on his face and snapped his neck, ending his life. She didn't wait as she took the knife from her calf and hacked into his head, breaking open his skull in the same way she'd done it to Damon to find their source of life. Getting small chunks out, she held them in her bare hand.

Eating one, she handed another to Yafe and the third to Miriam. Miriam stared at her awkwardly before slowly reaching forward and taking it from her. "Are you sure?"

"Confident."

Miriam put it between her lips and swallowed. "Take the rest. I have more."

"Fifty percent, Miriam. Don't fuck around with me."

"You know I won't."

Jerry finished decapitating her victim and shoved his head into a bag the guards had brought. As soon as she had everything tied so it wouldn't leak all over her, she put it under her jacket and straightened her spine.

"Until next time, Miriam."

"Likewise."

They left. Each step into Raegina and toward the harbor, Jerry felt lighter and better. They'd done what they had to do, as much as Jerry hated it.

CHAPTER 9

he brain was gone by morning, but Jerry knew there'd be more. The crew had devoured it, needing the sustenance to make it through to the next day. Jerry hadn't told anyone where she'd gotten it, but Azar had shared a knowing look with her.

She shuddered as she lay flat on her back in her cot and stared at the ceiling. She needed a ship, and she likely needed one that was bigger than *Yarrow*. Her options seemed to be slim in terms of what she could get without causing too much fuss. Ursula was annoying her, not wanting to leave port to do anything, which meant they weren't making money and Jerry was just losing it by sitting.

A quiet had fallen over the vessel and crew, and Jerry wasn't sure how to deal with it. She'd seen it before, when the virus had first struck, and so many had died in the meantime. She didn't want to end up like them again. With no credits to buy another ship, she was stuck with stealing one. Pressing her lips hard together, Jerry went through the mental list of vessels she knew would be easy to snag, but none of them were quite what she wanted.

Blaise would expect an attack. Probably not from her specifically but from someone. No pirate went out into the seas without thinking someone was looming around a corner ready to take the bounty. That had been Jerry's first and only miscalculation when it came to *Yarrow*. She had relaxed too much in order to celebrate the haul they'd stolen.

She wouldn't make that mistake again.

Jerry rolled onto her side and stared at the far wall. Most of the ships in the harbor would be pegged in an instant as one trying to take Blaise on. She scratched her head, an idea forming, but she wasn't sure she wanted to run with it. Either way, perhaps a bigger problem than finding a ship was finding a crew. She'd need enough to fly two vessels home, *Yarrow* and whichever one she wanted to steal. Perhaps even three if she took *Wench's Dream* and refused to give her back or didn't sink her in the process. Maybe she would even kill Captain Blaise and eat him for dessert to celebrate ruining his plans.

Laughing at her ridiculous thought, Jerry turned onto her back again. She knew she had Azar, Yafe, and Sacha who would go with her. They'd all asked the night before when they were leaving again. They could no doubt feel her restlessness along with the quiet and depressed mood of *Calluna* and her captain.

Jerry was going to have to steal members of Ursula's crew, poach them right off the vessel. Still, they did all technically work for her, so it shouldn't be too much of a problem. Especially since *Calluna* wasn't doing anything. Standing sharply, Jerry pulled down on her tunic and stepped out of her cabin and into the thin corridor.

She took a few steps to Sacha's door and opened it without warning. "Get up. We're having a meeting."

Sacha groaned, but Jerry didn't give her more than two seconds to start moving before she walked to Yafe's and Azar's cabin. Once again, within a couple minutes, they were all seated, staring at each other. Jerry had to lead the conversation on this one.

"I want *Yarrow* back, and I'm going to get her. This is one more chance for you to back out if you want and not come with me on what may be a fruitless mission." She wasn't sure she wanted to look at them, to see their reactions, but she had to.

"Of course, Cap," Azar's deep voice nearly boomed through the room.

"We'll be there," Yafe added.

Jerry glanced at Sacha, who raised an eyebrow at her. Sacha was confident when she said, "I don't understand why you keep asking us if we're with you or not."

"Because I'm not sure we'll make it back to port."

"Ah." Sacha pressed her lips together firmly. "Well, *Yarrow* is the only home I've had since my parents kicked me out, and you are the only family I've had, so I'll go with you. I want her back, too."

"Right." Jerry nodded. That had been far easier than she'd expected—though she probably should have, given the way the conversations had been going since they returned. She knocked her head into the wall and closed her eyes, thinking deeply again about how they were going to get a ship. "We're going to need more crew."

"I'm sure we can hire someone," Sacha added in.

She was so naive about the way the pirating world worked, but Jerry had to hand it to her, she tried. They would hire some new folk, but they would likely take most of their crew from Ursula. Pay dependent on their success. Looking Sacha over, Jerry flicked a glance to Yafe and Azar to see what their opinions were.

"Where will we get a ship?" Azar asked. "And in what condition?"

Jerry shook her head. "I'm working on that one still, but we'll need enough crew to fly two vessels. When we get *Yarrow* back, Azar, I want you to captain the second one."

"Understood." She trusted him, implicitly. She probably should have given him *Calluna* when she bought it, but she enjoyed his company so much that she wanted him nearby.

"Who else?" She knew the implied question was there.

The silence that rang through the cabin was more than she could handle. She stared each one of them down, trying to figure out why they weren't answering. Surely they had to have some idea who they might want to bring with them on this heist on a heist on a heist. Jerry sat up a little straighter, trying to keep her body tension low.

"What are you all not saying?"

Yafe shook her head slowly. "What about Vivian?"

"Vivian?" Jerry looked directly at her. "I'm not sure Ursula will let her go."

"So…" Azar started slowly. "We're not bringing Ursula?"

"No." Jerry furrowed her brow, trying to figure out what he wasn't asking in that question.

Azar kept his eyes on her, those dark eyes drawing Jerry in as if he held all the answers to the world. She wished he did, because she was more confused now than ever about her life. All she knew was she wanted *Yarrow* back and she would go to the ends of Penum to get her. Azar rolled his shoulders and turned to his sister.

"Vivian would be a good choice. Also Cathal."

Jerry squinted at Azar. "Why Cathal? He doesn't seem all that with it, honestly. I need people who are going to move quickly."

Azar's pink tongue touched his full lips right before he answered. "Cathal has a strong back. If we're going to take on a ship where there will be a battle, having him around will be more than helpful. I've seen him win his fair share of bar fights."

Jerry pointed her finger at Azar. "As much as I don't want to know about those, you'll have to talk to me about how he fights."

"Yes, Cap."

Silence filtered through the room. Assuming Vivian and Cathal agreed to transfer to whatever ship Jerry could come up with, that still left them quite short on crew members. She should just take everyone from *Calluna* since they weren't going anywhere, or at least try to convince them. Though she was pretty sure leaving Ursula with a skeleton crew would be a battle in and of itself. At least these people knew how to work together, mostly.

Yafe caught Jerry's attention with a small wave of her hand. "What are you thinking, Cap?"

Jerry flicked her gaze by each of them before landing on Yafe again. She shook her head, not wanting to answer out loud. It would be so easy to take *Calluna* except that she wasn't fast enough or maneuverable enough to take on *Wench's Dream*. Jerry rolled her shoulders and pushed back into the wall she sat against. They needed a ship and a plan more than they needed crew at that moment, but perhaps if she told them they would have connections to ships she could use.

"Cap?" Yafe pushed.

"Answer me this, Azar." Jerry turned on him, giving him a firm look that told him she wouldn't broker with him this time. He had to respond. "Why don't you want Ursula to come along?"

Azar's lips parted in surprise. She was willing to bet he hadn't anticipated that she was going to go back to that conversation. But she wanted an answer. Jerry had her own opinions of Ursula, prior to the virus, when they had been in Joab and since then. Ursula had given her help when she least expected it and always been a friend she could call on, though with that help came expectations and strings Jerry had never been able to anticipate.

Azar sighed, nodding toward Sacha. "Sacha can say more than I can."

"I asked you. I'll ask Sacha next." Jerry held the silence by sliding her thumbnail under each of her other nails, cleaning the dirt that inevitably got caught up there when she worked on ships.

He groaned and rubbed a hand over the back of his head. "She doesn't lead well, Cap."

"What do you mean by that?" Jerry knew she was pushing him, but she wanted answers. *Calluna* was hers, and if she had to force Ursula to step down from her position as captain for the betterment of her business, then she would. Though she didn't have much of a business at the moment because they had no proprietors to give them legal jobs.

"This is a conversation you should have with her," Azar tried to deflect again.

Jerry shook her head and pinned him with an annoyed look. "No, tell me what's going on."

"The crew talks," Sacha butted in. "And they don't talk too kindly about Captain Ursula."

Jerry realized, probably far too late, that Sacha was the first and only person to refer to Ursula by her title, and that should have been Jerry's first major giveaway. Not only did Azar and Yafe not refer to her as that, but Ursula's own crew didn't, which meant there was very little respect for her authority.

"What do they say?"

"They say she's a tyrant one day and the giver of all things the next. They can never predict when she wakes up which version she'll be."

Jerry hummed, her voice so soft she didn't think the others heard her.

"They say she makes them do things...things they don't want to."

Snapping her head up at that, Jerry waited for more of an explanation, but she didn't get one. She wanted to know what they were all thinking because she hadn't seen the dissonance in Ursula's personality.

"Ursula also doesn't do a lot of the work. She makes everyone else do it."

Jerry inwardly shrugged. She wasn't the kind of captain who would make her crew do all the work for her, but she had certainly seen other captains like that out there. If Ursula was one of them, she couldn't completely fault her for it. Jerry pressed her lips together hard. "You're going to have to come up with a lot better than that for me to trust what you're saying."

"She's not a captain, Cap." Azar finally said something, his voice echoing with strain. Yafe reached over and touched his arm lightly to comfort him.

Moving her focus from Sacha to Azar again, Jerry waited. "What does that mean to you?"

"It means her interest isn't in the crew, but rather in her own benefit. She makes the crew do things she would never do, but she's hard on them. She never brings them up or teaches them how to work together. She doesn't have a crew, she has people who are her slaves."

Fuck. That put a lot of what Jerry had been thinking into perspective. She knew what they were saying without saying it, but all three of them had confirmed what Jerry had suspected for a while. She had to get rid of Ursula. It was more a matter of when and how because she couldn't take *Calluna* out to find *Wench's Dream*. She could trade her, though, for something that might be better suited to their needs.

"You can't do that," Yafe interrupted as if she could read Jerry's thoughts.

Startled, Jerry locked gazes with her closest friend. "Why not?"

"This is the only home they have, and if you get rid of it, they'll have nowhere to go. No ship will be able to move as swiftly as you want it to will be able to hold the crew on this vessel."

Damn Yafe for being right. Jerry threw her head back into the wall and closed her eyes, thinking. She had already decided a normal ship wouldn't be to her advantage. She needed to find one they could use as a decoy, something to confuse Blaise into thinking they weren't a threat. Jerry swallowed hard, knowing Yafe was right even if she didn't want to admit it.

"Fine." Standing sharply, Jerry smoothed her hands down her front and eyed each of them. "You figure out the crew."

She left without another explanation. Walking the corridors on *Calluna* with that conversation in mind tainted her view as she went. Crew stopped talking or hushed their voices as she slipped by them. It wasn't unexpected, but she also wondered what they were saying that she needed to hear. She didn't want *Calluna's* crew to suffer because she was too stupid to get rid of a tyrant in charge.

Jerry found Ursula in the wheelhouse, standing at the dash and leaning on the wheel doing absolutely nothing. *Though what the fuck is there to do when you quit the only job you have?* Jerry squared her shoulders as she stepped onto the deck loud enough to catch Ursula's attention.

"How's it going?" Jerry asked, not wanting to wade into the conversation she'd just left yet.

Ursula shook her head. "We're going to need more…brains."

"I know." Jerry nodded and stepped up to the wheel, placing her hands over the smooth and worn wood. She'd never felt *Calluna* was hers. Not like with *Yarrow,* but she supposed at the moment *Calluna* was all she had left, and she should start treating this ship like they were a team as well. "It's got a harder crash on it than the vestigen, so be warned. It'll hit swiftly."

"Duly noted." Ursula pushed her mass of fluffy curls behind her ear. "Can we talk about us?"

"Us?" Jerry frowned, shifting to look at Ursula. They hadn't talked about them in a relationship since Jerry got out of Joab and bought *Yarrow.* What the fuck could Ursula want now?

"We need to find jobs. Do you think Miriam might have anything?"

"I thought you had jobs with her." Jerry raised an eyebrow, wondering just what the hell Ursula had been doing for the last few weeks since they'd been marooned. How much of what she was told had been lies?

Ursula lifted and dropped her shoulder in a shrug. "We had a few."

"Why not more?"

"She...we didn't make it back in time from one so she cut us off."

Jerry knew there had to be more to that story. Miriam had practically raised her, been a second parent when her mother had been working, and she wouldn't so arbitrarily cut them off like that, not without reason. Not to mention, Miriam hadn't said anything since Jerry had been home and they'd seen each other more than usual.

"So, why not try to find more legal work?" Jerry leaned forward on the wheel, gazing out the front of the ship to see the pier.

"I don't own *Calluna*, so no proprietor was willing to work with me."

"Sounds like a bunch of excuses if you ask me." Jerry glared at Ursula and turned around, crossing her arms. "Why did you drop the contract with Mortimer Blair?"

"Salt isn't really my thing."

"Ursula," Jerry's tone was placating, she knew, but she couldn't quite manage to care. "When there's a shortage of jobs and ships and we need credits, you take what fucking jobs are offered. Morty's work was good. He paid on time, he didn't argue, and he's willing to work with women in business, which not a whole lot of proprietors are. The fact that you didn't even think to use that as an excuse tells me there's more to this than you're sharing."

Ursula's face pinched at being called out, but Jerry didn't ease up. If she had to step in and take over, she would, but she really didn't want to. She wanted her sole focus to be on *Wench's Dream* and finding *Yarrow* to bring her home.

"I'll talk to Morty before we leave."

"You're leaving?" Ursula chimed in, probably glad that Jerry wasn't going to push for more answers.

"As soon as I figure out the mess with a ship. You knew that. I want to get *Yarrow* back."

Ursula frowned and stepped in closer, not touching but

hovering her hand over Jerry's arm. She was clearly seeking permission to touch, but Jerry wasn't going to give her that satisfaction. They may have fucked on occasion when Jerry was stupider, but since she'd met Arloa she had very little interest in other women.

"I'm going to be asking some of *Calluna's* crew if they want to join me or stay here. It'll be their choice, and I don't want to hear any arguments from you. Unless I can secure us a contract with Morty again, you're not going to be doing much work anyway."

Ursula pouted. Jerry held back her sigh and stood her ground.

"If you hear about a smaller ship, let me know. I'm interested in using her."

Without another word, Jerry climbed down from the wheelhouse and disappeared into the bowels of the ship. She was going to have to pay far more attention to what Ursula was doing, or perhaps, what she wasn't doing.

CHAPTER 10

Jerry had gotten the message as she sat in the galley with a food packet and a vial of water. She'd immediately jumped up and walked out, much to the bewilderment of everyone else there. She grabbed her jacket and top hat, immediately leaving *Calluna* to head to the government building that sat on the hill in the center of Raegina.

She had been there a time or two before, the last time specifically to see Arloa. Jerry stepped into the government building, bypassing anyone who might be looking to kick her kind out like they had the last time. She swore she heard her name as if in a whisper, and when she looked up, Arloa walked swiftly toward the front doors, gaggles of men surrounding her as she went. Her head was buried in devices as they all spoke to her at once, and she didn't seem as though she had noticed Jerry at all.

Turning on her toes to follow Arloa's path, Jerry waited to see what would happen next. She was there to speak with Arloa Kauket, politician, the one person who had information that she needed in order to get her ship back. Flicking her thumb over her fingers, Jerry was about to step in when Arloa's chin jerked up, their eyes locking.

Arloa shook her head slowly, indicating Jerry shouldn't do anything. That brief second of eye contact lasted forever, and

Arloa mouthed the words, "Follow me" before stepping through the main doors and down the front steps.

It took Jerry longer than she wanted to admit for her brain to catch up with her body and tell it to move. Scurrying through the main doors, she caught sight of Arloa slipping into an electric carriage and the men who had been following her stopping to let her go. She was alone. Jerry's heart raced as she picked up her pace and started to run after the carriage.

How the hell was she supposed to keep up and follow like this?

Whipping into a free carriage, Jerry instructed the artificial intelligence to follow Arloa's carriage. She stuck her head out the small window several times to make sure they were going to the right place. Arloa's carriage came to a halt, and Jerry jumped out after pressing her thumb on the sensor to pay for the ride. Arloa slowly got out of hers but put her hand up to stop Jerry.

They were in front of another government building, one that was of lesser importance than the main building. Arloa slid her gaze from Jerry to the carriage she'd just exited. As Arloa walked away, Jerry stepped into Arloa's carriage and waited.

And waited.

And waited some more.

It was over an hour before Arloa came back, the entire carriage moving to the side from her weight as she stepped onto the stair to enter. As soon as the door was shut, Arloa sighed. She looked so overwhelmed.

"What happened?" Jerry asked, waiting expectantly for a response.

Arloa shifted her gaze to Jerry, worry etched into her face, her eyes with dark circles under them. "Senator Fudala has gone missing. It'll be all over the news accounts in the next twenty minutes."

Jerry's lips parted in surprise. "What do you mean missing?"

"He's gone. He was supposed to have a meeting with

Congress this morning, a special session he called, and he never arrived."

"Arloa…" Jerry trailed off but started again. "Did someone kill him or kidnap him?"

"We don't know anything beyond he's gone at this point. I've been heading off inquiries all morning."

Jerry's heart thrummed. "Are you in danger?"

Arloa shook her head. "I don't think so. I'm certainly not someone who doesn't make my views known, but I have very little power when it comes to actual changes."

Jerry nodded sharply. "I can see that, but you still have to have some concern for your safety."

"I have some information for you." Arloa brushed her hand against her cheek, moving the hair that had fallen over her shoulder. She looked worried, almost, but Jerry couldn't quite place the underlying tone to it. She'd seen Arloa worried before, when she was beaten, and this wasn't that same expression.

"That can wait a minute." Jerry reached over and covered Arloa's hand with hers, lacing their fingers together. It was probably the softest touch she had given her since they'd reconnected. Everything had been rough and heavy since Arloa had found her, fraught with Jerry's own struggles and Arloa's desire for more. That had been how they left the conversation, hadn't it? Frowning, Jerry leaned in and scooted closer, Arloa's skirts moving as they pressed together in the small confines of the carriage.

"It can't wait," Arloa murmured, her voice so quiet, Jerry could barely hear her as the carriage waited for input as to where they were going.

"It can." Following her instinct, Jerry pressed her palm to the side of Arloa's cheek and dragged her face upward so they could look at each other. There was that same flicker of something behind Arloa's gaze—it wasn't entirely fear, but she was definitely trying to mask something. Jerry just couldn't figure it out. Swallowing hard, Jerry brushed her thumb along Arloa's high cheekbones, finding the subtle freckles on her nose and cheeks endearing. "Are you all right?"

"I'll be fine, Jer."

She shuddered. She loved when Arloa called her that. Keeping position, Jerry held her still. "I want to make sure that you are."

"Why do you care? You've made it clear what we are to each other." Arloa could have sounded so angry when she said that. Instead, she was filled with desperation.

Confusion hit her first. Jerry didn't agree because she didn't know what they were to each other. Did they fuck? Yes. Many times over, and it was one of the highlights of Jerry's days since she'd been hit with the virus. Well, even before then if she was honest. Jerry moved her thumb from Arloa's cheekbone to her lips, that full lower lip damp from Arloa's tongue. Jerry was entranced with the way the lines were etched into the skin of Arloa's lips. It hit her hard that she wanted to kiss Arloa, wanted to feel those lines against her mouth. Her stomach fluttered at the thought of leaning in.

Arloa turned out of Jerry's grasp and tilted her chin down to break eye contact. Fear hit Jerry—she couldn't lose Arloa again. "Will you let me kiss you?"

"No," Arloa whispered. "I can barely stand to have you touch me."

Jerry's heart shattered. Shifting, she pressed her forehead into Arloa's shoulder and closed her eyes, drawing in her scent, the one that had carried her through so many days on that island, the one that had centered her for the last year. She breathed Arloa in, letting her soothe her soul for what she was about to say.

"I am not someone you have relationships with, Arloa. I can't even walk into the government building without being stopped for vagrancy." Jerry stayed put, wishing Arloa would touch her. "I'm not someone worthy of you."

Arloa hissed and in a second turned in to Jerry. Gentle

fingers at Jerry's cheek pulled her so they faced each other again, and Arloa's mouth was on hers as she murmured "kiss me." She was so tender in her touches. Arloa consumed her, and Jerry had to admit it. In all the time since they had met, Jerry wanted nothing more than to have her ship and be right here.

"I can't give you want you what." Jerry jerked back and closed her eyes. "I can't do that."

"What I want is you." Arloa's look was steady and firm. "That's all I want."

Jerry had no idea what to say. No one had ever wanted her. She was pretty damn sure her own mother hadn't wanted her, Miriam had seen her as a useful annoyance that she'd kept around, but no one had wanted her like this, with no strings, no expectations. Jerry moved in, pressing their mouths together firmly, with a desperation that wasn't physical for the first time. Jerry was wanted.

When they broke apart, Arloa eyed Jerry carefully. "You need to tell me what we're doing."

"I don't know what we're doing," Jerry whispered.

Arloa sighed and leaned forward to press her thumb against the sensor. "Tour the city."

Jerry's heart sank. She was going to be stuck talking about this until they came to some sort of conclusion, and Jerry had nothing to give. She thought she'd made that clear. Arloa leaned into the small seat they shared and stared straight forward. Jerry was pretty sure she had lost her.

"Captain Blaise Lotchski was seen in the Kigorlia Sea three days ago." Arloa's tone was void of emotion, and Jerry needed to know what happened in the last few seconds to cause the change.

"He could be anywhere by now," Jerry answered, still avoiding what she could of the conversation.

"Except this is the third time he was spotted there in the last week."

Jerry's heart rapped hard. "You said Captain Blaise was seen. Was he on *Wench's Dream*?"

Arloa turned slowly to look at her then, her eyes hardened. "No. He was on *Yarrow*."

The answer was there, and Jerry wanted to take it and run with it. She wanted to fly as fast as she could to find her ship and get her home, steal her back, cleanse her from that man who had taken her. Instead, she stared into Arloa's steel-blue eyes, wanting nothing more than to wrap the small woman in her arms and drag her into her chest.

Giving in, Jerry surged forward and pulled Arloa to her. She gave Arloa feverish kisses, sliding her hands into Arloa's mass of curly hair and tugging when her fingers caught. Arloa whimpered, her voice reverberating straight into Jerry's chest. In the carriage they were confined, but they were also outside of the view of the rest of the world.

Jerry broke the kiss. "I'm no one you want to be with."

"You're exactly who I want," Arloa answered. "You always have been."

"I don't fit into your life."

"I didn't ask you to." Arloa raised her gaze, her look firm and serious. "I didn't ask you to become part of my world. I don't want you to change, Jer. I want you to be mine."

Her heart raced as hope flew into her chest, but she didn't want to give in, worried it was false, that Arloa would take it back, that living separate lives wouldn't be what she ultimately wanted. But then again, Jerry was leaving to get her ship soon. She might not come back, and that would have to be something that they both lived with. Jerry slid down, her knees pressing into the floor of the carriage as they were taken through the heart of Raegina.

"Will you let me?"

"What are we doing?" Arloa whispered as if she was scared to once again voice the question that Jerry wasn't answering.

"I can't guarantee you anything." Jerry slid her hands up and down Arloa's thighs, moving her skirts as she went, but not in a sexual manner, in a comforting one. "I'm a pirate. I live for the thrill of the conquest, and I can't guarantee you I'll come back."

"I'm not asking for you to change your life. I know who you are." Arloa pulled her lip between her teeth as she smoothed her fingers over Jerry's cheek and behind her neck. Leaning down, Arloa swooped in closer as panic welled in Jerry's chest.

"You don't want me."

"I do want you. I don't know how many other ways I can say that." Arloa kissed her delicately before leaning back. She shifted, spreading her legs even more. "I want you against me every night I can have you. I want you to make me feel what no one else has ever accomplished. I want you to be exactly who you are because that is the person I fell in love with."

"Love is a myth for the rich to carry around like an anthem."

Arloa wrinkled her nose. "You don't find love on the sea? I find that hard to believe. You love *Yarrow*."

"*Yarrow* is a ship."

Arloa's eyes lit up as though she'd found an answer to a question she hadn't asked. Jerry realized far too late the mistake she'd made. She fought so hard for *Yarrow*, to go get her, save her, treated her as though *Yarrow* was her first love, which in all likelihood, she was. But Arloa was real, warm, alive under her fingers.

Parting Arloa's knees, Jerry pushed up onto hers and raised up so they were more evenly matched. Arloa's chest rose and fell, her breasts pushing against the dark brown leather of her corset, her creamy white skin unblemished, unlike Jerry's own. Tracing fingers over the edge of the corset, Jerry's mouth went dry, unable to form words.

Arloa finally spoke. "I want you to make me feel what you're scared of."

"What?" Jerry shook her head in confusion.

"Make me feel, Jer."

It was permission to touch. Jerry understood that. Reaching

forward, she unhooked the small belts on Arloa's sides, loosening the corset as she went so it was no longer attached to the beautifully rich maroon skirts. Arloa reached behind her back and tugged on the ties. As much as Jerry wanted to feel Arloa naked against her, she knew she was unlikely to get that wish.

Jerking the corset down, Jerry pulled out Arloa's breasts and pressed delicate kisses all over them. Arloa slid back into the small seat as the carriage rocked while they moved throughout the city. Arloa closed her eyes and parted her lips while Jerry swirled her tongue around each perky nipple. She had wanted to touch Arloa like this since she'd been rescued. She'd wanted to let these soft touches turn into something more, into what they should be.

Arloa hummed and reached between her legs, pressing her fingers hard against herself through her skirts. Jerry moved her hand in, taking over the pattern Arloa had started and rubbing large swipes of her thumb against Arloa's clit. Still the question raged through her mind—could she be what Arloa wanted? She knew she could never be what Arloa needed, but to be wanted was such a strong and powerful call, one she had never experienced before.

Jerry pressed open mouthed kisses over the leather, bending lower to kiss across the tops of Arloa's thighs to her knees. She pushed Arloa's skirts up, revealing inch after inch of skin. Perfect skin that had no marks. Jerry scraped her teeth lightly, waiting for Arloa to tell her what to do next, to give her a command that would push both of them over the edge.

When Arloa said nothing, Jerry continued what she was doing, slightly confused. After another minute or two, she slowed her teasing and moved to sit next to her on the tiny bench again. Arloa cupped the side of Jerry's face and brought their mouths together before shifting to sit in Jerry's lap, her back pressed to Jerry's front.

"I want you to touch me like you touch yourself."

"Arloa," Jerry murmured into the back of Arloa's shoulder, a small protest as she pulled up Arloa's skirts. She would do anything so long as Arloa commanded her to. "I can't get enough of you."

Arloa curled her legs around the outside of Jerry's, using her feet to hold herself in place. Jerry smoothed her hand down the front of Arloa's undergarments, finding her clit swollen and her lower lips slick, as if she had been waiting for this moment.

"I want you," Arloa whispered. "I want no one but you, Jer."

Jerry said nothing in response, needing to keep those words in her heart and learn to trust them. She needed to know that Arloa wasn't lying, that perhaps there was genuine love to be found between them, or at least that Arloa loved her. She slid one finger inside Arloa's warm body, curling it upward as she started the same slow swipe with her thumb as she did before, only this time, with nothing between them.

Arloa sighed heavily, her head dropping back onto Jerry's shoulder. "I want you to find Blaise."

"Why?" Jerry asked as she continued the same pattern. "It would mean me leaving."

"Yes." Arloa whimpered as her hips moved in time with Jerry's hand. "But it would mean you finding your home again, which is something you need."

Jerry's heart hammered. She loved pleasuring this woman, she loved talking with her, she loved being with her in any capacity—even if they weren't fucking. Arloa knew what she wanted, and that was something Jerry had pegged from the beginning. Arloa was strong-willed, and she would do anything to get what she wanted with very little expectations of Jerry herself.

"But you need me."

"I do." Arloa moaned, clasping her hand around the back of Jerry's head to hold herself in position. "But I need you to want me just as much."

That was it, wasn't it? Jerry needed to know if she needed or wanted Arloa and in what capacity. They used each other for information, for doing odd jobs, but was it more than that? It had been at one point. When they'd first met, Jerry hadn't wanted to need Arloa in that capacity. In fact, she had resisted it. Yet here she was, with her fingers deep inside this woman she couldn't get enough of.

"I dreamed of you on that island," Jerry confessed. "I dreamed of what I would do to you if I saw you again."

"When you saw me."

"Yes."

Arloa's breathing increased, her nipples hard little points that Jerry wished were still in her mouth. Jerry increased her speed, firmed up her swipes to heighten the friction. She needed Arloa to come apart on top of her, again and again and again.

"I wanted to come home to you."

That was Arloa's undoing. She tightened sharply, pleasure searing through her, and Jerry got to watch it all. The beautiful tightening of her face, the grip of her hands against Jerry's wrist, her entire body at Jerry's command. Jerry had never thought about it like that before. They both commanded. Arloa with words, as she often did in the government, and Jerry with her crew.

Sliding her hand from Arloa, Jerry licked her fingers and savored the flavor. She sighed and pressed her forehead into the back of Arloa's shoulder. "I want to come home to you again."

"Then do that, Jer. Because I'll be here waiting."

Arloa slid off Jerry's lap and hunched over as she stood awkwardly, trying to fix her skirts and corset. Jerry just sat back and watched, her own clit humming and begging for touch. She wasn't sure she wanted to ask though. She wasn't sure she could handle it after what they had just confessed.

When Arloa sat next to her, offering her back, Jerry pulled the laces of the corset to tie her up again. She dropped kisses as she quickly put Arloa together again so she could return to finish out her day. As soon as she was dressed, Arloa leaned forward and told the artificial intelligence to take them to the government building. Jerry sighed and was surprised when Arloa clasped their fingers together.

"My work is going to become busy with the senator missing."

"I imagine." Jerry wanted to say that she was worried, that she didn't want Arloa to be a victim to whoever was doing this, but she didn't even know if Arloa was a target or if this was a one-time thing for one particular person. Also, it would be too much of a confession for Jerry's heart to handle. "I don't know when you'll see me again."

"I realize you're not one for making promises you can't keep, Jer, but do promise me this."

Jerry looked into Arloa's steel-blue eyes, seeing so much in them and scared to put words to those feelings.

"When you come home, come home to me."

Jerry found herself nodding before she could think about it. Arloa's lips curled up into a smile and she leaned in to kiss Jerry one more time.

"I'll see you when you return."

One last kiss, and Arloa stepped out of the carriage as it stopped in front of the government building. Jerry slipped out a full minute later, walking straight back to the harbor.

CHAPTER 11

Jerry stood in *Calluna's* wheelhouse, readying her systems to go out for the day. She hadn't even asked Ursula or told her what she was doing, and she figured as soon as the engines started full force, Ursula would make her way topside to see what the fuck she was doing.

But Jerry was tired of sitting around doing nothing. Rolling her shoulders, she pushed the necessary buttons and pulled back on the throttle to reverse out of the slip. The conversation with Arloa that morning plagued her. She couldn't get it out of her mind, not only the fact that she'd once again been taunted with information she wanted and needed to meet with Arloa in person, but the fact that someone might actually want her.

What would have been between them if the virus hadn't happened? Jerry doubted they'd have stayed together, but the fling they had begun then had only just started, and Jerry had been so afraid she would give Arloa the virus that she'd made the cruel decision to leave her the hell alone.

Azar climbed the ladder, his heavy boots echoing on the wood planks as he walked up to her. "Where are we going, Cap?"

"To find us a damn ship," Jerry muttered through gritted

teeth. She wasn't mad at him. She was mad at herself for not being able to adequately figure out what the hell the conversation had been earlier that day or the last time Arloa had begun it. Jerry had no idea what to say either time, but this time, she at least understood more of what Arloa was expressing.

Still, she didn't see how any of it would work.

She wasn't someone people wanted. Jerry rolled her shoulders as she gently took *Calluna* out into the harbor and away from the pier. She had spent the last few hours formulating a quick plan. All they had to do was go out to see, find a ship that would suit their needs, and steal it. It was going to be the best option they had. She wanted *Yarrow* back, and to do that, she needed a ship that could function in the way she needed it to. She could always give it back if she had to.

"Cap?"

"Yes?" Jerry faced Azar, worried she had missed something.

His gaze on her was quiet and serene, as if he could read the inner turmoil she was going through, which she supposed he might very well be able to. He knew her well enough by that point, but it unnerved her at the same time. Jerry had prided herself for years on being a lone pirate, someone no one knew everything about—not even Miriam.

"Where are we going?"

"To steal us a ship, I told you that." She wrinkled her nose, turning *Calluna* so they were facing the open sea and no longer dodging other ships in flight.

Azar clicked his tongue and took up the second wheel to help Jerry maneuver out of the harbor. "So what's the plan?"

"Find something suitable. Steal it."

Azar turned and raised one bushy eyebrow in her direction. She knew she was doomed and that he had her pegged for lack of planning, which was so unlike her. She never went into anything without weighing all the possibilities and typically asking him and the others their opinions. But this time, she'd just taken control and gone with it.

"Ursula?"

"Belowdecks, I suppose." Jerry looked out the front window, staring at the sea. It felt so good to back on the waters, flying above them, ready for something other than sitting in port and doing absolutely nothing. She couldn't fathom how she'd managed the last weeks without it, honestly. The sea had been her life for so long that she couldn't live without it.

Yafe and Sacha joined them next, leaning against the dash to look out. They each had wide eyes as they kept their silence, and Jerry suspected it was the same for them. They lived by the ocean, waters they could never touch, but waters that gave them so much life, love, and passion. Finally, as soon as they were well out of the harbor, Yafe stepped back and said, "It's about time, Cap."

"What is?" Jerry fired back.

"You taking control of her."

Jerry shook her head. "That's not what I'm doing. I'm going to get *Yarrow* back."

"Someone needs to be here," Yafe murmured, always willing to say more than Azar would when it came to the interpersonal relationships of the crews. "Ursula needs the help."

"I need help?"

They all shifted to look over their shoulders or spin around, finding the redhead glaring at them.

"Were you going to tell me you were stealing *my* ship?"

"She's mine," Jerry responded, straightening her back and looking Ursula up and down. "And from what I've seen of you lately, you're not fit to be her captain."

Ursula snorted. "You don't know what it's been like this past month."

"I know you haven't tried." Jerry crossed her arms. She was vying for a fight, and she was going to bring herself right into one, whether it was with Ursula or a ship she wanted to steal. She needed to release the emotions pent up from the conversation with Arloa. She needed to do something.

"That's shit," Urulsa spat, coming in closer.

"Captain?" Azar's voice echoed through the wheelhouse.

"Yes?" Both Jerry and Ursula responded at the same time.

Azar looked at them both but focused on Jerry. "There's a ship coming in."

"Perfect. One we want?" Jerry was already walking toward the dash to read through the sensors they had even before he answered. Her mind was now completely focused on what they were there for and not on Ursula and her problems.

"Looks like it, Cap."

The nickname had a bit of force to it this time, and Jerry could tell he was as annoyed with Ursula as she was. But while she didn't have a ship to run herself, and she owned *Calluna*, it was her prerogative to do whatever she wanted with the vessel they were on.

Jerry sped *Calluna* up, pushing her to the max so they could head off the incoming vessel. They were still in Raegina's waters, and she would much prefer to be out of them before trying to steal a ship, but she would have to take the chance the authorities wouldn't find them. They were in completely open water, with no islands or shore to drive them up on.

They would need to find a way to corner it somewhere, and that would likely mean giving chase. Jerry squared her shoulders and pushed the engines harder. Vibrations shook through the ship, ricocheting up through her boots and into her legs. She felt them in her hands against the wheel as she steered, right along with Azar as they would if they were flying *Yarrow*. Fuck she missed that ship.

She needed her home back.

Urusla pushed between them, leaning against the dash to see out the front, as if that would tell her exactly where the other vessel was. It wasn't within range for them to see it yet, but they would come up on it quickly since the other ship was coming their direction.

"Azar, remember that run-in we had when we were on our way to Crasmere?"

"The time with the cargo vessel or the one with the dart?"

"The dart," Jerry confirmed. "You remember the tactic?"

"Like it was yesterday." Azar had a glint in his eye, the excitement of doing something finally catching up with them.

Jerry grinned at him. Ursula turned on her. "What are you doing with *my* ship?"

"Watch and see." Jerry grabbed the communicator and called out to the rest of the crew. "Battle ready, now!"

Jerry waited to see what would happen, though she suspected the crew wouldn't know much of what to do. They hadn't been properly trained from what she could tell. Jerry glanced at Sacha and Yafe. "Will you two go check?"

"Check what?" Ursula screeched, but Yafe and Sacha were already dipping belowdecks as they had been told.

Jerry shook her head. "To make sure you have properly trained your crew on what to do. If we want to steal a ship, then we need to work together as a team."

"They're *my* team, not yours."

"I don't think they're yours, either." Jerry mouthed off. "Shut up and let us work."

Azar turned them starboard. Jerry set the cannons ready to fire, only to realize they had none in reserves. She would argue with Ursula on that one later. For now, she needed a backup plan that still might net them something. They moved into place, where the other vessel would run directly into them, and she put *Calluna* down, keeping her hovering just over the water.

Jerry's heart pattered hard as she faced Azar with wide eyes. "Get a weapon. We're going to have to do this the old-fashioned way."

"What?"

"There's no cannons."

"Shit," he mumbled as he spun on his toes to do as he was told.

Jerry worked fast, ignoring Ursula hovering over her shoulder. She and Azar raced through the wheelhouse as they prepared and played dead in the water. Yafe's sweet voice came over the communications.

"Uh…Cap? They don't know what they're doing."

Jerry raced over and slapped her hand down on the dash. "No cannons. We're on to the back-up plan. Get everyone up here so we can play hide-and-seek."

Yafe didn't answer, but Jerry trusted that she understood what was happening and would do exactly as she had asked. That was what a good crew should do, one that worked together, one that lived together, one that stole and thrived together. Jerry sent Ursula a quick glare over her shoulder as she slid a pistol into the holster at her hip.

"There's no bullets," Ursula murmured quietly, as if she was finally recognizing the problems they were about to face.

"What?" Jerry's eyes went wide. She hated using weapons if she didn't have to, especially guns, but to not even have that as an option to defend herself was another story.

Ursula pursed her lips together and raised her chin defiantly. "I sold the ammunition for credits to purchase vestigen."

Jerry stared at her in awe. That should have been something discussed prior to their leaving, but Jerry had been in a rush, and Ursula had been less than forthcoming about what happened while Jerry and the others had been marooned. They were going into an ambush with nothing on their side except excitement, anticipation, and perhaps numbers.

"We're going to get back to harbor and have a serious talk about this." Jerry pointed a finger at Ursula and stepped her way out of the wheelhouse and onto the open deck. Azar followed her. The ship was coming right for them, and she could finally see it if she raised her hand over her eyes to shield the sun and squinted.

"Not much longer now, Cap," Azar stated.

"No, not much longer." The excitement and anticipation that

she'd had when they first saw the ship came surging back, and Jerry could barely contain herself to take action. The rest of the crew filtered out and onto the deck slowly. Yafe instructed them to crouch close to the wheelhouse or right along the edge of the ship and behind the wall to stay hidden.

If they were going to play dead, they didn't need anyone revealing their numbers. Jerry was already working through plans to train up this crew. She wasn't going to want to take anyone with her who didn't know what they were doing or had a sense of belonging and family among them. They weren't a charity house. The crew was expected to work.

The ship came closer, and Jerry held as still as possible. She nodded to Yafe who went into the wheelhouse, no doubt to put out the call for assistance so the other vessel would stop to help them. They shouldn't be marked as a pirating vessel since the ship was legally owned and operated—well, it used to be operated.

Jerry swallowed hard as she waited to see what was going to happen. Yafe stayed in the wheelhouse while she and Azar stood outside and watched. The ship was in clear view now. It was a sleek small vessel that could probably carry about twenty crew regularly. She had hoped it was slightly smaller, but this would have to do for now.

Clenching her fists, Jerry said, "Think she'll do?"

"Do we have another choice?"

They didn't. They both knew it. She had information on Blaise's whereabouts that week, which mean they would have to get to him swiftly before he moved again. Pirates rarely stayed in one place for long. Jerry had managed to avoid that issue since she also ran a legal business from both her ships, although Ursula had fucked that plan up royally. Finding those connections was not what Jerry wanted to focus on. At least they would have some income from Miriam and the new market she had created.

"Cap, they're coming," Azar stated firmly, drawing Jerry's attention back to the problem at hand.

They were close enough to potentially see Jerry and Azar should they step out of the wheelhouse. Jerry raised her hands and wildly moved them, trying to get their attention and state without speaking that they really did need help.

The ship slowed, but it was still coming in so fast. Jerry's stomach tightened, her gut telling her that they weren't going to stop. She stayed put for another thirty seconds before cursing and racing toward the wheelhouse. She shouted orders as she went.

"Stay down. Azar!"

Jerry thrust her hand out to wrench open the door to the wheelhouse, but by the time she got to the dash and the wheel to hit the thruster, the ship was already turning and speeding around them. *How the fuck had they been made?*

She hit the thruster hard just as Azar slid into place behind the second wheel. Yafe stepped back to give them the space to fly as they needed. Jerry didn't bother with maneuvering as she flew as fast and straight as possible to make up some of the distance, but it was next to impossible. She knew they wouldn't be able to catch up. *Calluna* didn't have the thruster power to manage it.

They sputtered behind the other ship. Jerry slammed her palm against the wheel. "Fuck!"

Ursula unwisely stepped forward, her hands on her hips and moving her skirts to reveal her thick thigh. "I told you we've been struggling."

"Don't start with me." Jerry pointed a finger directly at her. "This crew is untrained. This crew is nothing more than a fucking charity case, and you are nothing better than a head on a platter. You've done nothing to train them, teach them, and the only reason this ship is still here today is because you still had funds—my credits mind you—to live off freely."

Sacha stepped inside, her eyes widening at the tension she

found. Jerry didn't even give her a full look as she pinned Ursula with the entirety of her fury.

"You aren't worthy of the title captain. You're not worth anything to me anymore. I should throw you off this damn ship right here and now."

Ursula's lips parted as if she was going to say something, but Jerry held up her hand to silence her.

"I don't want to hear anything from you. If I so much as hear one fucking word out of your mouth, I will likely do something I might regret. *Might*, because at this moment, I'm pretty sure it'd feel damn good to watch you sink into the waters."

Yafe stepped forward as if she was going to stop Jerry from doing just that, but Jerry jerked around and out of Yafe's reach. She was beyond angry. Ursula's lack of everything had put them in jeopardy and now Jerry had even less hope that they'd be able to get a ship in time to find *Yarrow* and get back on their feet.

"You're dismissed," Jerry spat. "Get the fuck out of *my* wheelhouse before I take action you'll regret."

Ursula was stunned. She stood there for a few seconds, likely debating what to even say, but eventually, she turned and climbed the ladder down to the lower decks. Jerry spun on her toes, put her hands on her hips, and stared out at the water as they flew toward Raegina. She eased up on the thruster to take them back to regular speeds so they wouldn't overburden the engines.

"Azar, when we reach the slip, I want a full evaluation of *Calluna*. Everything that's wrong with her, I want to know about it. Use whatever crew you have to in order to get it done tonight. Yafe and Sacha, you evaluate the crew. Tell me what the fuck they can do. I'm sick of knowing what they can't."

Silence was her only answer, but she knew they had heard her, and she knew she was asking a lot of them but what had just happened was embarrassing.

"You two can start now. Don't let them in unless they can tell you who the captain of this ship is."

"Yes, Cap," Sacha and Yafe stated together.

As soon as they were out the door and topside, Jerry slapped the wheel hard, the shock of pain reverberating up through her arm and into her shoulder from how hard she had hit it.

"Fuck."

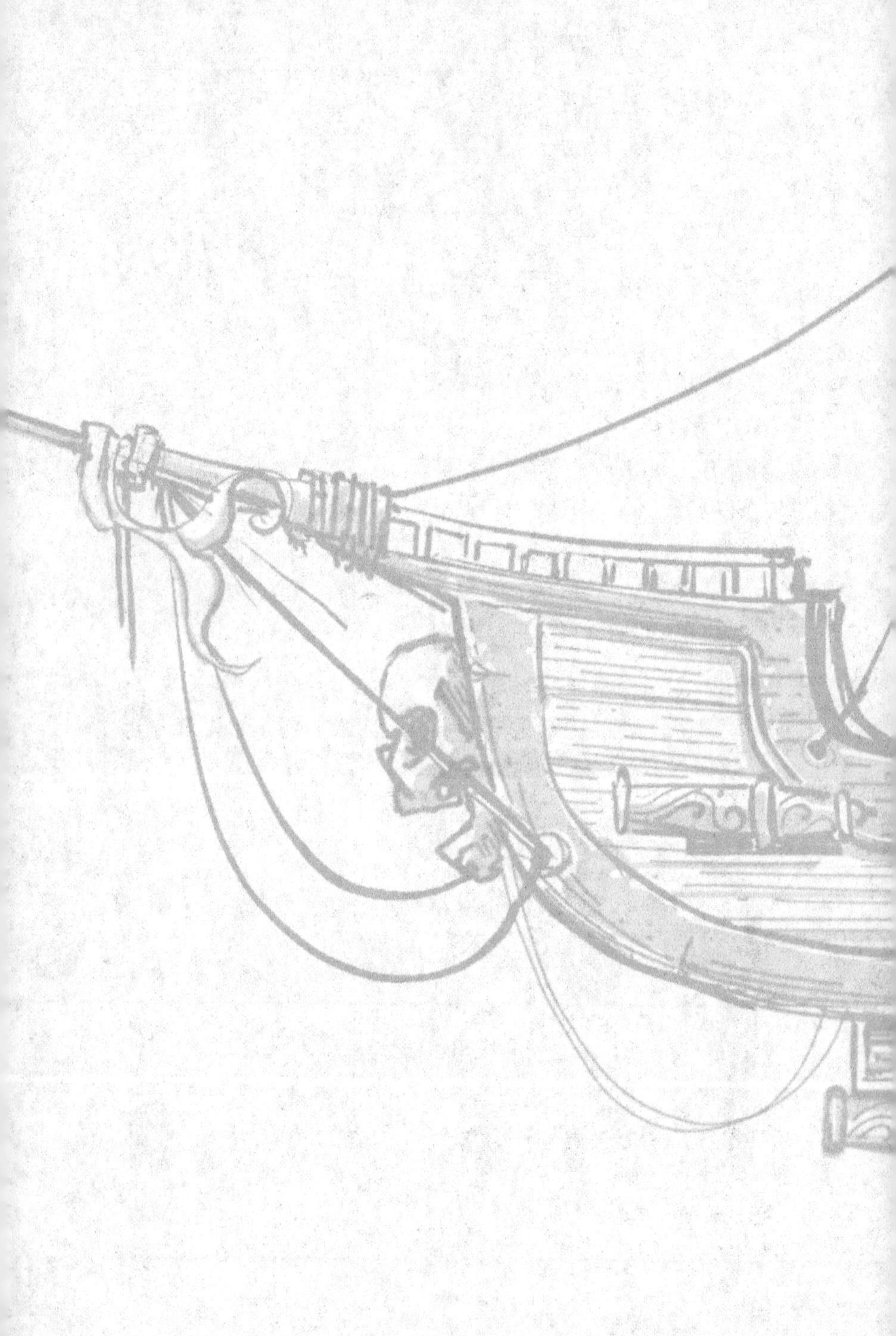

CHAPTER 12

They limped into port, Jerry ducking her head for their flight of shame. It had been stupid of her to try and hijack someone in Raegina's seas. The authorities could come after her any second, and everything she had long fought for would be at risk. Rolling her shoulders and her neck, Jerry settled *Calluna* into their silo and let out a sigh.

Everyone had abandoned her in the wheelhouse, so she could lick her wounds in solace. Yafe had stopped by once, telling her that Ursula had been hiding out in her cabin the rest of the flight home. Jerry had snorted but had thought *good*. She didn't have the brainpower to deal with that disaster yet.

Once *Calluna* was settled, Jerry stepped away from the dash, a sense of dread in her stomach. She had calmed considerably since they trudged back to port, but she still couldn't help but realize that she would have managed to stay much calmer, plan better, if only her brain had been working the way it used to. She hated that she couldn't even begin to think like she used to.

No matter how much they had searched for a cure, all they had found were stopgaps. There was no way to fix the virus. She was doomed to live with the pain that was this craving every second of her life for the rest of her life. Stepping onto the top rung of the ladder, Jerry took her time going belowdecks until she found herself standing in front of the captain's cabin. She almost went inside, but at the last minute, she stopped.

She wasn't able to deal with anyone yet. Not in any fashion that would allow her crew to stay alive should she get ahold of them. Bypassing Ursula's cabin, Jerry made her way to the galley, finding her main crew—the only people she trusted perhaps—and waving them into the hall.

"I want you to start everything we talked about, immediately. I won't stand for what happened today to repeat itself."

"Aye, Cap."

"I'm going to be out. I'll be back with more *medicine* and hopefully a plan to figure this mess out."

Yafe looked as though she was going to protest, but Jerry just shook her head. She didn't have time for it. Jerry stalked out of the corridor, down a level, and to her own cabin. She grabbed her jacket and discarded most of her weapons—not all, because she never left without all, but if the authorities were to find her with a gun, she would be sent straight back to Joab before she could speak one word of defense.

Jerry didn't even bother to check herself in the mirror in her small washroom. She knew she looked like shit. From that morning in the carriage, to the windblown disaster of an attempted steal, to her anger at the entire situation, there was nothing that would make her look good.

Her first stop as she traversed the cobblestone streets was to the proprietor's building, where Mortimer Blair held offices. She'd been there so many times throughout the last year, that she practically had it memorized. Her plan of staying dead was all going to be damned to hell because her people needed to eat and she needed the papers to prove she had legal business in Raegina in order to cover for pirating.

Swinging through the door, Jerry narrowed her gaze as she looked around. There were far less proprietors than the last time she had been. The new phase of the virus must be hitting harder than she'd thought, though she hadn't paid any attention to the news information being broadcast. Not that it was reliable.

The small desk that sat at the center was usually her first stop, but it was completely empty. Jerry brushed aside the idiotic idea that perhaps Ursula could take over working there just to get off *Calluna*—and no longer captain any ship that she would no doubt run aground.

"Jeraldine?" Morty's usually boisterous voice had a hint of surprise to it.

Jerry swung around, finding him in the entrance to the hall that would lead to small rooms they could do private business in. Jerry softened her gaze, needing his help more than to piss him off. She bowed her head slightly in a sign of respect for his position over hers. "The one and the only."

"I thought you were dead."

"So did I." Jerry walked in closer, but he stepped back as if he was afraid of her. She cocked her head to the side in a question.

"Do you have the new strain?"

"No, sir. I've been marooned on an island for the last two months." That little fib wouldn't kill her. "I didn't even know about the new strain until I returned."

Morty's puffy cheeks relaxed, and he jerked his head up at her. "You're lucky then."

"Seems it." Jerry kept her hands at her sides. "I've been informed by my colleague that she reneged on the contract we had discussed."

Morty's eyes darted around the room, and with the jerk of his head toward the back rooms, Jerry followed him. He was a short pudgy man, well-off, and more often than not he wanted to have a personal hand in his dealings, which was why it was rare that Jerry didn't find him at the office. She preferred dealing with him straight to dealing with one of his lackeys.

As soon as the door closed to the small room, Jerry leaned over the table. "I apologize for anything she did without my express permission. I would not have squandered our contract had I been here."

"But you weren't here," Morty stated, his words harsh.

"Not by choice. I took a secondary job to Potelia, and on my way back, we were hit by a band of pirates on *Wench's Dream*."

Morty's nose turned up at that, and she knew that instant that he had heard of that particular ship. She was curious what he knew of it but wasn't sure yet she wanted to press.

"They left me and my crew marooned on a small island. It was only by luck that we were discovered by a medical vessel. He still has *Yarrow*."

"I know of Captain Blaise Lotchski," Morty started, anger lacing his words. "I've dealt with him many times throughout the years. My condolences to your lost ship."

"I have one remaining vessel," Jerry started. "And she is more than capable of handling the contract we previously had, if it is still an open contract for the taking."

"Salt is not in as high demand anymore."

Jerry frowned. She knew it wasn't. With the massive death of people, the government had resorted to throwing them into the oceans instead of burying them, fearing the virus would still live on after death. While there had first been an uptick in the prices, they had sunk shortly thereafter.

"I can only give you half of what we previously agreed upon."

She didn't want to agree to that, but what other choice did she have? Legal work was so hard to come by with captains vying for the same jobs, and equally with the prices on everything plummeting. Jerry hadn't been able to take a good surveillance of what was viable and what wasn't. She had been out of the loop and so focused on surviving and finding her next fix of vestigen that she had little option for anything else. And no one wanted to hire an ex-convict.

"Deal." They shook on it. "But I'm also in need of a secondary ship. Would you happen to know of any for purchase? I'm looking for something small, to rival *Yarrow* since she's no longer in my possession."

She would die before she told him what her plans were with the new ship. Morty raised an eyebrow at her, folding his hands over his potbelly that had definitely lost roundness. She wondered if it was from stress or from the lack of credits to pay for his previously lavish diet.

"I do have a small vessel in my possession I would sell to you —and only you," he added at the last minute.

Jerry understood what he meant. He didn't want Ursula to be flying his ship, a sentiment she very much agreed with. "How much are we talking?"

"Thirty thousand five hundred."

Cold washed through Jerry. She'd had time to look at the store of credits she'd managed to keep for the ships business when she left, and Ursula had burned through most of it to keep herself afloat. Jerry shook her head slowly at him, glancing at her boots under the hem of her pants. "I'll have to live without, I'm afraid."

Even what she earned from Miriam's newest line of business in the underground wasn't going to sufficiently fill that gap fast enough to catch Blaise while she was ahead.

"When would you like the first shipment of salt?" Jerry changed topics.

"Three days."

Jerry nodded sharply. "We can do that."

They spent an hour drawing up the contract and signing it. Jerry knew she wasn't ready to enter back into that partnership, but she had no other choice. Her crew had to eat. She needed fuel for the one ship she still had, and she would need the business to keep her mind off the fact she wasn't sure she'd ever get *Yarrow* back in her possession.

The walk away from Mortimer's offices at least had lifted her spirits slightly. Dusk fell, and she knew she was hitting the perfect time to find Miriam in a decent mood. It had only been a few days since she'd seen her last, but Jerry could already tell that her crew were struggling to keep up with the change in their prescribed sanity.

She also wanted to check in and see how much Miriam owed her. Jerry rubbed a knot in the back of her neck as she walked down into the cellar and took the stairs two at a time up to Miriam's new hideout. She wasn't fan of it, much preferring the dank basement of the bar much closer to the pier—and fewer stairs. It was really all about having to climb so many damn stairs.

As Jerry entered Miriam's small hidey-hole, she let out a breath and shook her head. "Fucking stairs."

Miriam snorted but kept her head down in whatever she was working on. "This new line of business is slow to take off."

"I thought it might be."

"If it's the only way to survive, one would think they would be open to the how."

Jerry grunted and put her hands on her hips as she straightened her back. "We have been taught, morally, *do not harm* from the day we were born, Miriam. It's ingrained in our society that we must rely on each other's aliveness in order to survive. The idea that we must kill, harm, end a person's life, in order to live is counterintuitive to what we have been taught. That is not an ethical boundary many are willing to cross easily."

"They will." Miriam's voice was calm, but Jerry knew she was right. As people became more desperate, the sale of brains would pick up, and Jerry would be a rich woman. Rich from the death and destruction of others. Not the way she had thought she'd go out. She could only imagine what they would do to farm out those who needed to die for others to survive.

"How many credits?"

"Not many. Here." Miriam slid a small device over for Jerry to glance at it.

Miriam had only managed to clinch the sale for three brains. Where those brains had come from, Jerry had no idea, but her stomach clenched at the thought that someone had died—most likely unwillingly—in order to provide life. Her life, which wasn't worth much of anything was one of those.

"I need another one."

Miriam frowned and finally looked up. She had aged in the last week, well really, the last few months since Jerry had seen her. She hadn't noticed it before, but the lines around her eyes and mouth were deeper than they had been before. Jerry held her gaze.

"You have a large crew."

"I do, and I have plans in place to take them out, so we need enough to get by."

"You're asking for a lot."

"That's nothing new."

Miriam quirked an eyebrow at that. "Do you want your discount?"

Jerry's stomach twisted at the thought. Using sex to get what she wanted was something her mother had taught her from a young age. Hell, Miriam had taught them both that lesson, and Jerry had willingly given in to Miriam's requests to get her off in order to have a cheaper cost to herself.

Yet with the conversation with Arloa lingering in her mind, she wasn't sure she could do it. Arloa wanted her, not for this, not to get off and provide a service to each other but for so much more than that. Arloa had willingly given her the information about *Wench's Dream* without asking for anything in return. In fact, that had been the case with just about every piece of information or connection Arloa had given her.

Jerry's lower lip quivered as she debated what to say, how to get out of it. Miriam let out a wry chuckle as she leaned back in her chair, putting one booted foot up on the edge of her desk, her skirts sliding down, nearly revealing what was between her legs. Jerry's stomach was still in knots as Miriam slowly shook her head back and forth.

"Gone and found yourself love, have you?"

"Hardly," Jerry answered. "But a regular fuck is hardly anything you can fault me for."

"And I don't," Miriam answered. "Your mother found one of those once."

Jerry knew where Miriam was going with this. The regular fuck had been Jerry's father, someone she had never met because as soon as her existence had been revealed, he'd gone racing the other direction.

"He was a handsome fellow. Looked just like you."

Jerry hated when Miriam went on this rant, so she stood quietly by, waiting to see how much two brains was going to cost her and if the three they had managed to sell was going to be enough to cover the costs. Two should last her crew long enough, should it? She would hate to take captives solely for the purpose of killing them on a longer journey.

"He paid handsomely, too."

This was the connection Jerry had been waiting for. "And what will it cost me for two?"

"For you, love, I think what you've already put in should pay for it."

"Sure." Jerry dropped the device back onto the desk. "Where are they?"

Jerry followed Miriam down the flights of stairs until they reached the cellar door. Jerry hadn't known what she expected, but it was more than to be handed a burlap bag at the entrance. She stared at it before untying the top and opening it. The scent of blood hit her first, and she knew instantly what was in there. She swore she saw two and instantly closed it up again, not wanting to stare too long.

"Thanks for this." Jerry bowed her head.

"Come back when you need more." Miriam leaned salaciously against the wall, no doubt trying to test Jerry's resolve to not take the deal on a discount.

"I'll see you soon," Jerry answered, ducking her head as she climbed out. She didn't want to be there any longer than necessary. She needed Miriam in order to survive, but that didn't mean she had to like that fact. Her walk back to *Calluna* was swift, and when she reached the vessel, she was glad to see Yafe was running drills with the crew and getting them into shape.

She would check in with Azar before the night was over to see how much damage there was. At least she had a contract that would bring in credits again, even if it was less than before. It seemed no matter how much she tried to get ahead, she was only ever sliding backward. Tossing the goods she'd gotten from Miriam into the galley and locking them down in the cold storage, she went to find Azar and Yafe to get a well-rounded picture for when she had to talk to Ursula.

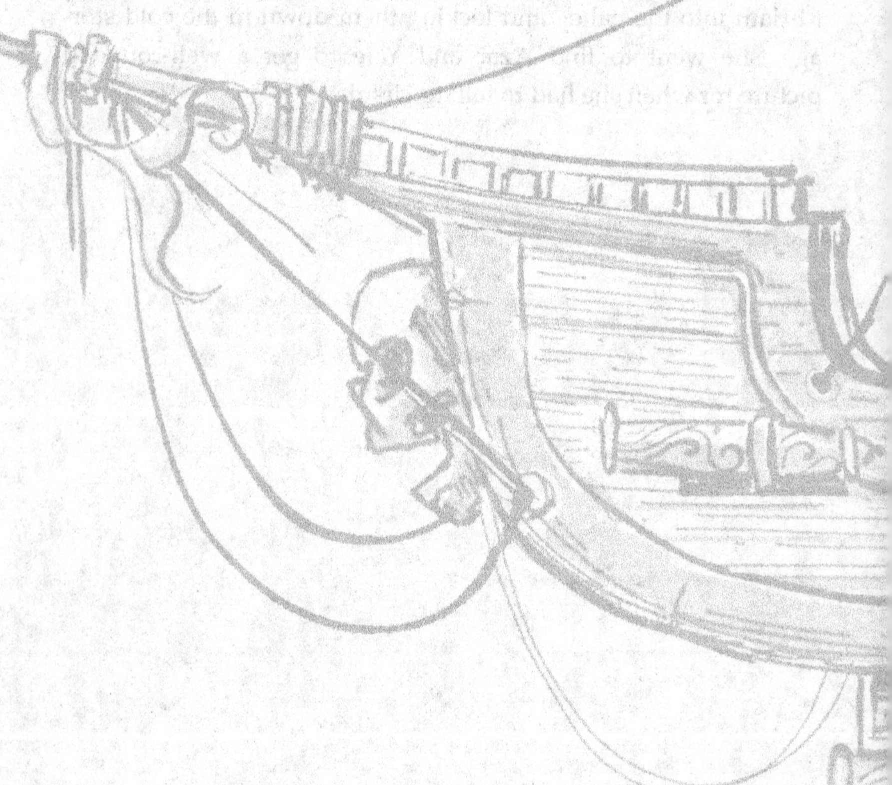

CHAPTER 13

They stood topside, staring at Raegina's harbor. Jerry had told Ursula to meet her up there, and yet once they were in the same vicinity, waiting for the inevitable to happen, Jerry wasn't quite sure where to begin. She leaned against the railing and held herself up so she could maintain eye contact in the distance.

"Are you going to give me the boot?"

"I haven't decided yet," Jerry responded, glad to see Ursula understood how serious this was. "I didn't expect to come back and find this. Yafe's been poring over the financials, and you started this before we were marooned. Did you think I wouldn't notice?"

"I didn't think it would matter."

At least it was an honest answer. Jerry still didn't want to look at her. Sighing, Jerry straightened her back and crossed her arms over her chest. "You squandered *all* the funds."

"I know," Ursula murmured. "I didn't have a choice."

"I can tell you if you do stay on my crew that you won't have access to those funds any longer. I'm half tempted to just give you the boot to make my life easier." Management was the part of this job that Jerry hadn't been thrilled about. When it was her and the crew from *Yarrow* it was so easy, and she barely had to worry about anything, but buying the second ship and putting Ursula in charge had been her undoing.

"Understandable. I'm sorry, Cap. Really I am."

That was the first apology Ursula had given her for this particular blunder, and Jerry took it to heart. She at least sounded remorseful. The problem with the virus was that it made humanity impulsive, so when they were low on vestigen, things tended to get tricky. Maintaining and controlling themselves was difficult, but add in the hormone deficiency and they were all as good as lost from the start.

"I want you to work with Yafe on training the crew today. I'm tired of not having people do anything and not knowing what they should be doing. You've done a shit job at that."

"Aye, Cap."

Jerry pursed her lips. "Azar discovered some issues with the engines, which we nearly killed yesterday. He's pulling a few of the crew to help him work on those, and there is a crack in the hull."

Ursula's eyes went wide. Jerry had figured she hadn't known that one, but it would easily explain why the ship wasn't flying well to begin with and why their fuel had leaked massively as they tried to steal a ship they were ill-equipped to.

"So I'm not getting the boot."

"Not for now." Jerry clenched her jaw, still not sure that was the right decision, but she didn't have anyone to replace Ursula yet. "But you're no longer captain while I'm on board and perhaps even after I leave."

"You're leaving?"

Jerry raised an eyebrow at her. "Yes. I'm going to get *Yarrow* back."

"Are you sure that's wise, Cap? I mean, we have *Calluna*."

"Which can barely make the run tomorrow to Beren Island for salt." Jerry put her hands on her hips. "I got the contract back, Ursula, and I plan on keeping it this time. Your idiocy made me lose half the income on that, but at least it's still income."

Ursula's lips parted in surprise. Perhaps she didn't realize how angry Jerry still was about the entire situation, how mad she was that she was there cleaning up this damn mess to begin with. Jerry shook her head and clenched her jaw.

"Go help Yafe. I don't want to see you for the rest of the day. If I do, I'll make you scrub this entire deck on your own."

"Aye, Cap." Ursula didn't hesitate as she turned around and left Jerry on her own.

That conversation had gone better than Jerry anticipated, although the addition of a few grams of brain matter might have helped it along. She'd put Yafe in charge of distributing that, too. Rubbing the back of her neck, Jerry knew she was going to have to start swinging some responsibility Sacha's way. She was still slightly bitter over the Damon-betrayal that landed them marooned and partially blamed that on Sacha even if it wasn't her fault entirely.

She would deal with that another day. For the rest of that morning, she had a crazy idea that she needed to follow up on and an aristocrat she needed to visit. Jerry checked with no one as she left. She would see how much work they would get done while she was gone. She knew Azar would at least have the hull fracture fixed because they needed that in order to make it to Beren Island. The engines could wait so long as they didn't push *Calluna* too hard.

Rolling her shoulders, Jerry stepped onto the dock. She tipped her hat down to hide her eyes from the rest of the world, not that there were many people out and about like there used to be. Since she'd been gone for months from the time she left to go to Potelia, she distinctly noticed the difference in the number of people wandering the streets now compared to before. It had dwindled slowly, but now it was so obvious.

The dockmaster barely even came to visit. The stark difference between here and Potelia, where the government provided medication for its citizens, was stark. She stepped off the dock and onto the cobblestone streets. Her boots were sure as she took the most direct path into the center of Raegina.

Jerry hadn't had much reason to travel into the center of the city before she met Arloa, and it seemed as though she was making this journey far more often than she'd ever anticipated. Except at one point, she had expected it. She'd even wanted it. Back when she'd first met Arloa, she had thought their fling would last longer than her usual. Arloa was such an intriguing woman.

She was strong but presented as meek. Her tiny form lent itself well to that. She wasn't beautiful by the standards of society, but Jerry saw beauty in her every moment of the day. Her lips were not full, her face was slightly askew, and she often left it bare of paint, which Jerry appreciated. They had met in a place where a rich aristocrat did not belong, and yet multiple nights in a row, Arloa had been there waiting.

Now Jerry was once again trekking her way into the city to see her, into the government building that had tried to throw her out the last time she'd fully made her way inside. This time she didn't even look like a woman, didn't present how she was supposed to, and she had no doubt that she would face the same discrimination as she did then.

Jerry passed through the tall wrought-iron gates to the inner part of the city. They were left open except at night, when she would need permission to slide from one area to the next. During the first phase of the virus they had been completely closed, but as the months had passed, the gates had been reopened since it was rare the rich fell ill. Jerry snorted at that. Something was in their blood that prevented it, something they all had access to that Jerry and her unsightly crew of unmentionables didn't have.

Whatever that was remained a mystery, but she didn't have the time to look into it deeper. Not yet anyway. Perhaps one day.

Walking confidently to the front of the government building, Jerry made sure to keep her hands out of her pockets and her chin raised confidently. She would not let them turn her away. At least this time, Jerry knew where she was going to find Arloa's offices. They were hidden away in the back corner of the building like any *good* woman should be. Wrinkling her nose at the thought, Jerry stepped into the extravagant building and immediately turned to walk down the hallway toward Arloa.

She had two aims for this meeting, and she would accomplish both of them. She only hoped the second covered up her real aim. Someone shouted at her to stop, but Jerry ignored him and moved forward. She was close to Arloa's offices. As soon as she reached the door, the man caught up with her. Jerry cocked her head at him and rapped her knuckles against the door. Arloa would answer, and she would take care of everything by letting her in.

"What's your purpose in being here?" he asked.

Jerry shook her head. It was the same damn thing every time. "I'm here to speak with my representative."

He glowered. "There are other methods of communication you could use."

Jerry grinned broadly. "Actually, I believe Senator Kauket quite likes my methods of communication."

She was probably saying too much, and it would give away too much about their relationship. It certainly suggested some things that Jerry wasn't sure Arloa would want implied, but she couldn't help herself. It had been too easy, and she wanted to push back at him. She was tired of being treated like the scourge of the planet.

"Senator Kauket isn't in her offices this morning," he responded, as if he knew absolutely everything.

When the door suddenly opened, revealing a very petite and

fiery Arloa Kauket, Jerry's grin grew broader. "Oh, really? She looks like she's here."

"Is there a problem?" Arloa came out and stood nearly between them. Jerry wondered if she thought Jerry might do something unbecoming.

The man didn't budge, which was surprising. Jerry had figured facing the wrath of Arloa would be a good indication he should leave. "*She* should not be here."

"And why not?" Arloa did move between them. "She has every right to be here—as you do—if not more, since we represent her in the law."

He didn't cower. This was going to be a game to Arloa to push him until he backed off. Jerry was going to enjoy it. She stayed quiet, letting Arloa handle the mess of classism that she was born to deal with. Jerry could put it out all she wanted, but since she was the scourge of Penum, she wasn't someone who could easily change another's mind on it.

"She is not welcome here. She'll infect us all."

"Now, Canteron, why would you think that I wouldn't be the one to infect you? Hmm?" Arloa stepped closer to him, as if a threat of her presence was going to give him the virus they were all afraid of and Jerry lived with. "Does she look infected to you?"

Canteron lifted his gaze from Arloa to Jerry, and his gaze hardened. "Unregistered citizens, if she even *is* a citizen, aren't welcome to the building."

"She is a citizen. You can check if you're *that* concerned about it. And she is registered."

Jerry was surprised by that confession from Arloa because she certainly had not registered for a visit that day. Canteron seemed put off, and he gave each of them a stiff look before acquiescing and bowing his head slightly. "My apologies."

"You owe them to her, not to me," Arloa pushed, apparently not letting him off the hook.

Jerry enjoyed this side of Arloa, the protective part, the

person who was forceful in her defense. Jerry loved that side of her in an entirely different situation, too. Though she wasn't about to share that with their audience. As soon as Canteron left, Arloa dragged Jerry into the offices by her hand and shut the door quickly.

Again they were the only ones in there, the office small and unbecoming of the status Jerry felt Arloa deserved. Then again, she was a woman in a man's world, and despite what the laws said, women didn't have innate rights like men in Penum, and especially in Raegina.

"What are you doing here?" Arloa hissed, locking the door to ensure they wouldn't be interrupted like they had been in the hall.

"What did you mean that I've registered?"

Arloa cocked her head to the side, her tender curls of hair bouncing from the move. Jerry rubbed her fingers together, resisting the urge to reach up and touch them. They stood a respectful distance apart, but she wanted to move in closer, wanted to touch. "I have you on my permanent list, so anytime you need to speak with me, you're welcome here."

"Interesting. He didn't even ask my name." Jerry gave in and touched Arloa's hair. It was so soft against her bare fingers.

Arloa stepped closer, plastering her body against Jerry's as she dragged Jerry's mouth down to hers. The kiss was sweet, not heated like in the carriage, but Jerry was sure that was because Arloa had no idea where they stood with each other.

When Jerry broke the kiss, she asked, "Did they find the missing senator?"

"No," Arloa murmured, her gaze turning down. "I don't expect they will."

"Pity."

"For some. For others it's likely a better situation all around."

"And Canteron, what is his position exactly?"

"Pain in my ass." Arloa giggled lightly. "He shouldn't have spoken to you like that. I apologize for him."

"Don't. He's not worth it." Jerry kissed Arloa again, still not sure how she would answer the questions from before. She knew Arloa held back because she needed to know where they stood with each other. "I was wondering if you had an update on *Wench's Dream*."

"From yesterday?" Humor lit Arloa's eyes as she stepped away and leaned against her desk.

Jerry frowned. "I guess it hasn't been that long."

"Why do you want to know?" Arloa reached out and grasped Jerry's fingers lightly.

"I want my ship back. I want revenge."

Arloa hummed softly, taking Jerry's hand and turning it palm up. She traced her fingers lightly over the skin, tickling. But more than that it was the tender touch of understanding, something Jerry had never experienced in her life. It had always been fucking for pleasure and to get what she needed or wanted, or what someone else needed and wanted. It had never been simply because gentle touches showed a softer side of herself and others solely for the purpose of comfort and love—if Jerry believed that's what Arloa truly felt for her.

"Revenge is such a cold way to live," Arloa commented. "But I do understand its tendency to grasp a heart and not let go."

Furrowing her brow, Jerry looked up at Arloa's steel-blue eyes. "You do?"

"Yes, Jer, I do." Arloa didn't elaborate, which had been Jerry's hope.

Instead, they stayed standing next to each other. Jerry knew she needed to turn the conversation, but she wasn't sure exactly how to make that shift. The real reason she had traveled all the way to the center of the city to visit Arloa in the first place, and it wasn't for sweet kisses and understanding, although that was pleasant enough to warrant the trip.

"I need a ship," Jerry stated. "*Calluna* has more problems than I thought. Azar found a hull fracture, and the engines are shot. We tried to go out yesterday and failed."

"I know you did." Arloa rubbed her temple. "I received a communication…"

"You what?"

"Something about a pirate ship in Raegina's seas trying to play dead in the water."

"We *were* dead in the water." Jerry frowned. It was only a small lie, one that would hopefully get her what she wanted. Arloa would either accept it for what it was or she would allow the lie to stand. "And we weren't pirating. I secured us our old contract that Ursula spurned, and we needed to test the vessel."

"I see you made it back to harbor well enough."

Jerry snorted. "We made it back. *Well enough* is subjective."

Arloa's lips parted. "Why not purchase a new ship?"

"I don't have the credits."

"I could—"

"No." Jerry cut her a sharp look. "Absolutely not."

A stillness came over them. Arloa was about to speak when there was another knock on the door. She glanced over her shoulder, then to Jerry. "Excuse me a moment, would you?"

Jerry stepped back, allowing Arloa the space to move. She reached the door and looked over her shoulder before she opened the door. Canteron was back. Jerry had to hide the smile as Arloa stepped into the hall and shut the door behind her. Without hesitating, Jerry pulled up Arloa's permanent device and slid the small piece of technology Vivian had given her onto the thumb pad. She waited until it clicked through the security and searched for Arloa's codes. She knew it was a stupid idea, that it would put everything between them at risk.

Arloa's voice raised, and Jerry worked quickly. As soon as she found the code, she committed it to memory. She closed everything down after erasing her trail and stepped to stand by the window. She didn't want Arloa to know what she was doing. When the door clicked shut, Jerry turned to face down the beautiful woman in front of her.

"Canteron?" Jerry asked.

"He's quite insistent you don't belong here."

"Well, he's correct. I don't belong here." Jerry crossed her arms. "And I should leave you to do the work you were elected for."

Arloa eyed her suspiciously but dropped the gaze when she came in to stand close. "I'm still waiting for an answer, you know."

"I know," Jerry whispered. Because she did. She had to tell Arloa one way or the other, and it would either end what they had or continue it. Jerry wasn't sure what she wanted. She'd only just started to come to terms with the fact that she couldn't stop thinking about this woman.

Cupping Arloa's cheek, Jerry brought their mouths together. She took it slowly, exploring not only Arloa's mouth but her own feelings in the process. Together they stood for what seemed like minutes until Jerry pulled away and pressed her forehead to Arloa's with her eyes closed.

"I just don't see how this will work."

"You don't have to," Arloa answered. "Because I don't know either, but I would like to try."

"I can't even come here without someone trying to kick me out. Our lives are so different."

"Different doesn't mean not compatible."

"True." Jerry straightened her back. "I'm still thinking about it, Arloa, but know this, if there is anyone who could sway my mind, I'm sure it's you."

"That will have to do for now, I suppose."

Jerry bowed her head slightly in acknowledgment before stepping around Arloa. "I'll leave before Canteron comes back with reinforcements."

"When will I see you again?"

"Don't know," Jerry answered honestly. "We start our runs to Beren Island tomorrow."

"Please find the time, soon."

"I'll try." It may have been the third lie she told that day in that office, and Jerry was determined to make it the last. "I am obsessed with you, Arloa."

Without another word, Jerry shut the door and left. She needed to get out of there and breathe clean air, and the only way that would happen would be if she left Raegina entirely.

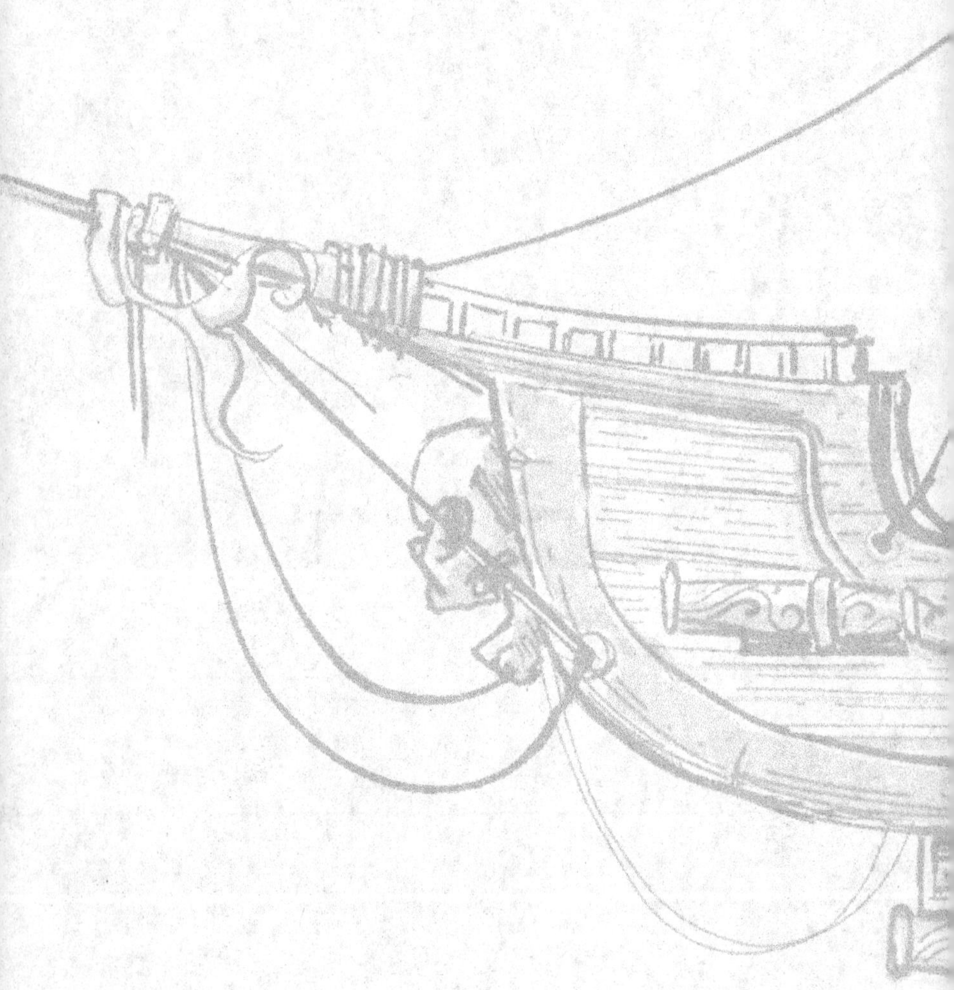

CHAPTER 14

Jerry shimmied the brand-new corset she had purchased the day before over her chest. Yafe helped her pull the laces tight, tying it as she made sure the crisp white undershirt was perfectly in place.

"Are you sure about this, Cap?"

"It's the only way I can think of getting this done quickly. She won't mind."

Yafe's frown in the mirror told Jerry that she disagreed with that assessment and it would be an argument for another day—one Jerry was willing to fight if it meant she had *Yarrow* in her possession. Yafe tied the skirts up, making sure they were tight against Jerry's slim hips.

It would make it harder for Jerry to move quickly and efficiently, but she needed to look like a well-off woman if she were to sneak into the pier where the sleek white medical vessel was held. She'd stolen ships from dock before, but it wasn't her preference. There were far too many variables that she wouldn't be able to control.

"I'll remind you when we finish this, Cap, that you chose a ship over a woman."

Jerry's nose wrinkled in a smile. "I will choose a ship over a woman any day, and if she doesn't understand that, she's not the woman for me."

"Tell that to Arloa." Yafe finished tying the skirts up and stepped back.

Jerry looked herself over in the mirror, her dark hair neatly braided down her back to the dark brown leather of the corset she had chosen. It was a beautiful one, nothing as fancy as Arloa's with its subtle erotic embroidery, but she'd been limited on time and flat-out broke. She smoothed her hands over the deep blue skirts that brought out the color in her eyes. It was perfect. She could easily pass for a woman of some means in this.

"Thank you for the help, Yafe."

"Anytime, Cap."

Jerry stepped out into the main part of her cabin. "Do we have a crew ready to leave with us?"

"We do. It'll leave Ursula with a skeleton crew, but if she's just making salt runs, she'll manage to survive."

"We'll be back before she knows it, and if she's got income, she can hire a few extra hands on her next trip back into Raegina."

Yafe frowned. "Are you sure you want to do this, Cap? There's no going back from it if you do."

Jerry locked her gaze on Yafe's deep brown eyes. She was a beautiful woman, inside and out, all that black curly hair that haloed her face and her dark skin that glowed in the sunlight when they were on the waters. But mostly it was her kind heart that had never managed to be polluted by the grime of Penum— her everlasting compassion for others. Jerry took a moment to mull over her words before nodding. "I'm sure."

"Then let's get *Yarrow* back."

Grinning, Jerry clasped her hands on Yafe's shoulders. "I'll meet you at Beren Island."

"You better. I don't need to be forging a plan to break you out of Joab."

Jerry's smile faltered slightly. She would die before she went back there, and if Yafe didn't understand that yet, then she never would if it ever came to that. "See you soon."

She stepped out of her cabin and down the hall toward Vivian's. Yafe went the opposite direction to get Ursula ready to leave for Beren Island. Her boots clicked on the wood plank flooring as she made her way down two more levels in *Calluna* to Vivian's door. Knocking, Jerry waited for an answer, trying not to itch the new clothes against her skin.

As Vivian opened the door, Jerry was impressed. She looked everything a young lady of society should. Jerry had splurged a little more on the outfit for her young counterpart, needing her to be able to run distractions while Jerry broke into the ship. Vivian was younger by a couple years, but more key than that, she looked younger because Jerry looked far older than she should for her twenty-three years.

Time in Joab had weathered her beyond what it should have. Still, Vivian's light brown eyes and matching light brown hair was perfect, and she'd done it up in a curious little bun at the back of her head with tendrils of curls on the sides of her face. No one would suspect she was brilliant, and no one would suspect that she was really Jerry's weapon of choice.

"Ready?" Jerry asked, her voice lower and deeper than normal.

"Aye, Cap."

"Good." Jerry led the way out of *Calluna*, closing up the door to the vessel as soon as they were on the dock. Yafe glanced out at them through the wheelhouse, nodding and bowing her head before Azar and Ursula took *Calluna* upward and out to sea. It was just Vivian and her now until they managed to join them at Beren Island.

"Cap, I've got the coding ready."

"I knew you would," Jerry mumbled. The pit of her stomach swirled with some kind of odd emotion she wasn't sure she wanted to name, but the last conversation with Yafe hadn't done anything to help her on that front. She was more worried now than she had been before.

They walked slowly, which was against Jerry's nature, meandering their way inside the city. They stopped at several stores, playing as if they were there to shop instead of waste time. The plan was in place, and it was ready to go. Jerry's entire body was ready for it to happen, for some type of movement to begin so that she could get *Yarrow* back and exact revenge on Blaise Lotchski for leaving her to die on an island with a usurper.

"What do you think?" Vivian called to Jerry.

Jerry spun to find Vivian's dark fingers on a beautiful cloth. Jerry narrowed her gaze at it, a memory tugging at her. She moved in closer, touching the cloth, and realized belatedly that this must be where Arloa had gotten her embroidery done. Jerry couldn't escape that woman no matter how hard she tried.

"It's beautiful," Jerry answered, knowing Vivian was still waiting for her, and that she would have to say something to get her off the topic and onto something else.

They eventually moved into a small store filled with jewelry. Jerry recognized some of it immediately as the jewels they had stolen months ago before she'd even gone to Potelia. It sent a thrill of satisfaction through her at the capture, but at the same time, pity because it hadn't sold yet, which meant Miriam had been absolutely right to barter the price down.

Taking Vivian's hand in hers as they finished, Jerry walked with her toward the docks. Surely it had been long enough at that point. They stopped to surveil the ships harbored in their individual slips. Jerry knew exactly which one they were going to, and it wasn't anywhere near where they stopped. She pressed her lips together hard, deciding once again that this was the plan in place and this was what she wanted to do. It was the only way to get a move on rescuing *Yarrow*.

"Thank you, Cap," Vivian's sweet and soft voice reached her ears.

"For what?" Jerry turned to her shorter companion,

wondering where this sudden expression of gratitude was coming from.

Vivian slowly looked up at her. "For everything really, but I didn't know what a ship was supposed to be like until you took over *Calluna*."

"That shouldn't have happened. Ursula—" She stopped short of disparaging her captain in front of her crew. If Vivian were to continue on *Calluna*, she shouldn't have a tainted view of Ursula if Jerry were to allow Ursula to continue on. And thus far, Jerry hadn't decided one way or the other. She would leave her in control for now because it was necessary until they retrieved *Yarrow*.

"Ursula was overwhelmed," Vivian started.

Jerry worried she'd already done too much damage. "She was. Doesn't excuse how she treated the crew or *Calluna*, however."

"Will you end her contract?"

"Perhaps. I don't know yet. We'll see how she does while I'm away this time."

Vivian's eyes crinkled at the corners. "I'm excited to work with you, Cap."

Jerry couldn't fathom why someone would want to work with her, not now. Perhaps when she had started her business and was doing everything legally, but now, all she did was risk them death. Their run-in with the island and Blaise were all too clear in her mind as to what they were risking.

"Are you ready?" Jerry asked, bypassing having to comment on that.

"Yeah, I am."

"Good." Jerry took Vivian's arm and looped it in hers.

Together they walked down the harbor, skipping quite a few piers to the ships that were for the rich. They were smoother, cleaner, and newer. Jerry spotted the one they were going to well before they reached it. The small white medical vessel that had rescued them from the island really was the perfect choice for their hijacking of *Wench's Dream*.

A lump tried to form in her throat, but she swallowed it down. She led the way as they maneuvered down the pier toward its dock. Jerry made sure to keep her gaze on the planks in front of them, not wanting to alarm the harbor master that they were there for any other purpose than a walk along the water.

Vivian made idle chitchat while they moved, which Jerry was quite thankful for. Her mind was a web of disasters coming from every direction, including Arloa miraculously showing up and finding them in the midst of stealing her ship.

They took a few turns down the pier to the dock they wanted. No one was on it. Jerry resisted the urge to look wildly for anyone who was going to stop them. Instead, she slowly lifted her chin, narrowed her gaze, and found absolutely no one in the vicinity.

Jerry stood next to the ship and stared at the small device that needed her palm print in order to open the door. Each one of her ships had one as well. She pulled open the small number pad next to the hand sensor and pushed the code she had spent all night memorizing. The sensor blinked three times before it clicked and stayed lit.

The door to the ship lowered down to allow them to walk across it. Vivian still held her arm wrapped tightly in Jerry's, as if they were a couple out for a stroll or perhaps two very close friends. They stayed silent until the door lifted and shut, locking in place. Jerry released of a breath she hadn't known she was holding and immediately stepped away from Vivian. They had a lot of work to get done.

Jerry immediately stepped to the interior of the vessel and made her way to the wheelhouse. She hadn't been there when Arloa had rescued her, but she knew the way. She would in just about any ship as she'd been in so many growing up and frequently roamed them throughout her tenure.

As soon as they were in, Jerry immediately stared at the dash in absolute awe. It was beautiful. Perfect lines, buttons and knobs that would lift and drop, turn and maneuver. It was stunning to see how clean it was. Vivian didn't wait as she got onto her knees at the base of the dash and pulled out a panel.

Vivian started her work, pulling apart wires and plugging in the small device that she had hidden in her purse. Jerry turned everything on to make sure the ship ran. She couldn't believe they had made it inside with no problems. She was so close to finally getting what she wanted.

She stared out the front window, seeing the dock ahead of them and finding the authorities standing at the top of the pier. Her heart stuttered, and air balled up in her throat. She had no idea what to do, or if they were even coming for it. It wasn't uncommon for authorities to patrol the areas, but to do it that day at that time was too much of a coincidence for her to feel secure in staying long.

Perhaps Arloa had noticed she'd stolen the codes and had called the authorities on her. Pulling her lip between her teeth, Jerry glanced down at Vivian who lay on her side, half under the dash as she worked her magic. Jerry didn't want to worry her just yet, so she held the knowledge inside and didn't utter another word.

She ran scans of the vessel, making sure no one else was on board with them even though she was pretty sure they were alone. Except…they weren't.

"Fuck," Jerry muttered as she hit a few more commands into the system to find out exactly who was there and where they were.

"What?" Vivian called from below.

Jerry shook her head, not ready to answer that question just yet. She was about to hit a command when a cold, angry voice startled her.

"Who the hell are you?" His accent was strong, thick, as though he hadn't been in Raegina very long.

Jerry spun on her toes, every nerve in her body telling her

she was going to have to fight her way out of this one. She was going to have to win and pray to whatever damn deity was out there that the authorities didn't catch on or that he didn't hit a signal before saying something.

"I'm Jeraldine Adelric." Her voice was so calm that she wasn't sure how she'd managed to keep it that controlled, because she felt anything but. "I'm here to take this ship."

"Like hell you are!" He shouted at her, his hands raised as if he was going to sock her in the side of the face.

Jerry ducked, grunting as she stepped to the side and accidentally hit Vivian's leg in the process.

"Keep going, Viv!" Jerry ordered as she side-stepped another attempted hit. This guy was hardly worth his salt in security, and not for the first time, Jerry wondered who he was.

He swung at her again, only this time, Jerry grabbed his arm and twisted under his reach behind his back, pulling his arm with her as she went. She held it at an odd angle as she reached to her side and grabbed her long knife, shoving it up against his jugular.

"I told you, I'm taking this ship."

He growled, but he didn't say anything else, which was wise. Jerry shoved him toward the door that would lead to the lower decks and pushed him against the wall right next to it. She found rope and tied his hands and ankles together. As soon as she had him done up, she put away her knife. He stood at the door, glaring at her.

"This is a Kauket vessel, you know. They'll ruin you when they find out."

A shiver ran up Jerry's spine, but she held her ground with him, giving no outward sign that what he had said bothered her. She raised an eyebrow at him and stepped in closer, sweeping her boot under his tied up feet and knocking him to the deck with a loud thud.

When she glanced at Vivian, her face was pale, and fear filled her gaze. "Ignore him."

"Kauket?" Vivian's voice wavered. "You didn't tell me—"

"I told you to ignore him," Jerry spat.

"The Kaukets are a powerful family," he tried again.

Jerry hissed before kicking him in the face to knock him out cold. She was tired of listening to his voice, and since she had revealed her name, there was no turning back now. He would certainly come in handy later.

Stalking to the dash and the wheel, Jerry crouched down and gave Vivian a sincere look. "I have pull with the Kaukets. Trust me, they won't kill us for it."

"That's not what I'm afraid of," Vivian answered before turning back under the dash and completing her work.

Once they hacked into the systems, Jerry took control of the wheel and pulled the ship out of the slip. Vivian stood up and moved to stare at the man who was still passed out near the door. "Who is he?"

Jerry shrugged. "Look in the manifest. He was probably left here to make sure the ship stayed secure."

"That makes no sense."

Unless Arloa knew someone was coming, then it makes perfect sense. Though Jerry didn't say that out loud or share that tidbit with Vivian. She didn't need to know who Jerry fucked and who she didn't fuck. However, the thought that the ship wasn't actually Arloa's but the Kauket family vessel was a different issue entirely. She didn't mind stealing from her girlfriend who pretty much spurned her family name except when useful, but to steal a ship off the very people who founded, ran, and funded the glorified prison system in Raegina? That was a different story entirely. One Jerry was not comfortable being a part of.

Yet it was too late to change her mind now. Jerry competently steered the ship out of the harbor and toward the open sea. The authorities never came closer to the dock, and by the time they were out of sight, Jerry breathed a sigh of relief.

"He's a vagrant," Vivian muttered.

"What?" Jerry turned on her.

Vivian kicked his boot lightly. "He's not on the manifest, and I took his print to scan for his identification. He's a vagrant."

"Well, I guess that's a bonus for us." Jerry snorted as she picked up speed and headed straight to Beren Island.

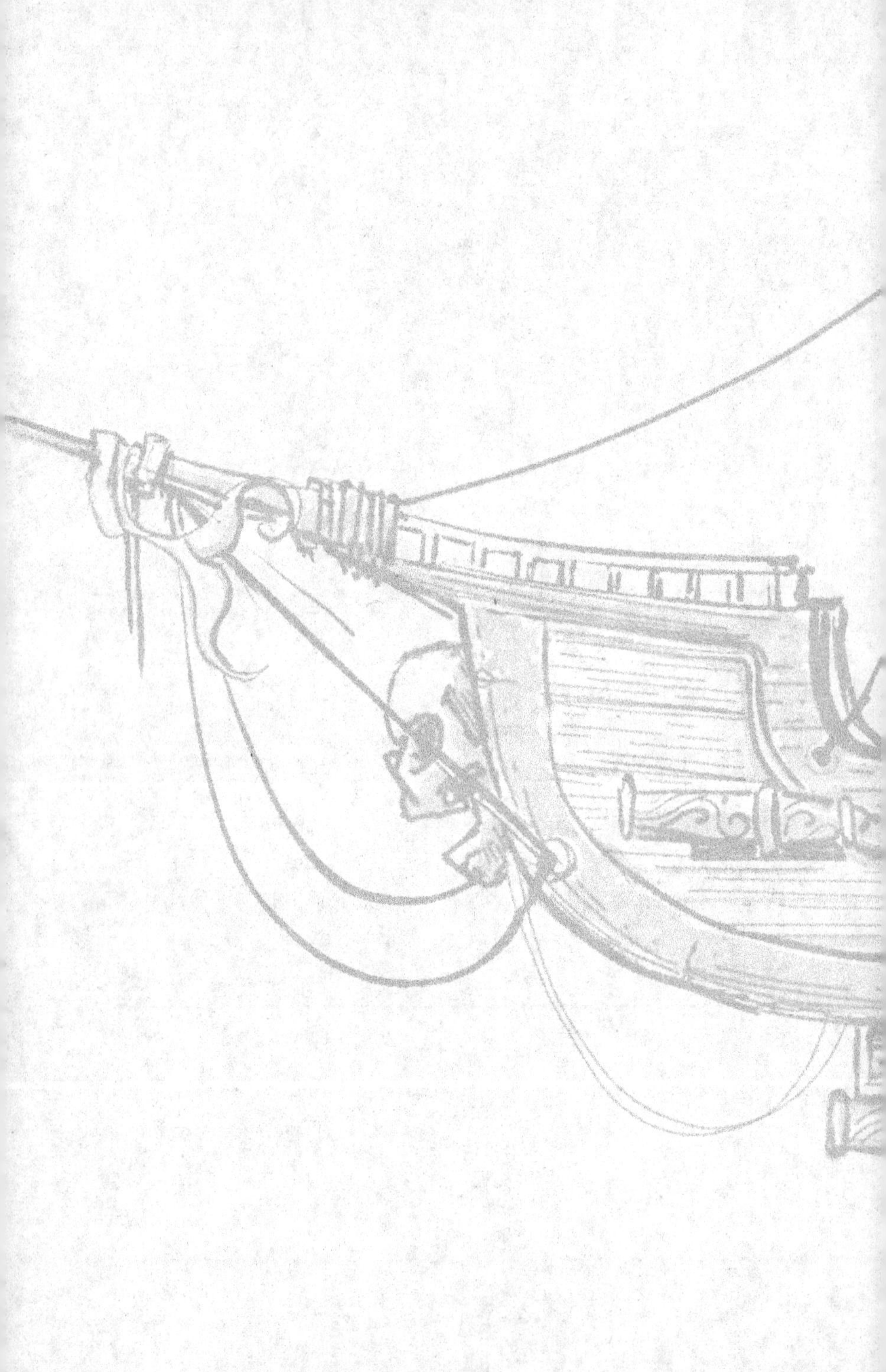

CHAPTER 15

Rendezvousing with *Calluna* took less time than Jerry had anticipated. The ship they'd stolen had a good speed on her, far better than *Calluna*, so it was already looking up. As soon as they were out on the open seas and beyond Raegina's borders, she and Vivian had taken the man into one of the empty cabins and left him tied and locked up.

Vivian kept eyeing Jerry suspiciously, as if whatever image she'd had of Jerry prior to the man's coming up and catching them had been shattered. Jerry didn't envy her in that moment, though she'd learned throughout the years not to build up images of those she surrounded herself with. It was part and parcel of why she was never disappointed when someone fucked up.

She settled the ship down right next to *Calluna* and hovered her over the water. She was too high up for the makeshift dock they had built in the last few years, so they would need to transfer everyone from the island to *Calluna* and then to the medical vessel. Which would be faster than any other plan she could come up with. She took off her jacket and rolled up her sleeves, eager to see how far they had gotten in filling *Calluna's* storerooms with salt.

After they double-checked to make sure the man was still

locked away securely, Vivian followed her across the vessel's open door to *Calluna's* deck. It felt good to step on her, as if she was getting one step closer to home. Jerry kept that tidbit of information to herself as well, not needing to be reminded again what a disappointment she was to Vivian.

Azar met her on the deck, wiping grease from his hands as he stepped out to nod at her. "I see you were successful."

"Yes," Jerry answered. "And have you been?"

He gave a nod but had a slightly pained expression, which told Jerry there was far more to that story than he was letting on. She would have to get it out of him later.

"Getting the ship was rather uneventful, though we did end up with an extra passenger in the process. Seems a vagrant was staying onboard and was as shocked by us being there as we him."

"What did you do with him?" Azar tucked the greasy cloth into his waistline.

"Locked him up for now."

"What will you do with him?"

Jerry knew the answer to that, but with Vivian acting as oddly as she was, Jerry wasn't sure she wanted to answer that question so vividly. She didn't want to make death as stark as it was when there were innocent minds around.

Vivian tried to step around them and down into the ship. Jerry sighed heavily, letting her go. She would figure out the plan for later. As soon as the young woman was out of ear shot, Jerry pinned Azar with a serious look. "I plan to eat him, and so do you."

His face fell, but he didn't argue. They both knew they could be gone for a number of weeks, and they would need the sustenance in order to get through it.

"How's the mining going?"

"They should be finished in a few hours, I believe."

"Good. Are you done with maintenance?"

Azar frowned. "As finished as I can be. They'll need a few

more parts in order to completely solve the problems, but we can order those later when we have the credits."

"Very well." Jerry sucked in a deep breath of the freshest air she had breathed in days. This was what she missed about the open waters.

Azar led her inside, where she found Ursula waiting. Jerry was slightly miffed that Ursula wasn't down helping the crew with the salt like she would have been, but then again, Ursula wasn't her and she led in a very different way than Jerry did. Jerry nodded toward her.

"Azar says she's all fixed up."

"For now," Ursula answered, that slight petulant tone back in her voice, but she seemed to school it quickly enough. "The crew will be done in a few hours."

"Good. Then we'll do the transfer, and we'll be on our way."

"Will I still be in charge?" Ursula asked it as though she was afraid of the answer, which she very well might be.

Jerry held all the power in this situation as the owner of *Calluna*, but at the same time, what choice did she have? She needed Azar and Yafe with her in order to take back *Yarrow*. She had no idea if she was going to be coming back with two ships or three or just one, and she needed two people who were competent and understood orders well to make this trip a success.

"Yes," Jerry finally answered, giving in to Ursula's nerves. "For now, at least. But I'll be taking most of the crew with me in order to get back *Yarrow*."

Ursula nodded sharply and crossed her arms. "I'll let them know."

"No, I will, once they've finished bringing in the salt for Morty." Tension filled the air as there was another battle over control and power, but ultimately, Jerry won out. She would no matter what, because if she had to, she would delay the salt and leave *Calluna* stranded on the island if she had to. There was no doubt in her mind about it. Or better yet, she'd take them both.

Jerry ignored her as she stepped up to the ladder and slid down it into the lower decks. She had to find Vivian, see if she wanted to continue with Jerry or if what she had witnessed turned her stomach. It didn't take her long to find the young woman, already changing out of the beautiful dresses Jerry had purchased for her into something far more reasonable for a pirate. Jerry stepped up and helped her with the laces.

"I wanted to check in before our next leg of the journey," Jerry said, her voice soft, almost muted. She didn't understand why she could be so gentle with Vivian, but with just about anyone else she was rough and pushy. She had no soft bone in her body except somehow Vivian managed to reach it. Though if she thought about it, others did too—Arloa, Whitney, Yafe, Azar. Cursing her own tenderness, Jerry clenched her jaw and pulled the corset from Vivian's body.

"You wanted to see if I still think I should join you," Vivian stated succinctly.

"Yes." Jerry was glad that for once someone else was as straightforward as she was.

Vivian's lips thinned as she raised her gaze to meet Jerry's eyes, a smattering of freckles along her cheeks and shoulders that Jerry hadn't noticed before. "I know what you're going to do to him."

"He can be useful to us."

"Not in that way." Vivian's eyes filled with water.

Jerry understood the sentiment, even if she hadn't said it. That had been her greatest struggle since they'd returned from the island. It had been necessary while marooned, but why in the name of a civilized world was it necessary elsewhere?

"I know," Jerry whispered, clasping Vivian's shoulders. "I'm not happy about it either."

"I'm not unhappy, Cap. I'm disgusted, with myself, with you, with every single one of us."

Jerry nodded her agreement, not able to look into the sweet girl's gaze again. "I know. It makes me hate myself even more."

"Then why are we doing it?" Vivian's voice became low, barely audible in the closed cabin.

"Because we don't have another choice aside from insanity and tearing each other apart. What is one life for the survival of many? Hmm?"

Vivian gasped, her full lips parted, and Jerry finally looked her in the eye.

"Do you want to live or do you want to die? That's the only question you need to answer. And believe me when I tell you that I will make his death as painless as possible."

"I suppose that's a blessing in disguise."

She sounded so forlorn, and not for the first time did Jerry want to wrap her arms around her and hold tight, but she resisted the urge. She hadn't been given permission, and she certainly wasn't going to ask for it. Which reminded her—Jerry removed her hands from Vivian's shoulders and pressed them down to her sides. "Do you need any more help undressing?"

"No," Vivian's voice was gentle this time, a hint of something in it that Jerry was scared to label. "Do you?"

"Oh." Jerry's cheeks heated, and she looked toward the small door. Yafe was still on the island, mining salt to bring back for credits, so it was going to be either she stayed dressed until Yafe returned or she acquiesced and allowed Vivian to help her. "Sure."

Turning around, Jerry waited for Vivian's skilled fingers at the ties of her skirts and corset. She could likely have gotten them undone by herself if she tried hard enough, or took a knife to it—which was her preference—but the dress was nice and she didn't want to have to buy a new one. Since she'd been in it nearly all day, Yafe had made sure to tie it tightly.

As soon as the material was loosened, Jerry turned around and held it against her front so it wouldn't sink lower. The thought struck her that Vivian was not the person who should be doing this. She wasn't the one Jerry wanted to be helping her undress.

"Thank you. I'll see you topside as soon as the others are back so we can start."

"Aye, Cap," Vivian answered.

Jerry walked out of the cabin as swiftly as possible. She went straight to her own, struggling to hold her corset together as she climbed the ladder up one level. When she was changed into her normal garb, she packed up what little belongings she had and transferred them onto the new medical vessel. She repeated the actions, with Azar's help, for all of the crew who would be joining her on the next part of her mission.

Hours later, Yafe and Ursula joined her topside, and they sat around while the others changed and cleaned up to get ready for the journey. Jerry gnawed on the inside of her cheek as she raised her gaze to meet Vivian's eyes. It would be so easy to take her, and she was pretty sure it would be welcomed, but at the same time, she realized fully then that she didn't want Vivian. She wanted Arloa.

"Vivian, will you be able to work on a virus?"

"What kind?" She was back to her cheery calm self.

"One that will stop the engines on *Yarrow*. I can give you her codes and back up codes. I doubt they've changed everything over yet since we usually work on the fly."

Vivian nodded. "I should be able to do that with the codes. We'll have to get onto the ship in order to implement it."

Jerry frowned. They would need a diversion to be able to sneak on board. At that point, it might be easier just to take the vessel by more traditional methods than to rely entirely on Vivian, though she would always have more than one plan in her pocket. "Work on it."

"Aye, Cap." Vivian stayed put.

Yafe raised an eyebrow at her, salt in her hair, showing the work she had done that day. "How far out do you think they are?"

"Our information tells us they were in the Jackimore Sea last. I'll need to double-check with our contact to make sure that's still true, but if they are, it'll be four solid days of traveling before we'll reach them. We don't know for certain if *Yarrow* is with them."

"So will you torture him to get information?" Yafe pressed.

"If necessary," Jerry countered. She would do anything to get her ship back at this point. She wanted her home in her possession as soon as possible. "Azar will need to run diagnostics on *Yarrow* as soon as we get a chance to set her down, just to be sure there haven't been any dangerous modifications made, or trackers placed."

She added the last part, making sure they were all on the same page, although she didn't plan on leaving Blaise alive long enough to take her ship back or follow her again.

Ursula was being persistently quiet, and it set Jerry on edge. Normally she had no problem inserting her opinion into the conversation. Then again, Jerry had been particularly hard on her since her return, and she had taken complete control over everything that involved Ursula's livelihood, giving her no choice except to submit or leave.

Azar spoke up. "So plan one is to insert a virus to stop *Yarrow* in her tracks. What is the backup plan?"

"We take her the normal way. Board her."

"And if we cause more damage?"

"Then we fix her." Jerry pinned him with a sharp look. Based on how they had left *Yarrow* it wouldn't be that hard. She would have to have been fixed up before she would fly again. Blaise had put at least five holes in her hull based on Jerry's memory of the capture. She remembered every vibration as it struck, as it ricocheted right through *Yarrow's* floorboards and into her bones. She never wanted to experience that pain again. "We do right by her, get her back in safe hands, and then we will heal her."

"You talk about her as though she is a person," Vivian commented.

"She's my life," Jerry responded passionately. "And I'll get her back and rescue her."

Vivian looked at her with a kind of awe, the same kind that had been dashed away earlier that day. Jerry held her gaze a moment longer before continuing on. "When we get her, we'll bring her to a nearby island, assess the damage and what needs repaired and take her home. We'll split the crew into two to bring the medical vessel with us should she survive."

"And *Wench's Dream*?" Yafe asked.

Jerry raised an eyebrow. She would very much like to plunge that ship into the depths of the poisoned sea below them, but it would be a waste to do that with a perfectly functioning ship. Unwilling to give a full answer, Jerry nodded. "We'll see."

"As soon as we're aboard, we'll continue more training routines," Yafe continued. "I want to make sure we're all working well together before we take on Captain Blaise."

"It'll be a necessity," Ursula finally spoke up. "Blaise is ruthless, and he won't let you go easily, especially considering this will be your second encounter with him."

Jerry wasn't quite sure where Ursula was getting that information from, but she knew it was true. It would be true of any pirate captain who truly lived on the seas, unlike her. She was a pirate by necessity. He was a pirate because it was in his veins. There was never another option for him except to captain his own vessel for the sole purpose of thievery.

"We won't lose this time." Jerry said confidently, yet there was a inkling in the pit of her stomach that told her otherwise. She would lose something in the process. She just didn't know what that would be yet. "Ursula, keep doing the salt runs. I don't want to lose another contract with Morty should we be able to avoid it."

"Understood." Ursula nodded, her arms still crossed as though she were protecting herself.

"Yafe, let's divide the crews."

Jerry stood up sharply, making her way over the small medical vessel. They were going to have to double up on a lot of the rooms until they managed to steal *Yarrow* back, but then they would be divided again and all would be well. She ignored the others as she went to the wheelhouse to completely familiarize herself with the ship's center. She needed to know the ins and outs of its controls and exactly how she could quickly maneuver it. They would do that during some of the training that Yafe would run.

She blew out a breath as her crew started to come aboard. The small device in the center of the dash rang. Jerry's heart stuttered, and she leaned in to see where the call originated from. She cursed under her breath when she saw it was Raegina's government building and had Arloa's numbers attached to it.

As much as she wanted to answer it, to see how angry Arloa was with her, Jerry couldn't let on where they were, not yet. She needed more time to find *Yarrow* and to get her back. Closing out the communication, Jerry straightened her shoulders, wishing her crew would hurry the hell up so they could get going.

Immediately, the communications sounded again. She wasn't going to win this one, but she was going to hold out for as long as she possibly could. Jerry cursed, "Fuck me."

CHAPTER 16

The communications device would not stop ringing. Jerry tried her damn best for hours to ignore it, but as they were finally out at sea and on their way to find Blaise, she wasn't sure if she could hold out any longer. Anger built in her stomach at the annoyance, and she knew that Arloa knew. There would be no other reason the woman would consistently call her ship that much unless she knew Jerry was on it.

Swallowing hard, Jerry straightened her back as another notification came up that Arloa was trying again. She was just about to slam her hand down to deny the communications when Sacha's voice hit her. "You should just talk to her."

Spinning around, Jerry's eyes went wide at the sight of the young woman leaning against the door to the wheelhouse. She'd been so distracted that she hadn't even noticed Sacha come up there, but it looked as though she had been there a while. "Talk to who?"

"The Kauket woman you fawn over."

Jerry frowned, guilt hitting her like a ton of bricks. From the conversation with Vivian about the Kaukets and who they really were, to the conversation with Arloa about what she really wanted, it was nearly too much for her feeble mind to handle. Did she want Arloa? Yes. But she again had been reminded that it would be impossible to separate the woman from her family in some ways.

"You should just talk to her."

"I don't know what to say," Jerry confessed, heat filling her cheeks to the point it was nearly unbearable. "Hey, Arloa, I stole your ship. Sorry. I might bring it back intact. That sounds oddly patronizing."

Sacha's lips curled slightly. "I like you, Cap, you know that. But sometimes you're dense."

Jerry cocked her head to the side and crossed her arms, not sure she wanted to take on the battle of finding out what exactly she was dense about.

"She loves you," Sacha whispered as if it was some sort of revelation.

"I know that," Jerry answered.

Sacha's lips quirked slightly. "You love her."

Jerry equally knew that, but she wasn't sure she wanted to admit that to her crew, especially when love was not a priority in her life. Survival was everything, which made love frivolous. Jerry stepped back to the dash and the wheel, making sure the vessel was flying as straight as it could and checking the sensors that there wasn't another ship hidden somewhere. She'd been fooled once by Captain Blaise Lotchski, and she wouldn't allow it to happen again.

"Cap?" Sacha stepped in closer, standing next to her against the wheel as the communications went off again. "Talk to her."

"No," Jerry stubbornly answered.

"Cap," Sacha started again, this time her voice gentle. She reached over and covered Jerry's hand with hers and squeezed lightly. "She's just going to keep calling if you don't talk to her, and she'll be royally pissed the longer you wait."

Jerry knew Sacha was right, as much as she didn't want to admit it. She squared her shoulders and knocked her head toward the door of the wheelhouse. "Get some rest, Sacha. Yafe is going to make you run rounds in the morning with training."

"Perfect." Sacha's eyes lit up as if she was actually excited for that possibility. Jerry couldn't stop her chuckle as Sacha practically flounced out of the wheelhouse to the cabins below.

The dark skies in front of her soothed her soul. It had been far too long since she'd been on open waters like this, in control, waiting, just moving through the air as though she had everything under her control. She didn't, but the world didn't need to know that. Rolling her shoulders, Jerry tightened her grip on the wheel wondering if it'd be advantageous to do a drill right then and there. It would at the very least distract her from all these impending communications from Arloa. Seriously, didn't the woman have a job to do that would distract her from making these fucking calls?

Slamming her hand down on the communications, Jerry growled out, "Don't you have something better to do?"

"Jer?" Arloa sounded exhausted, her voice slow and her words slurred.

Confused, Jerry narrowed her gaze and stared at the small holographic version of Arloa that was cast in light purples. It was only her face, but she looked tired in a way Jerry had never seen her, not even when she'd rescued them, although Jerry had been slightly confused and distracted at that point and hadn't been paying full attention.

"What do you want, Arloa?"

"Did you take my ship?"

Confusion swam into Jerry's hazy mind as she narrowed her gaze at Arloa's blurred image. "Of course, I did. You contacted me on it."

"Oh. Right." Arloa rubbed her temple and glanced at something beyond the scope of the communication device.

Jerry wasn't quite sure what to make of that comment. She'd never seen Arloa so despondent or confused before. She was always the picture of put together and sharp. "Did something happen?"

"No," Arloa dragged the word out, and Jerry sensed the lie before it finished.

When had they started lying to each other? She knew when she had, but when had Arloa begun lying to her was more the question. Sighing, Jerry adjusted their course slightly before putting the autopilot on so she could focus on Arloa fully.

"What happened, Arloa?"

"Why did you take my ship?"

"Because it was available, and I needed a ship." Jerry's words had a bite to them, but she wasn't sure she'd even wanted to hold it back. She wanted an argument. The amount of times Arloa had tried to contact her was obnoxious, and she'd only answered to put an end to the incessant communications. "Will you answer my question?"

"What question was that again?"

"What *happened*?" Jerry pointedly emphasized the last word. She put her hands on her hips and stared Arloa dead in the eye as much as she could, being in a completely different part of Penum. She wanted to know, and as much as the stolen vessel was between them, Jerry still felt the need to comfort her, to console her, to be that person for Arloa as much as she could.

"They found that missing senator dead, and it's been chaotic all day."

"Is that why you were contacting me?" Jerry raised an eyebrow, her stomach sinking at the thought Arloa could be next in line to be taken and killed. She still couldn't fathom it, but she wasn't going to bring it up again because the last time she'd done that, Arloa had shot her down.

"No. I was trying to see if you took my ship."

"I believe it's your family ship," Jerry snarked back, her tone sharp. "Which would have been good for you to mention at any time that I was on it previously."

Arloa's lips twitched, which Jerry took as a good sign. "Of course, it's my family's ship. Do you think I could afford a vessel on my own?"

Jerry shrugged. She honestly had no idea how well off Arloa was. They'd never discussed credits, and while she was a senator, she didn't exactly represent a rich part of Raegina either. Jerry had purchased her own vessels with credits she had earned, but they were also much older and not medical ships.

"Ah, I see," Arloa started. "You really do think I am my family."

"Most days you are," Jerry countered. "And then some days I see the real woman underneath it all."

"And what do you see today?"

Jerry frowned. She put both hands on the dash and leaned down to get a good look at the small communications device that lit up the face of her girlfriend—at least, she supposed that's what they were to each other at that point. "Did you call the authorities?"

"I had no choice," Arloa murmured.

"And so they'll find me as soon as I enter Raegina's waters again?"

Arloa frowned. "I didn't tell them *who* took my ship."

Jerry hummed, satisfied with that answer. She would have to report it stolen otherwise her family would call her out, she supposed. Still, that put them at an impasse, Jerry not quite sure what to expect from Arloa or when the authorities would find her at that point.

"Will you bring it back?"

"Do you want me to?" Jerry raised an eyebrow at her. "Because with the authorities now on my tail, I'm not sure I can get her into the harbor without being caught."

"You're smart, Jer. I imagine you'll be able to come home to me."

Jerry's stomach swirled with that same odd mix of emotions that she hadn't wanted to identify yet. She needed to be able to say the words because she knew they were true, but at the same time, what would that to do her to admit it? Jerry sidestepped that conversation and started another one. "I will try to bring your damn ship home. In the meantime, do you have any updates on Blaise?"

Arloa sighed and threaded her fingers through her hair. "The government has been in an uproar since Fudala's body was discovered early this morning."

So that answered Jerry's question—no. Arloa had no more information, or she was withholding it as a punishment for Jerry's taking the ship without permission. She rolled her shoulders and glanced out the front window of the ship, not that she could see anything anyway, and made some adjustments to her systems based on what the sensors were telling her.

"How are you going to take back *Yarrow*?"

"That's for me to know and you to find out. I don't share my plans readily, especially over insecure communications." Jerry clenched her jaw tightly. Arloa must be tired if she was making that slipup.

"Jer."

"What?"

"These communications are as secure as they get. You can't believe my family wouldn't put in the best of the best into our ships, and I have a direct line to them from my offices and from my home."

Frowning, Jerry glanced down at the small image. Perhaps Arloa was right, but then again, she would have to trust that she was telling the truth, though she had little reason to think Arloa wasn't. Rolling her shoulders, Jerry brushed that thought to the side.

"I suppose we can talk about whatever we want, then, can't we?"

"I can think of something much better to do with secure lines." The salacious tone took Jerry by surprise.

She nearly gasped as she looked directly into Arloa's eyes and shook her head. "I am in the wheelhouse."

"So?"

"Arloa, the answer is no, and I can't even believe you would suggest that. There's no privacy on a vessel like this."

"Do you not have your own cabin?"

"Not currently." Jerry frowned. It was partly why she was avoiding it, but at the same time, someone had to be in charge up here, and it was going to be her. "I'll bring your damn ship back to you, but I expect you to call off the authorities when I do."

Arloa clucked her tongue. "I can't do that. You'll have to figure out a way to get her back to the slip without being noticed."

Jerry nearly growled in her frustration. That would be next to damn impossible, but she would bring the ship close enough to harbor that someone would discover it and return it to the Kauket family. "This senator—"

"Fudala," Arloa added.

"Yeah, where was his body found?"

"Near the harbor. The authorities believe someone was trying to drag it to sea and failed, or was interrupted so he was discovered instead of being wasted into the waters."

Jerry agreed that throwing a body into the poisoned water was the perfect way to dispose of anything someone didn't want discovered. Fuck knew she'd done it more times than she cared to count throughout her years.

"Seems like a smart idea," Jerry commented before focusing back on steering the ship.

"I suppose," Arloa answered, seeming distracted. "Jer, what we talked about before you left—"

"Is nothing we need to continue to talk about," Jerry finished for her.

"It is. I need to know where we stand."

Jerry frowned and refused to look directly at Arloa. She still hadn't made up her mind on where they were together in a relationship or where they weren't. She needed time to sort out her own feelings and what she very well thought might be a possibility. Yet she hadn't even managed to find the words to say that to Arloa thus far, and no matter how hard she tried not to think of the damnable woman, she couldn't stop either. It wasn't the first time she had thought this, but it wasn't love between them, it was obsession. And Jerry was pretty sure that the obsession went both ways.

"I still don't see how it'll all work in the end," Jerry commented, trying to slide by the fact she still wasn't sharing what she was feeling. She could only hope Arloa would let her get away with it.

"I'm not asking for your hand in marriage."

"Aren't you though?" Jerry snapped. "If you want a relationship, that's what you're seeking."

"Hardly," Arloa fought back. "What I want is you and whatever you'll give me."

Jerry snorted laughably. "If you wanted me, then you'd take what I'm giving and not ask for more."

Arloa's lips parted in surprise, and Jerry knew she'd caught her in her own web of words. They weren't meant to be together. Jerry was no one. She'd been born under the radar, and she had positioned herself to stay there until she died. She was an unsightly creature with nothing going for her. Arloa had been born into the richest family in Raegina, a family that was quiet but made their mark on the country and the world. They were well-rounded, well-educated, and Arloa was well above Jerry's standards. The two should have never met, and some days— well, most days—Jerry still couldn't fathom why or how they had managed to.

"You're right," Arloa stated, her voice weary as though she was ready to give up the battle she had been harping on. "But I *want* more from us."

"Then you're the only one. I'm comfortable with what we have, and I don't need more."

"No, I don't imagine you do need much in life, do you?"

Jerry was taken back by the bitterness she heard. Arloa was

correct. She didn't need much, and perhaps how she was thinking about this was all wrong. She didn't need Arloa, but she certainly wanted her. Wetting her lips and her suddenly dry mouth, Jerry straightened her shoulders. "I suspect you feel the same."

"You're correct about that." Arloa sighed, the pause in the conversation elongating until it was unnerving and tense. "Please come home to me, Jer."

The ache in Arloa's voice hit her right in the center of her soul, though Jerry was remiss in not admitting that. They might live very separate lives, but somehow, they had become so entwined in each other that she couldn't imagine not seeing Arloa again. Which had been in her thoughts while she'd been marooned.

"I'll return your ship."

"That isn't what I meant," Arloa said sadly. "But if that's what you can offer at this time, I suppose I'll take it. At one point in time, I had thought you were one of the strongest women I knew. Perhaps I assessed you wrong."

"Perhaps you did." Jerry pushed the engines in the vessel, picking up speed. She had decided that she would wake up her crew for an unplanned training lesson. They would fail miserably, she was sure, but it would be a good lesson in the long run.

"Jer?"

"What?"

"I do want you."

Jerry sighed. "I'll return your fucking ship."

Arloa gave her a sad smile. "I care more if *you* return than the ship. I can always purchase another one."

Jerry snorted, heat rushing to her checks again that night, and her entire body warming at the sentiment. She'd forgotten what it was like to have someone care about her. Her mother had died so long ago that she'd been on her own and surrounded in her own isolation. She had friends, companions, yes, but never something like this.

"I mean it," Arloa added. "I don't know why you're the one my heart's chosen, but you are. When I first saw you in that bar, I felt it then, too. I just didn't realize what it was yet."

Jerry had felt the same way. She'd been instantly attracted to Arloa back then and had never quite been able to rid that from her mind. Still, she remained quiet, not sure she wanted to answer or share more than what she already head.

"I have to run some trainings, Arloa. I'll return—" she stopped herself short and finally said what she wanted to "—I'll return to you."

The smile that lit up Arloa's face was a balm to Jerry's weary soul. Saying nothing else, Jerry leaned forward and ended the communications. She set the ship to run on auto again, making sure she would do well to get them where they were going without too much intervention. There wasn't much in front of them anyway.

Instead of stepping out of the wheelhouse, Jerry grabbed the internal communications device and pressed it to her lips. This was going to be one of the rudest wake up calls her crew would get, aside from an actual emergency, but it would be worth it to make sure they were all well and properly ready for that emergency to happen.

She shouted, "All hands on deck! Incoming combatant!"

CHAPTER 17

Azar stepped next to Jerry, and instantly she relaxed. She had no idea why she was so tense or worried about this trip, but she knew she had to get her nerves under control sooner rather than later. Perhaps it was because she had failed so much recently. Not only had she failed in her mission to steal the cirax but she had failed to protect her crew.

That was really the issue, wasn't it? She wasn't able to do the most fundamental task of a captain. Sighing, she stiffened her shoulders as Azar made some minor adjustments on the control dash and then crossed his arms to turn on her.

"You're moping."

"I'm not," Jerry muttered. Usually it was Yafe who would call her out on something like that, but Yafe had been so busy with training the crew that she likely wasn't going to be able to do it.

Azar chuckled loudly right next to her. She turned on him, her eyes widening as she dared him to say more. She pursed her lips and rolled her shoulders, tightening her grip on the wheel.

"It's a good ship," Azar commented. "Your Arloa must be a woman of means."

Jerry realized far too late that in all the time she'd known him she had never told him exactly who Arloa was. She'd only ever referred to her by the first name and never her station in Raegina, but he had to suspect something, didn't he?

"She's a Kauket and a senator." Jerry pinned him with her gaze, needing to know exactly what he thought of that.

Azar raised a bushy eyebrow at her, his lips parted slightly in surprise as the only sign he hadn't known. "You're fucking a Kauket? Does she know you were in Joab?"

"Yes," Jerry murmured, heat hitting her cheeks in a rush of embarrassment. She had never told Arloa why she was in Joab, however. It seemed as though she had kept a lot of things to herself, probably too much in the grand scheme of things. However, she would be a stupid woman not to go searching for the records, especially considering the position she held.

Azar cocked his head in her direction. "How did you find a Kauket to fuck?"

Jerry wanted to correct him, to tell him it was more than just sex, but hadn't she been trying to convince herself that was all it was for the last few months? It hadn't started as more. She remembered when they'd met, that sweet pull of confidence and mystery that had intrigued Jerry to the point that she had to venture into a relationship just to know how it would end. And she had seen how it ended. Swiftly by her own hand. Except it seemed as though it hadn't.

"Does she act like them? Give to Joab?"

Jerry shook her head. "No, she doesn't associate with her family."

Azar didn't look as though he believed her, but he didn't add anything to the conversation. They stood in silence, Jerry steering the ship. Her back ached from standing upright at the wheel for so many hours straight.

"Yafe and Vivian want to talk to you before you rest, Cap. And I do suggest that you rest. I'll take the ship tonight."

"Thank you." Jerry's voice was soft as she stepped away from the wheel, his hands replacing hers. She was glad there didn't have to be more explanation about who Arloa was or how they knew each other. Surely he would have figured out by then that Arloa was where Jerry got a lot of her information, aside from Miriam. They were both good resources to have, ones Jerry didn't want to give up.

Walking through the small door and into the corridor, Jerry followed the familiar path to Yafe's cabin. She would have to start there, though she should probably find something to eat to sustain her. Her crew had brought her snacks throughout the day, but it had been few and far between, and her empty stomach was loud.

She found Yafe in her cabin, Vivian already with her. Bypassing the galley, Jerry stepped into the room and shut the door, stretching her legs along the floor and tilting her head back into the wall as she waited to see what the two of them wanted to talk to her about. When they didn't start, Jerry pinned them each with a serious look.

"Well?"

"Training is going much better today," Yafe started. "We're finally starting to work as a team."

"I agree," Vivian answered. "I skipped out on the last couple so that I could work on this bug you wanted me to create."

Jerry nodded at her, not needing any more explanation. She knew what her crew was doing when—that was her job as captain—and she was glad that her orders were being followed. "Who are our weak ones?"

"Amabel seems to have certain loyalties to Ursula." Yafe slid a glance to Jerry, one Jerry had seen before that meant there was more to that comment than met the eye. "Cassuis seems to be good for us, though. He's rough, but I think that might come in handy when we meet *Wench's Dream.*"

Jerry raised an eyebrow. Yafe wasn't exactly giving her a direct answer. "But who are the weak ones?"

"Pancho," Vivian supplied. Yafe sent her a sharp look, and she shrugged in response. "He doesn't like working with women."

"How did he manage to survive on *Calluna*?"

Vivian pressed her lips together hard. "He wasn't there long, and he was always upsetting the balance."

Jerry frowned. "Telford?"

"He'll do for now," Yafe answered.

"Okay." Jerry waited for the rest of the weight drop on her, but they were both silent. Jerry held the quiet in the room, knowing there was something else that needed to be shared with her but the two of them were hesitating. Finally, with her patience gone, Jerry glared at Yafe. "You better start talking."

Yafe sighed. "Vivian needs to share."

Vivian looked as though she was going to faint. Her cheeks were pale and her gaze downcast. "Yafe thinks you need to know what's going on over on *Calluna*."

"So speak," Jerry ordered. "I don't have all damn night."

She had never seen either of them look so nervous, especially Vivian. They were newer to knowing each other and working together, but Vivian wasn't someone who hid her feelings in general. Jerry envied that. Only people who had grown up in a stable home had that freedom. Worry and fear flashed through Vivian's eyes before she nodded to herself.

"Ursula isn't a captain."

Jerry snorted loudly. "That's for damn sure."

"Right, but she may listen to what you tell her to do, but she rarely does it."

"What do you mean?" Jerry stayed still, watching to see what Vivian would do next or if she would try to skirt around it. Calling out her captain wasn't an easy task, and if Vivian was willing to take the risk, then Jerry was willing to listen.

"She broke the contract with Mortimer Blair when you left to go to Potelia."

Frowning, Jerry sat up a little straighter, even though this wasn't new information to her. She flicked her gaze to Yafe to see if she was telling the truth or not, but Yafe nodded an affirmation. "Did she say why?"

"She was tired of hauling salt."

Laughing dryly, Jerry closed her eyes and smacked her head into the wall with a loud thwack. They were all tired of hauling salt. It wasn't an easy job by any means, and being covered in small granules of salt every day was not what Jerry had envisioned when she started buying up ships for her fleet. She sighed heavily and shook her head. "So what was she going to do instead?"

"Work for Miriam."

"Miriam won't hire her," Jerry answered without opening her eyes. "Miriam hates her."

"But she likes you," Yafe gave her two cents.

Jerry opened her eyes again and settled into the conversation. "Still, Miriam wouldn't hire her without my okay. What else does Ursula do?"

"She threatens to withhold our rations all the time—not that it really matters anymore because there's no vestigen to be found anywhere."

Jerry bit her cheek. "What would cause that kind of punishment?"

"Anything," Vivian answered. "Whatever suited her mood in the moment."

"Be specific." For some reason, Jerry needed to know. She needed the details and to be able to have all the complaints against Ursula in order to have the conversation she'd been avoiding. She needed to know if the crew she'd left on *Calluna* was safe or if she would have to send a ship to rescue them.

"It's really anything, Cap. If we piss her off, if we don't move fast enough, if we don't get out of her way, if we look at her wrong—anything."

Jerry's heart sank. What had happened to Ursula in the time since they'd met? She had once been Jerry's part-time lover, before she'd gone to Joab the last time, but this woman Vivian was describing was someone else entirely. "What else?"

"She'll beat us, sometimes. If we really step out of line."

"For what?"

"Talking back, threatening to talk to you, going to find a day job."

Nothing was worth a beating in Jerry's opinion, but she hadn't actually made that a rule Ursula had to follow. She probably should have, though she'd never seen that streak in Ursula before, and she'd kept it well contained while they had all been on *Calluna*.

Jerry stood suddenly, smoothing her hands down the front of her thighs and then across her stomach. "Thank you, Vivian."

"Cap?" Vivian stood up sharply, following every movement Jerry made. "What are you going to do?"

"I'm going to take care of this." She jerked down on her leather vest and rolled her shoulders. She stalked straight up to the wheelhouse.

Azar gave her a sharp look, but Jerry held her hand up to silence him. She said nothing as she input *Calluna's* code into their communicator and waited for Ursula to answer. When Ursula's face appeared on the small device, Jerry debated exactly how to start this conversation. She'd left Ursula with direct information of how to access brains for her crew, and she couldn't imagine Ursula withholding something necessary for survival. How many people had she killed because of her own animosity toward others?

"Hey, Cap," Ursula said since Jerry didn't start. "Something I can help you with?"

"How is the salt run going?"

"We're on our way back to Beren Island right now."

Jerry nodded at her and slid a glance to Azar. Not for the first time, she wished time that she was on *Yarrow* so she could track where Ursula actually was instead of having to rely on her telling the truth. It seemed as though her trust diminished rapidly. "How much did Morty give you for the last shipment?"

Ursula's face pinched before she relaxed. "Minimum."

"How much?" Jerry pressed, wanting to know.

"Twenty credits per pound."

Jerry nodded. It was slightly less than she had hoped he would pay, but then again, she'd have to check numbers when she returned to make sure Ursula wasn't lying about that, too. In that moment, Jerry knew any trust there was between them was broken, and she couldn't allow Ursula to captain *Calluna* any longer.

"There are rumors circulating."

"What rumors?" Ursula narrowed her gaze, and Jerry witnessed every single one of her defenses go up.

"That you withheld vestigen in the past for infractions."

"I would never..." Ursula's lips parted, but she stopped speaking, as if denying the accusation was too much energy to even put into it.

"Ursula," Jerry stated calmly. "Is it true?"

"It's an effective tool for motivation."

Jerry slammed her fist onto the dash, startling Azar from his position at the wheel. Jerry shook her head wildly and pointed at Ursula through the small device. "You don't fuck with people's life like that. You're not a god!"

Ursula's nose wrinkled. "I'll do what works on my ship."

"It's not your damn ship."

Ursula snorted, her head moving side to side slowly, and Jerry's stomach sank. She knew where this was going before the words were even out of her mouth.

"It's my ship now." Ursula ended the communication.

Jerry cursed and slammed her hand onto the dash again. Azar, wisely, kept silent next to her. She needed to throw something. The energy in her veins was about to burst, and Jerry needed to dissipate it before she did something she would regret. Spinning in her boots, she stared around the wheelhouse, trying to find the one thing she would be able to destroy that wouldn't fuck over their plan.

"Cap," Azar started, but she spun on him and held up her hand.

"Don't talk to me right now."

Jerry left the wheelhouse and Azar behind. She stalked through the corridors to the galley and immediately walked out. She walked through each of the storerooms, her boots heavy on the deck as she went. She made it through all the decks before landing in front of her personal cabin. Slamming her way inside, Jerry grabbed the small chest she had brought along with the new items she had purchased and threw it against the wall. The wood splintered and shattered, scattering onto the floor.

Life had thrown her for an unexpected loop, one she had never thought she'd face. Her friends abandoned her when all she had done was try to take care of them. Picking up the larger pieces of wood, Jerry snapped them and tossed them onto the floor again. All she had done for the last year and a half was take care of what she considered hers, and it stung and it hurt. It was a devastating blow that her crew, her people, hadn't felt the same way in return.

She destroyed her cabin, and then she spent the next two hours cleaning it up. Fuck, she wanted something to drink, anything to calm the raging nerves abounding in her body. She'd never felt so betrayed. She had given Ursula everything, taken care of her during one of the most trying times in Penum only to be treated like this?

Collapsing on her cot, Jerry covered her face and turned on her side. As much as she knew she needed sleep so that she could steer the vessel throughout the day while Azar rested, she couldn't force her body or her mind to stop. She officially had no ships. Blaise had stolen *Yarrow* and Ursula had stolen *Calluna*.

For the time she'd been back, she'd wanted so little to do with *Calluna* because all her focus had been on *Yarrow*, but to have no ships…to be a pirate with no home…that was worse than she'd ever imagined. She had spent so much of her time and energy in finding those two vessels and making them hers, learning their systems, rebuilding their systems, only to have them taken out from under her in the span of a few months.

Jerry landed her fist into the wall, the shock and pain ringing up her arm into her elbow and shoulder was a stark reminder that this was her reality. She had a crew with no ship other than one she had *borrowed*, and she had no way to keep them fed and housed longer than this particular trip would take them. How would she even tell them?

Cursing again, Jerry bit the sides of her tongue. When she walked out of the cabin come morning she was going to have to be strong again, confident and aloof. She couldn't let them see her break down, and she would never fall into the same traps as Ursula when it came to being captain. She would be honest to an extent, but for now, she wanted to keep focused on why they were out there, why they were flying to the Jackimore Sea, and what their first goal was.

Find Blaise.

Steal back *Yarrow*.

She would deal with Ursula and *Calluna* when she returned to Raegina and could confront her face-to-face. Ursula was a dead woman.

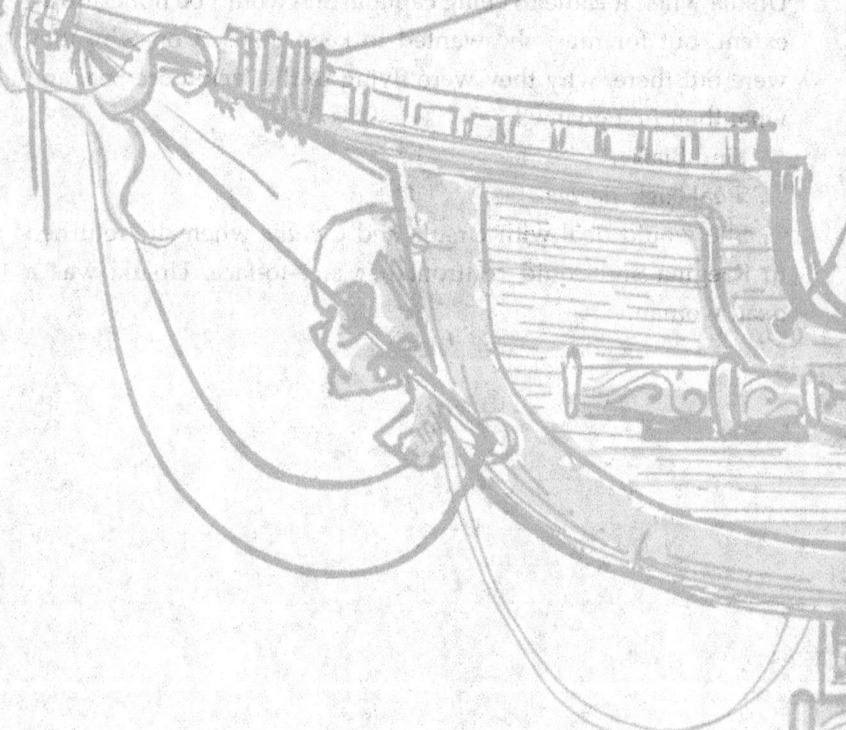

CHAPTER 18

When she woke up that morning, she was the most rested she had been in years. Every bit of energy in her body was ready to go, she was wide awake, and her mind spun with answers to all her problems. Dressing rapidly, Jerry raced to the wheelhouse, finding Azar's eyes drooping as he stood over the wheel. She grinned at him.

"Get some rest. She'll be here when we're ready to go."

Azar nodded slowly, saying nothing as he handed over the wheel. He updated her on their location, but shortly afterward he slunk away to catch up on sleep. For the last year, Jerry had lived in response to someone or something. She hadn't done anything to make Penum move because of her cause. All she had done in the last year and a half since she'd been struck by the virus was to respond and react.

Today, she was going to change that.

Rolling her shoulders, Jerry checked their position on the dash. They weren't all that far from the Jackimore Sea, another day's worth of sailing if they managed, although she did want her crew rested—in particular, Azar. She needed him.

It was odd to think that at one point she had relied on Yafe more than him, but since he had joined her crew permanently, she had always seen him as her second in command. Yafe was a close third, however, and was far more in tune with the emotional side of the crew than she was.

Jerry was just about to hit the communications to start a training tactic when she hesitated. A small blip on the radar lit up the screen in front of them. Her heart raced. It was a ship all right, but the question still remained if it was the right ship. She moved her hand back to the thruster and picked up speed, easing the vessel into flying faster and straighter. She wasn't going to win any awards for stealth for this one, but that wasn't her goal. She wanted to know if this was *Wench's Dream*.

They were in a medical vessel, one that from the first few glances wouldn't tip anyone off to them being pirates, and until Blaise was right on top of them, he wouldn't know who they were. Jerry pushed forward, following the tracker on the other vessel. It wasn't unheard of to find someone out in the seas—hell, that was how they pirated most ships—but they weren't even in Jackimore or anywhere near a harbor or on a main path to and from different countries.

The only people who navigated these parts of the seas were either seriously lost or they were pirates themselves. Jerry's heart thundered as she moved in closer. She couldn't be this damn lucky, could she? As they got closer, she slowed the ship so she could appear as though she wasn't flying straight toward them. She took a meandering path toward the other vessel and immediately grabbed the horn. "Yafe, wheelhouse. Immediately."

She was nearly out of breath. Jerry couldn't describe the giddiness rolling around in her chest. Who else would be out there? There weren't that many other pirates in these waters, not that many who would be here when *Wench's Dream* was controlling the seas. Jerry gripped the wheel hard as she impatiently waited for Yafe to join her.

The blip on the dash grew stronger, and Jerry's gut told her that it was Blaise, that it was *Wench's Dream*, and she was going to follow them to her death if she had to. She needed a bit of good timing and luck to turn her sails. As soon as Yafe appeared,

Jerry let go of the wheel, grabbed her telescope, and raced out to the deck. She said nothing to Yafe as she ran, full speed, right to the bow. Pressing the telescope to her eye, Jerry looked forward and tried to catch a simple glimpse of the ship.

"Please let it be them," she muttered as she eased the focus to try and get a clearer image of what was in front of them. Thankfully Yafe kept the ship steady as she looked so she didn't lose it and have to find the ship again.

Staring at the stern of the other vessel didn't give her much help figuring out which one it was, but suddenly, they turned broadside, and Jerry caught sight of the beautifully painted lettering on the side.

"Fuck." Gripping the telescope hard, Jerry raced back to the wheelhouse and slid in to replace Yafe. "It's them. Batten down the hatches."

Yafe grabbed the horn and gave out the orders. Jerry knew Azar would be up to join her as soon as he could drag his sorry ass out of bed. Guilt stabbed her side at having to wake him, but at the same time, he would be just as excited for the discovery.

"What are we doing, Cap?"

Jerry knew Yafe was asking about the plan, but before she could speak another small blip echoed on the screen south of their position. Jerry clenched her jaw, staring at it, the way it moved, the flight path it took. Her heart raced, and she moved her gaze up to Yafe, fear in Yafe's eyes as she stared back.

"Get Azar. Now."

"He's coming," Yafe said.

Jerry shook her head and pushed buttons on the dash to try and get a better readout of the ship coming their direction. It didn't move as quickly as *Wench's Dream*, but it moved in a much more straightforward, confident path. Jerry knew who it was without even having to see the ship. Sure enough, two more ships appeared shortly after it, some distance away, but enough that they would cause issues.

"Fuck." Jerry gripped the wheel hard and slowed their pace.

She would deal with them first and then get back to Blaise, but if he had any hint that the authorities were out there, he would run and hide like she would if she were in *Yarrow* or *Calluna*. Being in the medical vessel, there was no way to hide. She didn't have speed, and she was a beacon of *we don't belong here* shouting to the authorities her need for help. "Yafe, you need to hide all the contraband, and hide it well."

"Aye, Cap." Yafe got on the horn and made a second call to the crew, changing the direction of their actions.

As she ran from the wheelhouse, Azar stepped inside, his large form filling the doorway. "What is it?"

"We found *Wench's Dream*, and we found three authorities, no doubt after us."

Azar slid a glance to where his sister had been but stepped forward at the same time as he pulled up the readouts on the dash. "Are we hiding?"

"Where? There's no islands out here."

"We can outrun them."

Jerry slowly shook her head. "I'm not sure we should."

Azar gave her a confused look, and she knew why. Their goal was always to outrun and to hide from the authorities. They were always doing something wrong, but this time, they weren't. Aside from being in a vessel they didn't exactly have permission to be flying, they hadn't done anything wrong in it.

"I think we should let them catch us." It would be one of the worst tests of their relationship, and considering how they'd left off talking the other day, Jerry wasn't sure where Arloa would land, but it would be the easiest way to get rid of the authorities on a longer-term basis so she could focus on finding Blaise. "We'll be inspected."

Azar frowned. "I don't think that would be wise. We can't hide who we are."

Jerry drew in a deep breath and slid her gaze to him, locking her eyes on his dark brown ones. "No, but *she* can."

"Is this wise?"

"It's the best way to do this. We can't hide from three of them. They'll throw up a net and knock us out for days while we make repairs. I don't want to lose that time in our hunt for Blaise or be flat on our ass when he finds us."

"I can understand that, Cap, but—" Azar stopped sharply as the door to the wheelhouse opened.

Sacha stepped through it with Vivian hot on her heels. She gave Jerry a demure look as Vivian stepped straight into the room as if she owned it. "Who's coming?"

"Authorities." Jerry straightened her shoulders, not hiding from anyone what they were about to face or the fact that Joab was a strong possibility for all of them. "We're debating the finer points of running or staying."

"There's no point in staying." Sacha wrinkled her nose.

Jerry raised an eyebrow at her and immediately shut her down. "I don't believe anyone asked you for your opinion."

"You're fucking with all our lives!" Sacha screeched.

Jerry stepped in closer, towering over her much smaller frame and eyeing her as if she was a bug to be squashed. "I didn't ask for your opinion. You're on my ship, and I make the decisions here."

"Your decisions will get us killed."

"They very well might," Jerry answered, confidently, the surge of pride and truth filling her completely. "But you knew that when you agreed to be on my crew, and you knew that when you agreed to this mission. So your life, while it's in my hands, isn't entirely my responsibility."

Sacha's lips parted as if she was going to protest again, but Vivian stepped between them. "Cap?"

"What?" Jerry's nose wrinkled in a sneer.

"What's your plan?"

Jerry would be damned if she explained everything to these two who knew nothing. Sacha at least had some inkling what was going on, and she supposed Vivian did, too, since she'd helped with stealing the Kauket vessel. "I'm going to trust my instincts. Hide everything, and get the crew ready for an inspection by the authorities."

Vivian looked as if she was about to protest the lack of information, but she hesitated, something lighting up in her gaze, before she turned around and walked out of the wheelhouse. Sacha huffed and followed her. Azar gripped Jerry's arm and spun her around.

"You better be right about this, Cap."

Jerry knew it, because if she was wrong, the vast majority of her crew would die in the fight to avoid Joab. Jerry walked up to the wheel and prepared the vessel. She started flying east, slowing, and then west. She bent down and climbed under the dash after pausing and fucked with the navigation system, pulling wires and reconnecting them incorrectly. She pointed at Azar sharply. "You will fix that when they ask you to."

"Aye." He blew out a breath and held the wheel firmly while Jerry left the wheelhouse and walked down to her cabin.

Jerry stared at the ceiling from her prone position on the cot until she knew they were being boarded. It took everything in her not to get up immediately. She waited until Azar called for her, and slowly made her way up to the wheelhouse. When she entered it, Azar had the ship idling and three men stood around, imposing on him.

Jerry had the audacity to look surprised as she rolled her shoulders and raised an eyebrow at who she figured was their leader. The rankings on his shoulder were enough to tell her so. "I'm captain of this vessel."

"Your man here has been little help in answering our questions."

"He's been told to fetch me should anything happen." Jerry nodded at Azar as if he had done exactly what he was supposed to. She pressed her hands to her hips and eyed the main man again. "May I ask who you are?"

"Authority Commander Sheldon Mullins, ma'am."

Jerry inwardly cringed at the use of the salutation. She was only called that by misogynistic assholes, and it didn't bode well in their favor. She might have to rely on Azar more than she'd anticipated for this one, unfortunately. "I'm captain of this vessel. Why have you boarded us?"

"It's not your ship." He stated it so smoothly that anyone would believe him even if he'd told her she could jump headfirst into the ocean below.

"You're right." Jerry lowered her shoulders. "I was making a special run for a member of the Kauket family, and was allowed to use her family's vessel."

Sheldon narrowed his eyes at her in disbelief. "I don't take kindly to liars."

"I'm not lying." Jerry folded her hands behind her back, keeping an eye on the other two authorities who flanked their leader, muscles tight as if they were ready to come down on her. "Why don't you contact Senator Arloa Kauket of Raegina and ask her."

Sheldon didn't budge, and Jerry suspected she was going to have to argue with him to even get him to do that, but this was her only plan to get out of this, her only way to push aside the authorities so she could focus on her true mission—Captain Blaise Lotchski.

"Go on," Jerry pushed. "She'll tell you exactly what I've told you. Not to mention, you're beyond the borders of Raegina's waters, your power here is slim."

Sheldon frowned. "Not when it concerns government, ma'am."

Jerry clenched her jaw hard to keep herself from saying anything stupid. She was exhausted by all the backward drama in the world, the lack of ability to keep up law versus societal ruling. "Contact her."

"I plan to." Sheldon jerked his head toward the man on his left. "Do it."

He said nothing as he walked to the dash and started the communications system.

"What are you doing out here?"

"We were on our way to the Jackimore Sea to reach Teedo, where we planned to pick up a shipment." Jerry said it with all the confidence she had, hoping Arloa would be sly enough to avoid details if she could. That was the main place where they would get tangled and in trouble.

Arloa's beautiful face appeared on the communications device, and Jerry frowned at it. The lines looked deeper around her eyes, the bags under them dark, and she was exhausted. Sheldon stepped up to the dash and leaned down so Arloa could have a clear image of her.

"Ms. Kauket."

Jerry bit her lip hard. He wouldn't even call a senator by her title, which told her a great deal about the man himself.

"I'm a senator, and you shall address me as such." Arloa's tone was pure contempt. "Why are you interrupting me?"

"I have found the medical vessel your family reported as stolen."

Arloa's eyebrow twitched, which to Jerry said she was surprised by the discovery or by the report—she wasn't sure which without speaking directly to Arloa, but they could deal with that later. Either way, the change in her features was so subtle that Sheldon likely missed it because he didn't know her well enough.

"What would you like me to do with the unlawful who occupy it?"

"I suppose I should question which unlawful it is you mean." Arloa shifted something around in front of her, as if she as still working while talking to the lowly man in front of her. It was the perfect way to tamp him down a few notches without outright telling him he was below her. Jerry had to fight her desire to smile.

Sheldon turned sharply on her, probably realizing he hadn't actually gotten her name when he'd boarded the ship. Jerry could have laughed. They must have sent the greenest asshole possible after her. Or perhaps he was the only one willing to lead the low-class battalion beyond Raegina's borders. Not many authorities would venture that far, though she had seen it on occasion.

"My name?" Jerry's tone was quite jovial. "I'm Captain Jeraldine Adelric."

A darkness floated over Arloa's gaze, but Sheldon missed it because he wasn't facing the communications device. When he turned back to Arloa, she looked murderous.

"Leave my vessel at once, authority. They are on my ship with my permission."

"But ma—Senator...there was a report—"

"And I have told you, Captain Adelric has my permission to be aboard. If you delay her mission any further, I'll hold you accountable." Without another word, Arloa ended the communications. The wheelhouse was cast into silence.

Jerry waited for the verdict, but she already knew what it would be. For him to go against a senator would end his career faster than he could blink. Jerry waited patiently as he turned, still in shock.

"My men will escort you out," Jerry stated as she held open the door to the wheelhouse so they could reach the deck.

Sheldon listened to her, dumbfounded, and Jerry couldn't hide her amusement as soon as the door swung shut. Azar made sure to escort them off. As soon as the authority's ships left, Jerry dipped under the dash to put the navigation system back together, glad she hadn't needed to use that plan. Azar stood sharply at her feet, kicked her boots, and then waited for her to answer.

"What?"

"That was an unnecessary risk."

"But also the easiest way to get rid of them."

Azar hummed his displeasure. Jerry finally put the last wire into place and slid out from under the dash. "It was fun to watch him get a beatdown."

"That it was," Azar answered. "But what's the plan now, oh dear Captain?"

Jerry held out her hand, and Azar helped her to stand. "Now, we find Blaise. I'm sure with any sign of authorities that he ran and hid, the coward he is, so let's find him. We know he's nearby."

"And Arloa?"

Jerry's jubilation faltered slightly. "I suppose I should contact her."

"Probably." Azar glowered as he grabbed the wheel to get the vessel moving again. "And the sooner the better."

"Right." Jerry wiped her greasy hands on her dark pants. "Getting on that."

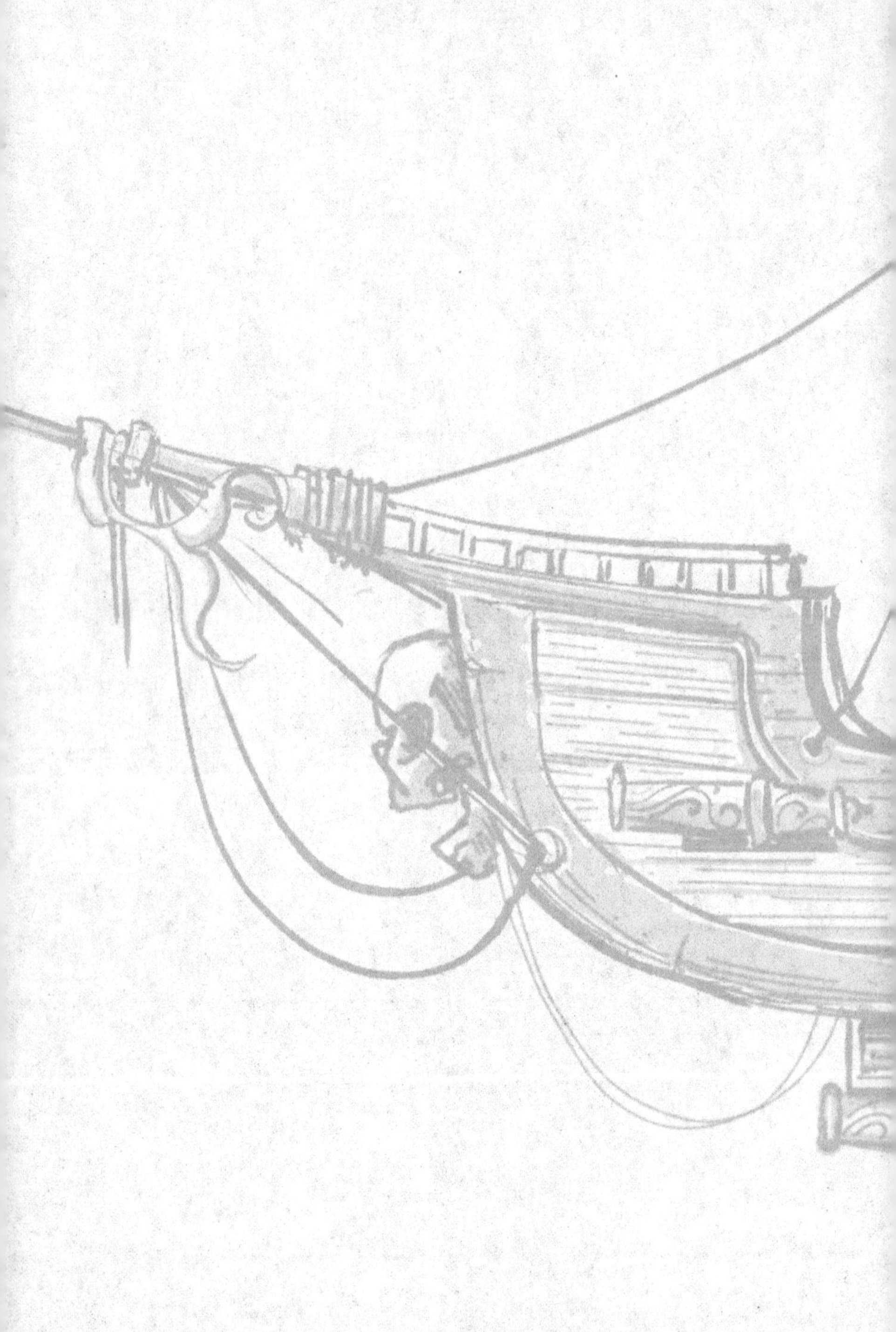

CHAPTER 19

erry had shooed Azar out of the wheelhouse again, urging him to rest. It had taken a few minutes of convincing, but eventually, he had wandered down toward his cabin. Jerry sighed as she watched Yafe and Sacha run another training simulation since they had the crew ready to go.

People moved around in front of her, Jerry giving commands from the wheelhouse as she would do during any battle or attack. Though she was equally as likely to find herself out on the deck and protecting her ship should they be boarded or attempting to board anyone.

She had sent Arloa a message hours ago, requesting a communication as soon as she had time. The poor woman had been disturbed enough throughout the day to have any other impending actions on her time. Jerry had yet to receive a response and had decided to give it only a little bit longer before she made the communication herself.

Yafe stepped into the wheelhouse, her hands on her hips. "They're looking better."

"They are," Jerry agreed. It was the first time she felt as though she could say that and not be lying. "You're doing well with training them."

Yafe hummed her agreement. "Sacha and Vivian have both been excellent help."

"What I'm trying to figure out is if Ursula did no training of her crew whatsoever, what did she do?"

"Nothing," Yafe answered. "From my understanding she did nothing."

Jerry frowned. "It was a mistake to give her that power."

"Probably." Yafe stepped closer to Jerry and put a hand on her arm to get her full attention. "But mistakes happen, and now is your chance to rectify it."

"She took *Calluna* and her crew. I'll have to board her like we're boarding Blaise."

"An easy feat with an untrained crew. She won't be able to put up a fight like Blaise will."

"True," Jerry spoke slowly. She knew it would be easy to take *Calluna* back, but that didn't mean it wouldn't be an internal battle on her part. Ursula had been her friend—they had built a relationship together for years—so to have it ruined so arbitrarily was not what Jerry had expected. "Who will I put in her place?"

"I can think of a few souls who might fit the bill."

"You?" Jerry raised an eyebrow in Yafe's direction.

"I could, yes, but I'm not sure I want to captain a vessel."

Jerry nodded her understanding. Yafe was such an empath that to put her in complete control over a ship would make her jaded or it would break her, neither of which Jerry wanted for one of her closest friends. "I'll figure it out after we have *Yarrow* back in our possession."

"Yes." Yafe leaned against the dash, her hip digging into the edge as she looked Jerry up and down. "Now, about your woman."

Jerry sighed. Even far out in the sea and beyond the borders of their home she still couldn't escape Arloa. She'd wanted to. When they'd been marooned on the island, when they were in Potelia, and the entire year before while she hadn't spoken a word of Arloa or seen her, she'd wanted to be rid of her memory and her presence, but it was impossible. Jerry's obsession ran strong and in a way that was impossible for her to escape.

Her slide back into Arloa's grasp had been slow and steady, and she had willingly given into it at each and every stage. Now she was left with nothing but Arloa to hold her steady, to keep her pointed toward home in a way that she desperately needed. Raising her gaze to Yafe's dark eyes, Jerry blinked away a sudden onslaught of tears.

"Cap?"

Jerry shook her head and put her hand up. "In some ways I've been a fool, Yafe, and in others, I have been the smartest pirate on the planet."

Yafe looked at her as though she didn't understand the contradiction, and that was perfectly fine. Jerry didn't want to explain it. Bolstering herself, Jerry rolled her shoulders and checked their navigation, keeping her eyes peeled for *Wench's Dream*. But Jerry suspected they would remain hidden for at least a day.

"I'm waiting for Arloa to contact me. I need to thank her for helping us escape the authorities."

Yafe nodded slowly. "And?"

"What do you mean?"

"What else will you speak to her about?"

"Nothing of consequence." Jerry turned to look out the front window, wanting the conversation to change topics or be over by that point. "We'll need to make sure everyone isn't struggling with the virus."

Yafe cocked her head slightly, Jerry catching the movement out of the corner of her eye. She didn't turn to face Yafe fully, still wanting to change topics and not talk about Arloa if she could avoid it.

"Cap? Is there a reason you can't say it for what it is?"

Jerry surpassed the shudder. There were many reasons she couldn't. The thought of eating someone still churned her stomach. The thought of killing someone only for her survival washed her in cold shame.

"It's natural—"

"It's not natural," Jerry interrupted on a hiss. "It's anything but natural."

"But the legends…"

Jerry sighed and pinched the bridge of her nose. "I know what the legends say, and I know this is what they resorted to when this virus first came about. But that was seven hundred years ago, Yafe. One would think we've made some advances in society since then."

As Jerry said the words, she knew it wasn't true. While their society had advanced with technology, and for a time, the laws had advanced toward equality, the overtones in the last fifty years had taken them backward.

Sexism, classism, and racism were rampant in their world, particularly in Raegina. She'd been surprised when Arloa Kauket had been elected as a senator. Then again, she was from the right class and race, although her sex remained a problem she had to overcome. Jerry frowned, focusing back on Yafe as she tried to remember the conversation at hand.

"It's disgusting."

"You believe you're disgusting for having to eat someone else's mind in order to sustain your own."

"Yes." Jerry flushed and stared down at the dash, really wishing Arloa would contact her or a blip that might be Blaise would appear. She would rather take this conversation back to the uncomfortableness it had been before. "Make sure everyone is well, please."

"We don't have any left."

Jerry groaned. "Why didn't you just say so?"

"Because I need to know what you want me to do about it."

"You'll do nothing. Stay here."

Jerry left the wheelhouse and stalked into the corridor. She rolled her shoulders as she slithered through the halls and into the bowels of the ship where she'd locked up the man they'd found on the vessel when they stole it.

She stopped outside of the door and pressed her palm fully to it, the cold of the metal door seeping into her skin and reminding her how aloof she needed to be for this to happen. She hated this. Morose, Jerry pushed open the door and shut it swiftly behind her. She would do this with no witnesses. They would all know, of course, but none would be able to testify to it actually happening.

The man looked up at her, a dead stare in his gaze as if he already knew his fate. It was different to kill in battle, to kill when protecting herself to survive. Then again, this was only another kind of survival, a passive one. Her heart thrummed steadily, and she didn't want to admit defeat into this lowest part of her world.

He scuffled around, trying to stand, but she hadn't fed him in days so he was weak. Jerry moved in, wrenching him around so his back was pressed to her front. She didn't want to see him, didn't want to hear or feel him struggle more than she had to. She pressed the blade of her short sword against his throat and made the slice quick and true.

He didn't cry out—that was a saving grace she hadn't known she needed.

The man bled out on the floor, and Jerry stood watch over him to make sure when it was done that she could collect his brain and take it to the galley. Her stomach churned at the mere thought of what they were about to do—what she had already done. With a parched mouth, Jerry used her sword and cracked open his skull. Using the hilt, she made the entry point even wider and pulled out the precious life-giving source they all needed to live.

Why was it that one had to die for many to survive?

Was that a fair trade?

As much as she would like to think so, Jerry knew it wasn't. A life for a life was never a fair trade. Cutting the cloth from his body, she wrapped the brain tightly to keep any blood from dispersing as she brought it up a few levels. Jerry left his body there, locking the door behind her. She would dispose of it later when the crew was sleeping and wouldn't have witness her crimes.

Entering the wheelhouse, Jerry handed the *prize* to Yafe with a grunt and took over the wheel again. "There."

"Where did you—"

"Don't ask questions you don't want answers to." Jerry couldn't look her in the eye. She couldn't even stand to look in Yafe's direction. Guilt consumed her.

"I'll distribute it accordingly."

"You do that."

Yafe, thankfully, left her alone. In the silence of the wheelhouse, Jerry struggled to keep her emotions at bay, and when the communications panel lit up with a connection from Arloa, Jerry took it as the distraction she needed.

"I hope I didn't disturb you with my request," Jerry started, her tone stiff and formal.

Arloa cocked her head to the side, her eyes tight with worry. "Are you all right?"

"They left without incident."

"I'm glad to hear that, but Jer... I'm not the one who contacted them."

"I didn't realize this was a family vessel when I took it."

Arloa's lips thinned as she pursed them. "Did you really think I was rich enough to have my own?"

"Yes," Jerry answered honestly, and she wasn't sure that she was wrong either. However, she could see why Arloa wouldn't need a vessel, especially if she had access to her family's. Arloa's life wasn't on the waters like Jerry's. It was only another reason why their relationship would never work.

"I don't need a ship."

"I did," Jerry answered. "So I took this one. Thank you again for dealing with the authorities."

"If they come back, I'm not sure how much more help I'll be. You need to bring the ship back to harbor in order to avoid them."

"I can't do that," Jerry mumbled. "My mission isn't complete."

"To get *Yarrow* back?" Arloa's features hardened, her jaw clenching and her cheeks pulling tight.

Jerry knew that look even from that distance. Arloa still didn't agree that this was the best course of action. Jerry couldn't disagree more. She needed a win, and at that moment, her win was going to be *Yarrow*.

"Jer, don't you think—"

"She's my home, Arloa. Whether you understand that or not, she is my world." The bite in Jerry's words was stronger than she'd intended, but she couldn't help it. She was tired of having the same damn argument. "Accept that and you'll accept me. I won't leave her in the hands of someone who would molest her."

"*She* is a ship!" Arloa's voice rose.

Jerry knew in that moment she'd made a wrong step, but she still couldn't stop herself from pushing forward. "She's more than a ship. She's the only one who's ever been there for me."

"Are you saying I haven't?"

Gritting her teeth, Jerry halted all forward movement of the conversation. That was a trap she had to decide if she wanted to walk into or not. She needed to know if it would be one she could get out of or if it was one she wanted to get out of.

"What I'm saying is my ship is my life, and if you can't accept that—"

"You don't mean that," Arloa interrupted.

"I absolutely mean that," Jerry confirmed, her tone brokering no room for argument. *Yarrow* would be her first love no matter what, and any woman who was with her would have to accept that. "*Yarrow* is my life."

"Then I suppose I know where I stand."

Yes, just below Yarrow. Though Jerry didn't say that out loud, nor would she ever. No woman had ever taken a place that close to her heart before, and it was likely the closest any woman ever would. The tug and pull Jerry experienced when it came to anything related to Arloa was back in full force. She wanted to soothe the hurt she had caused as much as she wanted to continue the distance she had created.

"Jer, tell me this one thing." Arloa's voice was softened, as if she truly was looking for an answer, something that was going to shift both their worlds and would alter everything from there on out.

Jerry wasn't sure she wanted to hear the request. This moment was monumental, and it was something Jerry needed to avoid, but her voice betrayed her. "What?"

"Do you love me?"

They locked eyes through the power that was technology. Jerry didn't want to answer this way. She wanted to say it with Arloa's hot skin against her, the feel of her in Jerry's arms, the power of being in the audacious woman's presence. Yet anytime she'd been in the position before, she'd balked at the idea and the words. Perhaps distance was the way to make this statement. "I don't see how that's relevant to this conversation."

Arloa nodded slowly, as though she wasn't sure what to say now that a confession had rung through the air. "Please return my ship to me."

"Call off the authorities," Jerry pushed back.

"You know I can't do that. Once the report has been filed—"

"You're a Kauket, and you're a senator. You can do whatever you want, Arloa. Don't try me on this. I know the power you hold."

"You think too highly of me." Arloa's lips parted in surprise. "Not everything is within my grasp and certainly not this."

"Call off the authorities. You know I'm here to do justice for *Yarrow*, nothing more. I'm not here to steal or maim—"

"But you will," Arloa countered, her tone angry. She softened as she continued, "You will, Jer. That's the point entirely. You will use that vessel you've stolen and break the law. The law which I'm bound to uphold."

Jerry snorted. "The law that is obtuse."

"It may very well be in some cases, but thievery isn't one of them."

"And how will the law hold Lotchski accountable? Hmm? The law doesn't care about anyone but itself, and you're a part of the problem, not the solution."

"I will always be a part of the solution!" Arloa's voice rose to a near yell.

Jerry had no idea what nerve she had hit in Arloa, but she had definitely hit one. Taking a moment to breathe and calm the conversation, Jerry started in again. "The law is for rich white men. Until it's truly equal in practice, there's no point in following it. Call off the authorities. I've not stolen the vessel, I've merely borrowed it, and I will return it."

Arloa let out a wry laugh. *"Borrowed?* In what world have you *borrowed* it?"

"In this one." Jerry put her hands on her hips. "Rescind the authorities."

"It's not within my power."

"Then find the power to do it." Jerry wanted to slap her hand against the communicator and end the call, but she couldn't force herself to move and make Arloa's beautiful face disappear. The obsession that was this woman filled her again. "I won't go back to Joab."

"Joab?" Arloa's brow wrinkled. "Is that what this is about?"

It was what this was always about. Jerry lived if only to escape, and escaping Joab was first and foremost in her mind.

"Jer, I won't send you there."

"You might not, but everyone else will. I have a record. I may have gotten my cards in order to buy *Yarrow* and *Calluna,* but I have a record. Surely you can't be so obtuse as to not know that."

"I know it." Arloa's voice dropped to a whisper. "I researched you when I met you. A woman in my position must know who she is seen with."

Jerry snorted. "Perfect. Do you know what happens in Joab? What *your* family funds?"

"Yes." Arloa said it so coldly, as if it made no difference that people were beaten, raped, and murdered in a facility that was labeled as rehabilitation.

Jerry shook her head slowly, realization dawning on her. She didn't know who Arloa was. Not truly. Arloa had more secrets than Jerry did. "How can you support—"

"To be absolutely clear on the matter, I don't support it."

"You don't fight it."

"As I've said many times throughout this conversation, I don't have the power—"

"You're a Kauket."

"And I have defied my family too many times for them to listen to a word I say. I'm not my family, Jer. I've told you that from the first moment I met you. I may have their name, and that may carry some weight, but I'm nothing of what they want me to be."

"You're an aristocrat," Jerry lobbed the accusation, knowing it would hurt.

"Yes." Arloa glared back. "And you're a pirate."

"I am, and that should tell you exactly how this will end."

"It very well may," Arloa countered. "But that doesn't mean we can't enjoy what we have for now."

"For now?" Jerry raised an eyebrow and held out her hands to her sides. "For now I've borrowed your vessel. I will return it. But right now I need to steal my home back, and you won't stop me from doing that."

"I know," Arloa whispered. "But I wish *I* was your home— not her."

Jerry's heart sank, realizing where the entire argument

stemmed from. Leaning in, Jerry moved close to Arloa's sweet image on the communications device. "But she *is* my home."

"I know, and I accept that."

"Then call off the authorities."

"As much as I might want to, I don't have the power to do that. You'll have to find your own way around them."

"Nothing I haven't done before," Jerry muttered.

"I should hope so." Arloa raised her chin. "When you return, Jer, I want an end to this."

"An end to what?"

"The question I've asked. I want to know where we stand."

Jerry wasn't sure how to answer that. She knew in her gut that she wanted an end and she wanted to never break that connection between them at the same time. "I'll see you when I return."

"As soon as you return. I'm tired of waiting."

Jerry nodded sharply and ended the communication. Stretching her back, she sighed heavily. She'd said it. Not in so many words, but she'd confessed her obsession for this intrepid woman. No matter how many times Jerry ran through the conversation in her mind, it still didn't sit well with her. The conversation had something underlying it that she couldn't put her finger on, some kind of urgency she hadn't been able to name, and it hadn't been on her side. It had been entirely on Arloa's.

CHAPTER 20

Jerry sat on the edge of the deck while they gave the engines a rest. She'd been circling the area for more than a day wondering where Blaise had gone to hide when she'd just given up and taken the much needed break—one her entire crew needed.

The tight confines on the ship with the extra people were beginning to be too much, so she gave them a couple hours to rest, relax, and do nothing except try to stay out of each other's way or have a bit of fun. Jerry sought the much needed quiet of the deck near the stern of the ship, the solace something she had longed for.

Her conversation with Arloa had twisted in her gut so many times throughout the last day, and she still wasn't sure what to make of it all. She'd wanted to confess she loved the aristocrat, the government official, the one person who couldn't be more her opposite in some ways even though in others they were so damn similar. Grinding her teeth, Jerry stared up at the darkening sky as the sun fell below the horizon.

What the hell was she supposed to do with it all? One minute she was captain of a ship, the next she had been marooned for five damn weeks, then she'd lost her other ship to the captain she'd hired. Within all of that was the drama of love, something

Jerry adamantly didn't want in her life, especially not with a government official. Too many things to trace back to her that could land her in Joab.

"Hey, Cap. Got a minute?"

Jerry tilted her chin down and spied Vivian, standing with her hands folded in front her, nervously brushing her thumb against the tops of her knuckles, and her lower lip pulled between her teeth. Instantly curious, Jerry raised an eyebrow and nodded toward the empty spot next to her.

Vivian sat, brushing her hands under her ass as she went. Jerry missed seeing her in the beautiful dress she had purchased for her, but pants were far more practical for what they were planning. Jerry stayed put, leaning against the back railing as if she had all the time in the world, which she supposed she did. The sound of wind rushing against the ship, bowing around it as it moved, the engines barely whirring as they held their position above the sea's waters, and the waves moving gently against each other was so damn soothing. She should sleep out there instead of in her cabin.

When Vivian didn't immediately start the conversation, Jerry let the silence linger. She was technically not on duty at that moment, but as captain, she was always in charge and there when one of her crew needed her. There was no off button in her profession. Jerry stretched her legs out in front of her, closing her eyes and focusing more intently on the sound of the water below them. Sometimes she could barely hear the raging waters of the ocean, when there was a storm or when they were moving swiftly for an escape from whatever chased them.

Jerry eased the muscles in her body, still wondering when Vivian was going to start talking about whatever it was she'd deemed necessary to break Jerry's silence. Finally, as the sun dipped all the way below the horizon, Vivian's voice filled the quiet space between them.

"I'm almost finished with the bug."

"And you think it'll work?" Jerry eyed Vivian curiously.

While engineering and mechanics had always been her forté, programming and the science behind all the technology that made ships run was not.

"I don't know."

Despondent, Vivian refused to look Jerry in the eye. For someone typically so confident in her abilities, it unsettled Jerry that she wasn't sure about this one in particular. They hadn't worked together for very long, but Jerry had been there when Vivian had been saved from the virus overtaking her body. It wasn't that long ago, only half a year by her memory, but Vivian had proven to be an asset to her little crew.

Jerry frowned and glanced in Vivian's direction. "What's wrong with it?"

"There's no way of testing it."

"But outside of testing it, it should work?"

Vivian's mouth pulled tight to one side, and she waggled her head back and forth. "Without testing it, I don't know if it'll work."

Jerry sighed. That was a bit of a conundrum because they certainly couldn't test it without *Yarrow* in their possession. "What's the worst that can happen?"

"Aside from it simply doing nothing, it can get into *Yarrow's* systems and destroy some of the coding already in place, making her unable to fly or at worse, sinking her."

Jerry's stomach flopped at that. She didn't want to sink the ship that she had spent so much time, effort, and money to save. To sink a ship was the end of a ship. The ocean below would eat it in a heartbeat, destroying everything in it, even if that was them. "Is there a way to stop it should it not be doing what is expected?"

"I haven't been able to program that in yet. I want to, but if we find *Yarrow* before I do, then there won't be a failsafe."

Jerry rubbed circles in her temple as a headache formed. Everything seemed to slip through her fingertips, and she wasn't sure she'd ever be able to get it back. First it was *Yarrow*—actually, it was her life. The life she had worked so damn hard to take back and have under her control. When the virus had hit, her life had taken a dive into the underground, a place she had emerged from and never wanted to return. But such was the way of things, she supposed. She still hated it.

"How much time do you need to create one?"

"A failsafe?" Vivian's light hazel eyes turned on her. At Jerry's nod, she continued, "Another week at least. This bug was a lot more complicated than I originally thought it would be. Keying it to a specific ship without being on that ship stretched my abilities."

"I understand."

"But I can do it, Cap. If you want me to, that is."

Jerry nodded. "I do."

"Okay." Vivian shifted, as if she was about to get up, but Jerry put her hand out in front of her to stop her. "Cap?"

"Would you mind…staying here for a bit?"

A flash of worry crossed Vivian's features, but she rested against the railing. "Sure. Any reason in particular?"

That had been what Jerry wanted to avoid. While the solace was nice, she really needed to talk to someone about anything other than the ship, Blaise, or Arloa. Vivian was the easiest option since she was there, but equally, Jerry figured she could outsmart her enough to avoid those topics. "Just want to get to know my crew better."

"Right." Vivian's lips twitched into a smile. "You seem to know Yafe, Sacha, and Azar well enough."

"They served with me on *Yarrow*, so of course I know them well. And Yafe I knew before I hired her."

"You knew Ursula before, right?"

"Yes." Jerry didn't hesitate to answer because it wouldn't matter if she told the truth. Enough talk had happened about her relationship with Ursula for it to be confirmed easily enough. "I met Ursula when I was fifteen."

"Really?" Vivian looked intrigue now. "How'd you meet?"

Jerry chuckled lightly. "She was trying to work for Miriam."

"What?" Vivian's eyes widened. "What for?"

"She wanted to be one of Miriam's whores." Jerry wrinkled her nose at it. Her own mother had taken that job, so it wasn't because she thought of it as a lowly or unworthy position, but the thought of selling her body for credits was beyond how she wanted to spend her life. It was never a safe position to be in. "Miriam wasn't too keen on her, something about the way Ursula spoke to her I guess? I'm not entirely sure, but after Miriam told her no, she and I became fast friends. I was working on leaving Miriam's inner circle at the time."

"You were part of her inner circle? That's hard to believe." Vivian crossed her arms as she stretched out her legs and crossed her ankles. She looked absolutely relaxed.

Jerry wished she could have that much ease in talking with someone, especially about her own past. She doubted very much that she'd ever succeeded in getting out of Miriam's inner circle, but at least she wasn't considered a regular employee any longer —although with their current arrangement for brains, that could be another mark against her. Should the authorities find out about that one, they wouldn't even bother to keep her in Joab. It'd be straight to the plank for her.

"Did you grow up in Raegina?" Jerry asked, changing the topic slightly. "Until you were infected, I'd never seen you around the harbors."

Vivian shook her head slowly, her curls bouncing with the movement. "No, I grew up in Cantren in the Kilgorii region."

"Really?" Jerry faced her. "I never would have guessed that. You don't look like you're from there."

"My family is from here, and my father wanted me to get a proper education, so he sent me to Raegina for finishing school. I finished." Vivian winked. "But I hated it."

"I imagine so."

"I used to make modifications to the center's artificial intelligence for the fun of it." Vivian giggled, the sound pure and innocent in a way Jerry envied. "Then some started to pay me to make certain modifications. That was how I figured out I was good at this kind of stuff."

They couldn't have been that far apart in age, now that Jerry thought about it, but Vivian had the innocence of growing up in a stable home with a family who cared about her where Jerry hadn't been given that opportunity. Her mother had done her best, yes, but that had still come with a great number of sacrifices and shattering worldviews.

"My mother was sixteen when she gave birth to me. She worked for Miriam until she died."

Vivian's eyes went wide. She hovered her hand over Jerry's forearm until Jerry nodded at it and she clasped Jerry's wrist. "I'm so sorry."

"Nothing that wasn't expected when you're in her line of work. She was one of Miriam's whores, which is how I knew Ursula never had what it took to be one."

"So you grew up—"

Jerry nodded and interrupted her. "Yes, I grew up with Miriam always around somewhere. Sometimes we stayed at one of her houses, but a lot of the times my mother would be leased to ships for weeks or months at a time."

"I've heard about ships having that, but I've never witnessed it."

"It was outlawed centuries ago, but the underground always finds a way to profit on what is outlawed." Jerry reached over and covered Vivian's hand with her own and squeezed lightly. She was thankful for the touch, but at the same time, speaking of how she was raised only pushed her to realize she wasn't like everyone else.

"Seems we fall into that category, don't we?"

Jerry hummed her agreement. "I used to think this was the way to live. I went to Joab for two years."

Vivian hissed.

"Exactly," Jerry concurred. "I got out and swore I'd never go back. I got my cards, I found legal work, I had enough saved up to buy *Yarrow* with some help from Miriam, and I swore I'd never pirate again."

"And then the virus?" Vivian surmised.

"The virus." Jerry snorted out her frustration. "I got it from a man named Matthew Laurier. He had fast become my favorite crew member, but before we could take our second run to Beren Island, he succumbed to the virus."

"So many people have."

Jerry ignored that sentiment. She felt it, but she didn't want to delve into that emotion more than she had to. To think of the life that had passed away because of this damn virus was too much, and yet, they still had to survive through it all.

"Captain?" Vivian's full use of her title caught Jerry's attention. "Why do you want *Yarrow* back so badly?"

Jerry blew out a breath and broke her grasp from Vivian's, realizing far too late that they were still holding hands. She centered in on herself, digging deep into that desire, to try and put it into words. It had been so long since she'd managed to truly say it. She'd touched on the subject with Arloa, but she knew without even having to think too hard about it that Arloa hadn't fully understood.

"Growing up the way I did, moving from whorehouse to whorehouse and from ship to ship, I never had a home. Miriam might have been called that, the underground for sure, but it wasn't one thing that I could distinctly call mine. *Yarrow* was that for me."

Vivian stared at her. Jerry knew it without even having to look over. The feel of her gaze on Jerry's face was so strong in that moment, the confession true as it rang through the night air that chilled faster than she had anticipated it would.

"*Yarrow* is my home, and when Captain Blaise stole that, he took everything from me. I will get her back. I have to save her."

"You speak as though she's a person."

Jerry faced Vivian then. "A ship *is* a person to her captain.

She has to be. We have to work in sync with each other, take care of each other. We live and breathe by each other. She's my first true love."

"And is the woman who owns this ship your second?" Vivian's eyebrow rose, but Jerry sensed she could avoid answering if she wanted or simply refuse and Vivian wouldn't push it.

"She is," Jerry admitted. "Though I know it won't last."

"How do you know? I've loved before and lost before, but I don't know, it all seems so strange at times."

Jerry smiled, but it didn't reach her eyes. "I know because I'm a pirate and I'm a captain. No one can love me for long."

"That's quite a fatalistic point of view."

"It's the truth."

"She works for the government, your woman, right?"

"She does. Which is another reason I know it won't last. At some point, she'll have to catch me."

Vivian chuckled lightly. "You wouldn't imagine what some of those government types get up to."

"What do you mean?"

"When I was in finishing school, I did a little more than modify the systems at the school."

Jerry narrowed her gaze and shifted to look Vivian full on in the dim light that shone from the moon. "What did you do?"

"I toyed with the government systems. I wanted to see how easy it would be to get into them. I had to sneak in through the sewers in order to hook up to their system, but there was a direct line from that little shop by the government building, the one that sells those fancy glasswares."

"I know the one."

"In the cellar, there's a tunnel that leads to the sewer system that used to be used centuries ago, and I would take that and walk right into the main government building." Vivian looked so damn pleased with herself.

Jerry could have laughed. For a woman who was set up to

succeed and be in the upper class, she sure had fallen, and it seemed as though she'd done that willingly. "What exactly did you do while you were there?"

"Oh, tinkered with a few things here and there, especially at night when the building was largely empty."

"And what did you discover?"

"There's a senator there who would frequently invite women into his offices only to fuck them."

Jerry laughed, remembering her own time fucking Arloa on her desk a few months prior or in the carriage as she went from one government building to the next. They had been some of the most pleasant and arousing experiences of her life. "That doesn't surprise me."

"Doesn't it? And if I told you all these women were from the lower west end?"

That peaked Jerry's curiosity. The lower west end was the poorest part of Raegina, but they weren't known for prostitution. "Why from there?"

Vivian lifted a shoulder and dropped it. "I don't know. Some fetish he must have."

Jerry didn't answer, the thought spinning in her mind.

"And you know what else I found?"

"What else?" Jerry usually wasn't one for gossip, but since the government was much closer to her now than before, she might as well take the information that she received and hold it close. Who knew, it may come in handy someday.

Vivian grinned broadly from ear to ear. "I've never told anyone this."

Jerry gave her a pointed but silent look to tell her to spill the information already.

"I was able to connect with Senator Riley's communicator, and I overheard him talk about this special project he's been working on. It sounded really big."

"When was this?" Jerry frowned, trying to put together any more information she could find.

"Two years ago now. But he was talking about how the equipment broke or something but that he couldn't order a replacement because someone would get suspicious. It was about that time the connection was severed, so I never found out what he was talking about."

"Interesting." Jerry wouldn't give it more weight than that until she knew there was something else to go with it. There were many government projects that she would expect to be worked on in secret so it didn't surprise her that something like that would happen, though figuring out the extent to which Vivian would go to find information was far more helpful to their current situation.

Vivian shivered, and it was the perfect segue to ending the conversation and taking over her turn in the wheelhouse. "It's getting cold outside. We should go belowdecks. I want to check with Azar anyway."

"Yes, Cap." Vivian easily shifted from the friendly conversation back into the roles they were prescribed.

Jerry nodded sharply after they stood and walked directly to the wheelhouse, not looking over her shoulder as Vivian followed. Jerry shook her head at Azar, still mystified by Vivian's audacity and curiosity. It would certainly come in handy someday.

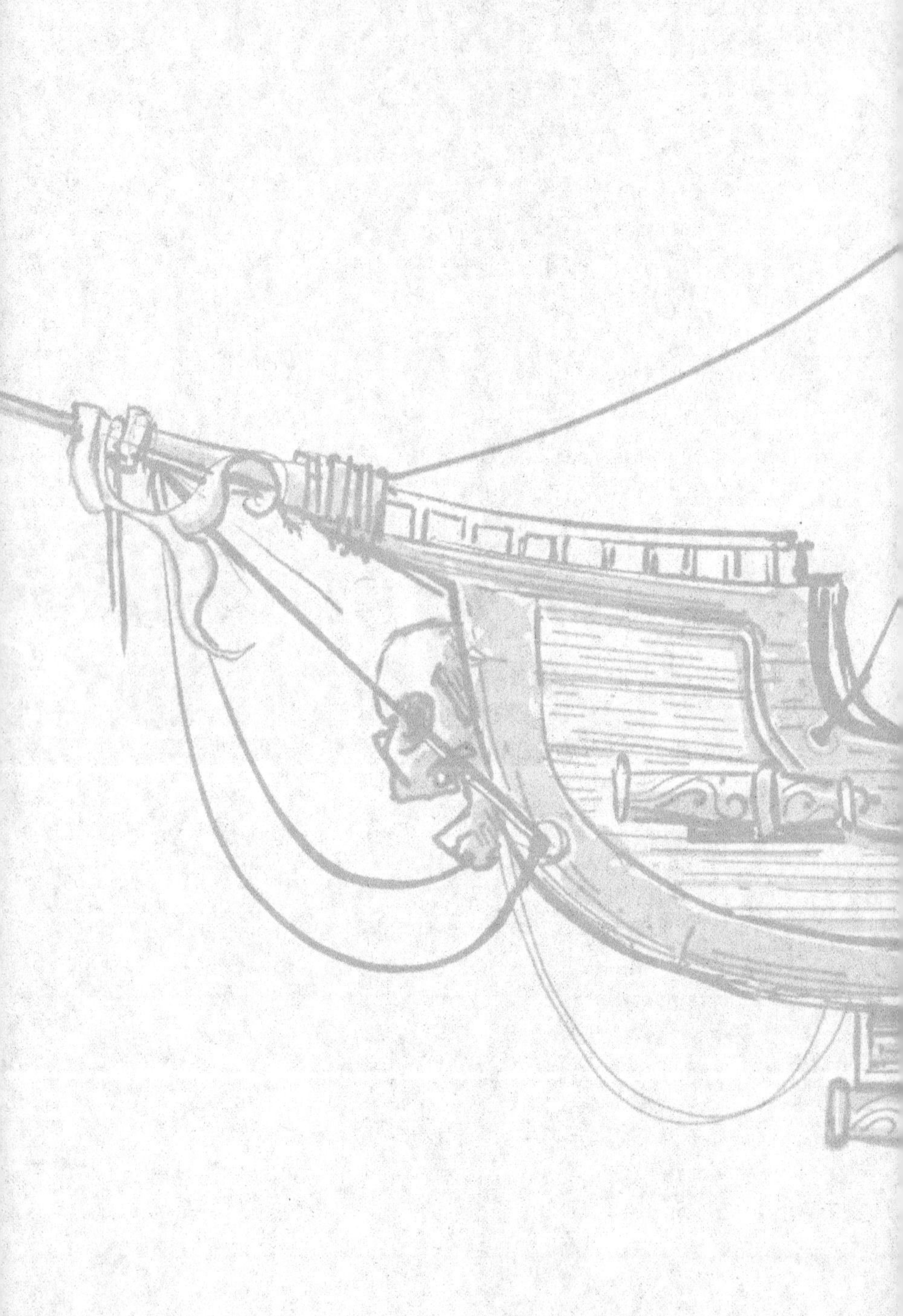

CHAPTER 21

n the silence of the wheelhouse, Jerry rolled her shoulders and cracked her neck. She was tired of waiting around. She wanted to find *Wench's Dream*, and she wanted to bring *Yarrow* home. Up ahead was a small cluster of islands—if they could even be called that. They weren't much bigger than a rock and certainly not big enough to hide a ship in, but Jerry had yet to find anywhere else on their maps where Blaise could have hidden.

Azar returned, a food packet to his lips as he ate his dinner and watched Jerry maneuver the vessel closer to the cluster. She was going to find *Yarrow* before they had to return to Raegina to restock on supplies because she wouldn't be able to do that without getting held up by the authorities.

"What are you looking at?"

Jerry scrunched her nose. "Something about this quarter here is off."

Azar narrowed his gaze and leaned in to look at the readout Jerry had pointed to. "I noticed that the other day."

"I've never flown this way before. Usually, I stick just outside the borders unless I'm on a run."

Azar gave her a knowing look, as though he was well aware

what she did with her ships, which was true. They'd flown together long enough at that point.

"Right, anyway, I thought I'd check it out. I can't see anywhere else they would hide." Jerry moved their vessel in closer but still kept some distance. She grabbed her telescope and put it up to her eye, looking through the small glass.

They had to be out there. Her gut told her as much, and it had rarely proven her wrong when it decided to show face. She had to get *Yarrow* and go home. She needed to see Arloa, talk with her, figure out what was between them without the distance and tension of the last several months.

"There," Jerry whispered.

"There what?" Azar asked, shoving another food packet between his lips.

"*Yarrow*." The name came out like a prayer, and Jerry's heart thrummed a happy rhythm.

"Are you lying?"

"Nope." Jerry removed the telescope and handed it over, letting Azar take his turn at it.

He held it up, moving it slightly from side to side until he stopped. Jerry's lips curled upward as soon as the grin cracked on his lips. "She's whole."

"They fixed her up, which means, they've been using her." That thought settled in the pit of her stomach in a way she hadn't anticipated. This was it. They were going to bring her home and save her from the pirates who had tried to kill Jerry and her crew. Tears stung Jerry's eyes unexpectedly, the relief at finally having found *Yarrow* after all that time. "Let's get her."

"What's the plan?"

"Get Vivian up here. I'm sure they haven't spotted us yet, but they will soon."

"On it, Cap."

Jerry took over the wheel while Azar disappeared belowdecks. He returned shortly with Vivian, Yafe, and Sacha. All of them looked as though they were about to burst with excitement. Jerry needed that energy. It had been so long since she'd felt it course through her veins, or felt the possibility that they were going to finally have a win.

"Is it really her?" Yafe asked, her voice thick with emotion.

"Aye, it is," Jerry answered. "And she's looking fucking good."

It pleased her to find *Yarrow* still flying and in service. It meant she had something to fight for because until then, she'd doubted from the start that it was even possible to recover her ship. Blowing out a breath, Jerry prepared herself to dole out orders.

"Vivian, get started on the bug."

"On it."

"Sacha, I want you to plan the party that's going to take *Yarrow*. Yafe, you and Azar are going to make the plans for *Wench's Dream*. I want you to make two plans each, one for if this bug of Vivian's lives and one for if it's dead."

They nodded at her simultaneously.

"I'm going to wander around, make as though we're lost and unsure of where to go. It'll help that it's nightfall. I want to try to lure *Yarrow* out. Since she's the weaker and more innocent of the two, I'm betting Blaise will send her before he sends out *Wench's Dream*."

"That's quite a risk to take," Azar answered.

Jerry cocked her head at him. "It's one I'm trusting."

He sighed but didn't argue any further.

"Vivian?"

Vivian had pulled out several different devices that Jerry had never seen before. She plugged the largest of them into the dash, the readout on the small screen at the top of it something Jerry didn't understand. Vivian didn't answer her, which irked Jerry slightly, but she realized Vivian was concentrating.

Yafe stood at the front window with the telescope in her hand again. "She looks gorgeous."

Jerry understood the sentiment. She had felt the same rush of love flood her as soon as her eyes had set on the shellacked wood, the single boom engine, the deck that had been her stomping ground for the year she had owned her.

A good feeling settled into the pit of Jerry's stomach, something she had rarely experienced in her life. The last two times it had been this intense had been when she'd bought *Yarrow* and when she'd met Arloa, as much as that may have pained her to admit.

"Let's do this." Jerry gave Yafe and Sacha sharp looks. As soon as they were out of the wheelhouse, she kneeled down next to Vivian. "How goes it?"

"*Wench's Dream* is going to be a problem, which we suspected." Vivian didn't even look up at her as she continued to tinker with the brass device. "We have to get closer to *Yarrow* to connect, but I think this is going to be it."

"Good. I'll get us closer and tell you when."

Straightening up, Jerry grabbed the wheel and steered right into the fray she had been searching for. Blaise would see her soon. He would find her and come to steal whatever wares she had, but little would he know what Jerry had planned for him.

Jerry took down the speed to slow, wanting to not seem in any rush, although that was an internal battle that she struggled to win. She wanted to fly as fast as possible to rescue her ship, her home, from the hands of pirates who had no doubt mistreated her in the time they'd held her captive. Bouncing in her boots to flush the excess energy from her body, Jerry clenched her jaw and her fingers, anything that would keep her focused and as steady as possible.

"Are you ready, Vivian?"

"Almost, Cap."

Yafe swung into the wheelhouse, out of breath. Her dark eyes were wide as she pointed at Jerry. "My team is ready."

"Sacha's?"

"Almost, a few stragglers."

"Perfect," Jerry muttered.

The last thing they needed at a moment like this were crew issues. Jerry pulled up the telescope, staring out at the exact place she'd seen *Yarrow* before, only this time, she wasn't there. Her heart ramped up as she moved the glass around to find her, to pinpoint where she'd gone and where she was coming from.

"There you are," Jerry whispered.

Yarrow looked even better out in the open. Her hull had been patched spectacularly. From what Jerry could see, it was a job well done, and she would expect nothing less from a pirate intending to use her ship. She hoped the inside looked just as good, but she imagined Blaise's standards were far lower than hers.

Sacha popped in. "We're ready, Cap."

"Good. Get your brother."

"I'm here."

Jerry smiled brilliantly. Everything was coming together. She kept the speed of the ship slow, acting as though she didn't see *Yarrow* speed around to her backside to hide in the wake of their vessel. Sacha's crew moved through the wheelhouse, crouching down as they stepped outside into the dark night and hiding below the rail so they wouldn't be seen.

They each had weapons on them, and they knew what the goal was. Take *Yarrow* by whatever means necessary. Jerry kept her eye out for *Wench's Dream* but didn't find her at all. She wanted to know where they were so they wouldn't be surprised when they showed up, but without any sign of the other ship, they were going to have to be on their guard.

"Vivian, are they close enough?"

"Yeah, give me a minute."

Once again, Vivian went silent as she focused. Jerry let her work.

"Cap, input your codes."

Confused for a second, Jerry bent down to find a second device in Vivian's hand. On it was a keypad. It wasn't the full handprint device she normally used, but the backup codes they'd coded in would work just as well. Jerry held her breath as she inputted them, hoping Blaise hadn't taken them all out yet.

"It worked." Vivian's excited whisper sent a jolt of energy through Jerry.

"It did?"

"Yes!" Vivian sat upright, staring down on the first device. "What do you want me to make her do?"

Grinning, Jerry shook her head. "You're fucking brilliant."

Jerry pointed at Azar and silently told him to take the wheel. She gripped her short sword on her side, pulling it out.

"Wait until they're just off our backside and kill their engines. Don't let them take them back until I'm on board and have control."

"Your orders, my command, Cap."

Jerry crouched down and moved out of the door and onto the deck. The air was cold against her skin, but the excitement burrowed through her. This was it. She was going to get her ship back, and she was going to prove to everyone that this had been worth it.

It took her some time to get to the stern of the ship, where *Yarrow* was. This was likely her one and only chance, and she was going to take it. Raising slightly to see her close up, Jerry shed one single tear. *Her baby.*

Suddenly the engines and lights went off on *Yarrow*. Jerry knew Vivian had cut the engines and the power. This was going to be one of the most dangerous boardings she had ever done, but they would succeed. Grabbing the rope on the side of the ship, Azar raised them up above *Yarrow*. Jerry stood up suddenly, not waiting another breath as she swung over the side of the vessel and landed firmly on *Yarrow's* deck.

Yarrow settled under her.

Jerry moved silently as she heard the thumps from her crew following. They all ran, thud after thud as they moved. Shouts from the wheelhouse reached her ears, and before she knew it, the door flung open. Jerry wasted no time. She flung her arm forward, bending her wrist only to flick it sharply right into the neck of the oncoming pirate.

His body collapsed onto the deck in the doorway, his head severed. She didn't spare him a second glance as she moved inside *Yarrow* and took out the two oncoming crew members and then held her knife right to the neck of the captain.

"Surrender and I'll spare you."

He swallowed hard. Another crew member came up the ladder into the wheelhouse, but someone from Jerry's crew stopped him in his tracks. She knew they had her back. The captain's lip curled upward, and he jerked his head back as if to ram his skull into Jerry's. She ducked, swiping her sword along his side and against his ribs in the process until she stood behind him. She grabbed his hair roughly and jerked his head back only to slice his throat and end any debate they might have had.

This was *her* ship, and she would do anything and everything in her power to save *Yarrow*.

The folly to *Yarrow* was there was only one way onto the main deck, and it was straight through the wheelhouse. She was a small ship, and Jerry had always intended to add a second escape route but had never managed to get around to it. It worked to her advantage this time. She hit the dash as the crew came out onto the deck. Her crew lined them up one by one, tying the hands and feet of those who surrendered and killing those who resisted.

Sacha stepped up next to Jerry, exuberance in her gaze. "That was way easier than I thought it would be."

"Finding *Yarrow* was always going to be the hard part. *Wench's Dream* will be a different story. She's much larger, faster, and has far more crew than this small ship can handle."

"Seems they had her packed."

Jerry agreed, which set the hairs on the back of her neck straight. They easily had twelve men on board, which meant some would be staying in the storerooms. It would be a shitty place to sleep and live, honestly. No temperature control, no air flow. It would be hell on a ship. She didn't envy them in the least.

"Mactar, what's your status?"

Blaise's voice sounded through the small communications device. Jerry bit her lip as she hovered her hand over it. Would it do well to warn him of their presence or would it do her better to hide that fact a little longer?

"We're five minutes out," Blaise answered.

Jerry sent a written response back, telling Blaise that audio communications, engines, and main power was all down. They were currently searching for the cause. As soon as she sent that, she contacted Azar on the other vessel.

"Be prepared for *Wench's Dream* to show face. She's a few minutes out."

"You were successful then?"

"Easy."

Jerry pressed her hand onto the sensor on the dash and immediately every single command on *Yarrow* reverted back to her. It must have been another one of Vivian's little bugs she'd added into the takeover. She'd have to thank her later with a handsome payout of credits as soon as she managed to get her hands on some more of those, though the brains from the crew they were about to kill would add to that nicely.

She kept the power turned off aside from the essentials. She had to work quickly. Sacha went out to the deck to give orders about the crew they'd captured and those they had killed— which aside from moving the bodies out of the doorways and away from the ladders, they were going to keep where they were for now. They could deal with them later.

Jerry set *Yarrow* to run stealthily, not making a peep as though she really had no power. It felt amazing to be back on her ship, to know every which way she worked and ran and to be at her command once again. Gripping her short sword tightly in her right hand, Jerry stalked out to the deck.

Narrowing her gaze, she could make out the lights from

Wench's Dream as she approached. They came swiftly, far more quickly than Jerry had thought they could fly. She'd have to ask the surviving crew about that and how to possibly make some modifications to *Yarrow* if it didn't involve a whole new engine system—which with her luck, it would.

Jerry stood still as she waited with bated breath for the inevitable. *Wench's Dream* would pull up either alongside her or alongside Azar. They would see what was happening, and they would either run or they would fight. Whichever their decision was would change her decision. So far she had what she wanted first and foremost, although the sweet revenge on Blaise she desired to inflict was going to be perfect.

She said nothing to her crew as they waited. They would do what needed to be done, but this thing between her and Blaise was personal. While she would ask her crew to risk for *Yarrow*, she would never ask them to risk for revenge. Loosening her muscles as she readied herself to go into battle, again, Jerry held her ground.

Wench's Dream pulled up port side. The lights of *Yarrow* flashed brightly, blinding *Wench's Dream*. It was the perfect addition to what she needed in that moment, and she would again have to thank Vivian for the improvisation. She hoped she and Azar were making nice because should everything work in her favor, she wanted to ask Vivian to join her crew permanently.

Jerry stood with one foot on the edge of the railing to *Yarrow* and gave him a hard stare. Blaise's eyes widened in surprise before he slammed his fist against the dash in front of him. *Wench's Dream* pulled up sharply. Jerry took a flying leap off *Yarrow*'s deck and landed hard on *Wench's Dream*.

It had been a stupid decision to make. She was alone, she could have fallen into the sea below and no one would have been able to save her, and she had to fight by herself against a group of men who had the advantage.

Blaise stepped out of the wheelhouse, his hands at his sides, palms facing toward her, sword at his hip that moved with each of his footfalls. He eyed her carefully as he walked closer. Jerry kept her head tilted down, wondering if he even recognized her. She hadn't been in his presence very long before he'd marooned her, and certainly a female pirate he had stolen from wasn't a huge blip on his radar.

"What have we here?" Blaise asked, his voice sickeningly sweet. "Is it none other than Captain Jeraldine Adelric? Though I suppose you're not captain of anything anymore, are you?"

The cold way he said the words washed through her. She wondered how he could have known that, but perhaps he assumed *Yarrow* had been her only ship. Jerry lifted her shoulder and dropped it in a shrug.

"Imagine my surprise to see how dumb you truly are."

"Me? Says the one who jumped aboard a vessel controlled by the sea's best pirate by herself, no crew to save her."

Laughing bitterly, Jerry raised her chin up. "Oh, that wasn't stupidity."

"No? What was it then?" Blaise stopped right in front of her.

"It was daringly brilliant."

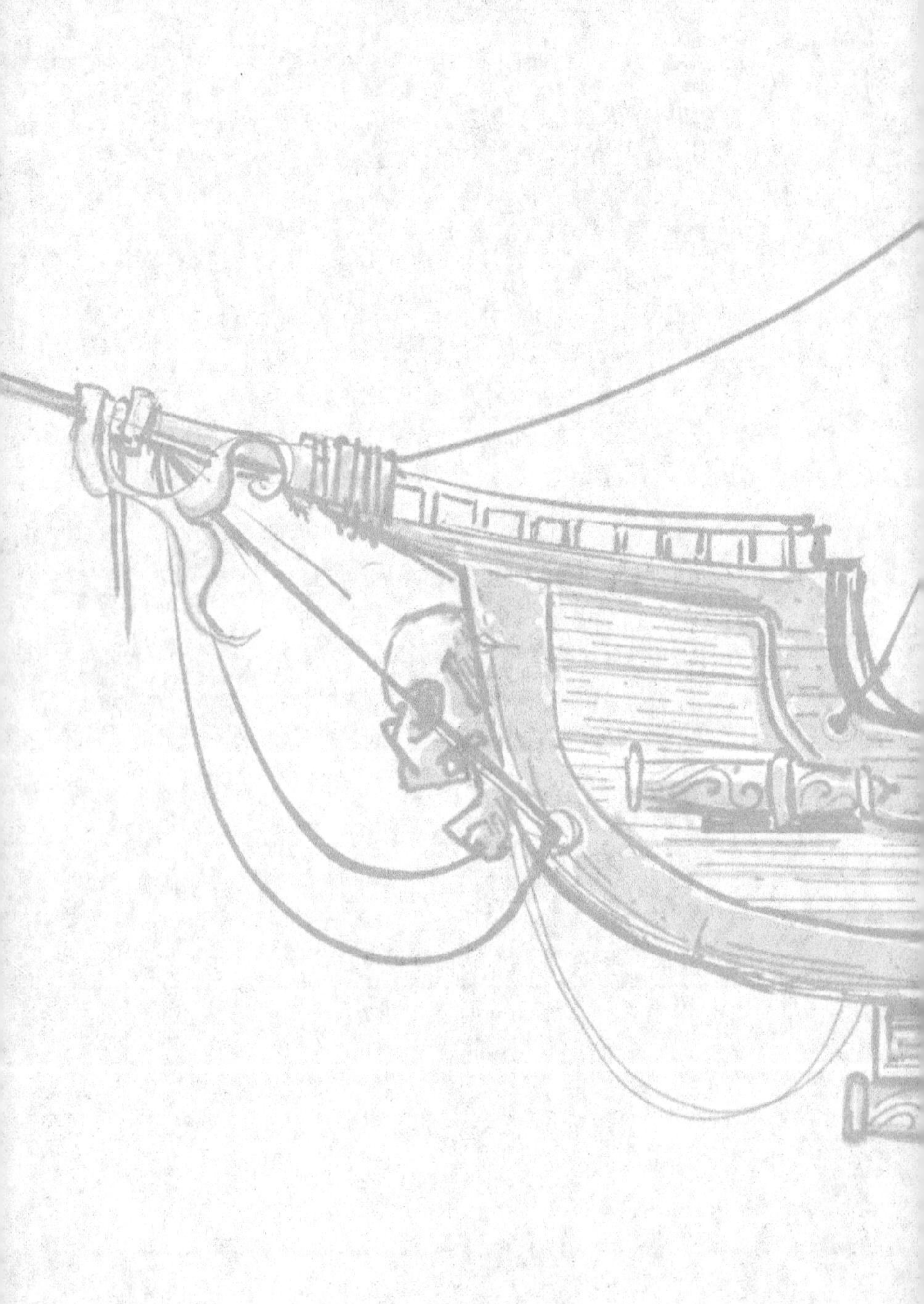

CHAPTER 22

Jerry jabbed her sword forward, slicing straight into Blaise. He dropped to his knees. Jerry wrenched her sword away and jumped over his prone form on the deck with a snort of a laugh. No damn pirate would have expected that one. Engines whirred behind her, and she knew *Yarrow* moved in closer. She strongly suspected Azar was coming close as well. To rescue her own stupid ass.

Charging forward, Jerry jumped straight into the struggle. Men emerged from everywhere, piling out of the ship and onto the deck to fight her and check on their precious captain. Jerry held nothing back as she dove into the fight headfirst.

She hit the deck with one knee, sliding her sword forward to cut at the knees of the first oncoming pirate. He collapsed to the deck, and Jerry stabbed him in the chest, ending his life. Fire was in her veins as she continued to kill, maim, and end anything that came near her.

Azar's loud scream echoed from behind her, and she knew her crew had finally joined her on *Wench's Dream*. She trusted they would have her back as she continued to push forward. She wanted control of the wheelhouse, which she knew they would defend with everything they had. Jerry pulled out a knife from her ankle, stabbing anything that came too close to her.

Azar touched her shoulder to get her attention, and when Jerry looked up at him, he had blood staining his tunic. "Where's Blaise?"

She turned sharply and pointed to where she'd downed him, the lump of a body on the deck still there. "Got him first."

"Good plan. The rest?"

"Take them down. We'll take them to Miriam when we're done."

They jolted sharply as *Wench's Dream* pulled upward, jarring their footing. Jerry dropped down and held onto the ground as she tried to hold tightly, not needing to lose her grip again.

Yafe and Sacha were across the deck, dealing with some burly men. Jerry pushed up on her toes and lunged toward them, wanting to protect her crew now that Blaise had been dealt with. She ran through the crowds of fighting men and reached Sacha first, jabbing her knife into the spleen of the man who was about to come down on her.

Laughing, Jerry ripped her knife out and sliced his head off with her short sword in the same fluid motion. Blood spattered across her face, and the scent sickened and pleasured her all at the same time. Fuck, she should have taken another piece of brain to keep her body going without this damn craving. She rolled her shoulders as she twisted on her toes to take on the man bearing down on Yafe, except Yafe had him handled in an unmoving pool at her feet.

"Nice work," Jerry commented before she ran back into the storm of pirates. Azar and the others were already working their way toward the wheelhouse. Jerry pointed at Sacha and yelled, "Grab that board! Block the door."

Sacha listened, dragging a large solid wooden board to Jerry and bracing it against the door to narrow the entry points onto the deck. *Wench's Dream* was a larger vessel and there were easily another ten crewmen belowdecks still.

"Block as many as you can." Jerry jumped up when a man swiped at her with his sword, missing her.

Jerry trusted Sacha was doing as she was told and charged forward. She was only a few steps away from the wheelhouse door when an arm wrapped around her neck and dragged her backward. The body behind her was thick and firm, someone who was strong and ready for work on a ship. Jerry slowed her breathing and focused her mind.

Lifting her fist, she jerked her arm backward and right into the man's ribs. He grunted, but it didn't make a lick of a difference. She then stomped on his boot, hoping to disrupt his concentration, but that didn't seem to work either. Her last-ditch effort, Jerry swung her left hand around and pushed past her side, the knife still clasped in her fist driving straight into the man's ribs, snapping them.

He dropped her in an instant. Gasping for breath, Jerry moved up on her toes and turned around. She screamed as she charged into him, using her short sword to slice his body up. He fought back, but with each cut to his skin, he fought a little less until he was a bloody mess on the deck. Sneering, Jerry pulled her knife from his ribs and reoriented herself back toward the wheelhouse door.

While the rest of her crew fought their battle, she raged forward. The door was open—shockingly—and she dove for it, hitting it with her shoulder to wrench it all the way open. Inside were two men at the wheels. The first one had dark skin, eyes the same color, and hair curled in a halo around his head. He came toward her, and Jerry held her hands up, ready for whatever fight he might put up.

"Surrender now and I'll let you live."

His white teeth shone in the dim light, and he belted out a harsh laugh. "You weren't much of a fight the first time we met you."

"A mistake I won't make twice." Jerry loosened her grasp on the sword, preparing for whatever step he might make. The other man, who Jerry assumed was Blaise's first, held firmly to the wheel. "Surrender or die, and to boot, I'll eat your brains first."

That caused him to stumble in confusion. Jerry took the opportunity and lunged forward. He was quick in his draw and held up a sword, the metal clanging against hers in the quiet room. Raging, Jerry cried out as she slipped in a circle to free her weapon and take another stab at him. The man put a stop to her again.

Jerry managed to get her knife into his arm, but he easily ignored it as he continued to parry her. Frustration reached into Jerry's chest, snagging hold of her as she continued to fight with him. The other man stayed completely still as he steered the vessel wherever they were going. Her heart raced, and she took another try at getting him, this time managing to slice along his leg with her short sword.

The click of a gun sent a shudder of fear through her spine. Jerry froze, the man looking over her shoulder. If there was a gun at her body, there would be little escaping it. The cold barrel pressed into the back of her skull hard, jerking her forward from the force of the movement.

She held her hands out to her sides to show her momentary surrender. Her mind whirred triple time as she worked through how to get herself out of this one, and when the man standing in front of her sheathed his sword against his side, she knew she had it. She just had to know who was behind her.

"Ugly thing like you won't be worth anything to the underground."

"Captain Blaise Lotchski," Jerry said, a sing-song quality to her tone.

Jerry snorted loudly. He had no idea who she was, did he? Blaise assumed she was a wannabe pirate, someone who didn't know what she was doing one too many times. She had more connections in the underground than he did, and no way would Miriam sell her to anyone.

Their crews battled on outside of the wheelhouse, and Jerry

couldn't catch anyone's attention, not that she wanted to. She didn't want them to die like she was about to. She wanted them to survive and fight for *Yarrow*.

He moved in, his hot breath against her ear. "Thought you'd killed me, didn't you?"

"Not really," Jerry answered, keeping her gaze on the dark eyes of the man in front of her. "But I definitely took you down a notch or two."

Blaise barked a laugh, but he had a definite wheeze in his breathing he didn't have before. Jerry had done that, she was sure, and she would end it all soon enough. She had thought for a brief moment she had at least injured him enough that he wouldn't be able to get up and would bleed a slow damn death. Apparently, she had been wrong. Jerry slowed her breathing, catching herself and becoming hyperaware of everything around her. She was ready for whatever was going to come next.

"Take her," Blaise ordered.

The man in front of her stumbled, and Jerry reached forward as she ducked down, grasping the sword at his side. The gun went off, the thump of the man in front of her hitting the deck loudly as Jerry flipped around and slid the sword straight into Blaise's heart. Jerry held his gaze as his lips parted with his last breath. She raised an eyebrow at him while his body went limp.

"Seems once again I've outsmarted you." Not giving the first mate a chance, Jerry spun on him with the sword in her hand. "Are you surrendering or choosing to meet the same fate as your captain?"

He raised his hands up by his head and released the wheel.

"Good choice." Jerry eyed him. "Call off your men."

"They won't listen." His voice was gruff as he spoke. "They only listen to Captain Lotchski."

"Then they'll be loyal to their death. Get on your knees."

He complied, and Jerry wondered if the rest of the crew would meet Blaise in the otherworld. She suspected they wouldn't if this man wasn't. Jerry found some rope and tied him up, bringing him out onto the deck.

She shouted as loud as she could, "Listen up all you pirates! Lotchski is dead! *Wench's Dream* is mine!"

Her crew cheered loudly, and *Wench's Dream's* crew dropped their swords in surrender. Jerry shoved the first mate into Azar's hands, letting him handle that situation. Within a few minutes, they had the rest of the *Wench's Dream* crew tied up on the deck. Sacha and Yafe took tally of what was in the ship's stores and how many were dead.

Jerry rolled her shoulders and supervised it all, but ideally, she wanted to get back to *Yarrow*. She wanted to get home and be among her family. Elation filled her, but that longing to be settled was still very much present in the forefront of her mind.

Vivian came aboard, having been on *Yarrow*, and flagged Jerry down. Walking toward her, Jerry wiped her hands on her tunic, realizing it was blood after blood and she would have to take some time in the washroom to get it all off. "What is it?"

"We just finished going through *Yarrow*."

"How many dead?"

"Sixteen."

"They had sixteen men there?"

Vivian frowned as she shook her head. "Twelve men. Four whores."

Jerry's stomach flopped hard. "And the whores? Are they dead?"

Vivian nodded. Jerry's stomach fell. She hadn't anticipated Blaise would still be one of those captains, though she probably should have. He was an asshole through and through.

Guilt hit her hard. That could have so easily been her and her mother. It wouldn't be the first time she had been in a situation like that. Pushing past the emotion bubbling in her, Jerry asked the next question.

"What else did they have on board?"

"Cirax."

"How much?"

"Nowhere near what you said it should be, though I would expect some to be used, but they were still missing some." Vivian dashed her tongue across her lips. "I hope you don't mind, but I gave the crew some if they wanted it. I didn't want to eat…the alternative if I could avoid it."

Jerry nodded sharply. "Just keep track. Cirax doesn't work as well, so you'll need more than you think you might."

"Understood, Cap." Vivian wrung her hands together, as though she was nervous. "What uh…do you want to do with the bodies?"

"Cut off the heads and store those. Throw the bodies over. We don't need them." Jerry caught the look of fear in Vivian's gaze and sighed. "If you can't stomach cutting off their heads, then someone else can do it."

"Okay." Vivian walked away, her steps heavier than when she'd arrived.

Jerry stepped into the wheelhouse, the floorboards still covered in blood from the battle that had raged in there. She'd get someone to clean it up if she didn't do it herself before then. Jerry messed around with the dash, working out their systems. Vivian would likely be better at this than she was, Azar definitely would be able to get her moving, but it would be Vivian who could give them easy control.

She'd contact Vivian in a bit and have her come over once she was done with *Yarrow*. Yafe stepped into the wheelhouse and put a hand on Jerry's arm. "We did it."

"We did," Jerry agreed.

"Now we have our home back."

Jerry's eyes crinkled as she smiled. Yafe was right. This had been what they had worked so hard for—getting their home back. *Yarrow* was more than just her home—it was her crew's home too. She had fought not just for herself like she had thought but for all of them. "How's inventory coming over here? Vivian just gave her report."

"Oh, it's going well. There is plenty in the storerooms, including some cirax."

"Vivian found some as well."

"Not surprising," Yafe answered. "That way they could all have access when necessary."

Jerry nodded as she ripped a wire from the dash, one that she hoped would reboot the system and delete the codes in it. "How many dead?"

"Twenty at least. I think Azar is still counting."

"Go find out, will you?"

"Sure thing, Cap." Yafe left her alone.

Jerry was about to get on the ground and crawl under the dash to finish some rewiring when she again noticed the blood. She was already drenched in it, but the prospect of burying herself in more was too much and her stomach clenched at the thought. Jerry cursed as she knelt down, blood soaking through the knees of her pants as she tried to avoid lying down fully in it. Blaise stared at her from across the room, and she wrinkled her nose at him.

She didn't used to be that way, and the fact that she had enjoyed taking his life should have told her she'd gone too far back into her old ways, perhaps even further to the dark side than she'd ever been before. Granted, Penum had become a completely different place from when she was growing up in the underground.

What would Arloa think of her now?

Frowning at no one but herself, Jerry rewired *Wench's Dream*, glad when her method of fixing the problem seemed to work. She had complete command of the ship where she hadn't before. Cracking her knuckles, she toyed with the commands and tested out what she could without going too far. She was already working on dividing her crew up. It would leave her with a skeleton crew on the medical ship and *Yarrow* which would put them at a bit more risk than she would like to gamble with. But she had promised Arloa she would return the damn ship.

Yet she still had one last stop before she reached Raegina. She was going to take back *Calluna*. It was her ship, whether Ursula thought so or not, and she wasn't going to leave *Calluna* in the hands of anyone that would mistreat her.

She would take *Calluna* the same way she had taken *Yarrow*. the backup codes she had insisted on programming into the systems would be to her benefit. Which reminded her, she would get Vivian to check *Wench's Dream* for anything similar that Blaise might have done, not that she was worried since his corpse was cooling only a few feet away from her.

Azar stepped into the wheelhouse and frowned at the bodies. "I'll take care of this."

"Thanks."

She didn't watch as he cut off their heads and dragged the remains to the edge of the deck where two more of her crew flipped them over the sides. Hopefully they would get a good rain soon so they could collect some water and clean the decks and ships properly.

When Azar returned, wiping his hands on his pants, Jerry gave him a firm nod. "I want you to command *Wench's Dream*. Go ahead and pick your crew."

"Who's going to take the medical vessel?"

Jerry pursed her lips as she stared out in front of her, seeing each of her crew in her mind. "I thought Yafe and Sacha might take that pleasure. They seem to get along well enough to manage it."

"I agree."

"Give them four others. You take who you need and give me six. From there we can work on a plan to steal back *Calluna*."

"Aye, Cap." Azar stepped out of the wheelhouse, casting Jerry into silence again.

She programed her codes into *Wench's Dream's* system, cursing under her breath at the damn name of the ship. She would have to change that as soon as they got to harbor and she took legal possession of the vessel, likely with some help from

Miriam. She wasn't going to give up this opportunity that had presented itself. Her fleet was increasing.

"Well, what shall we call you? Hmm?" Jerry patted her hand on the wheel lightly.

When the ship groaned back at her, Jerry's lips twitched upward.

"*Astilbe.*"

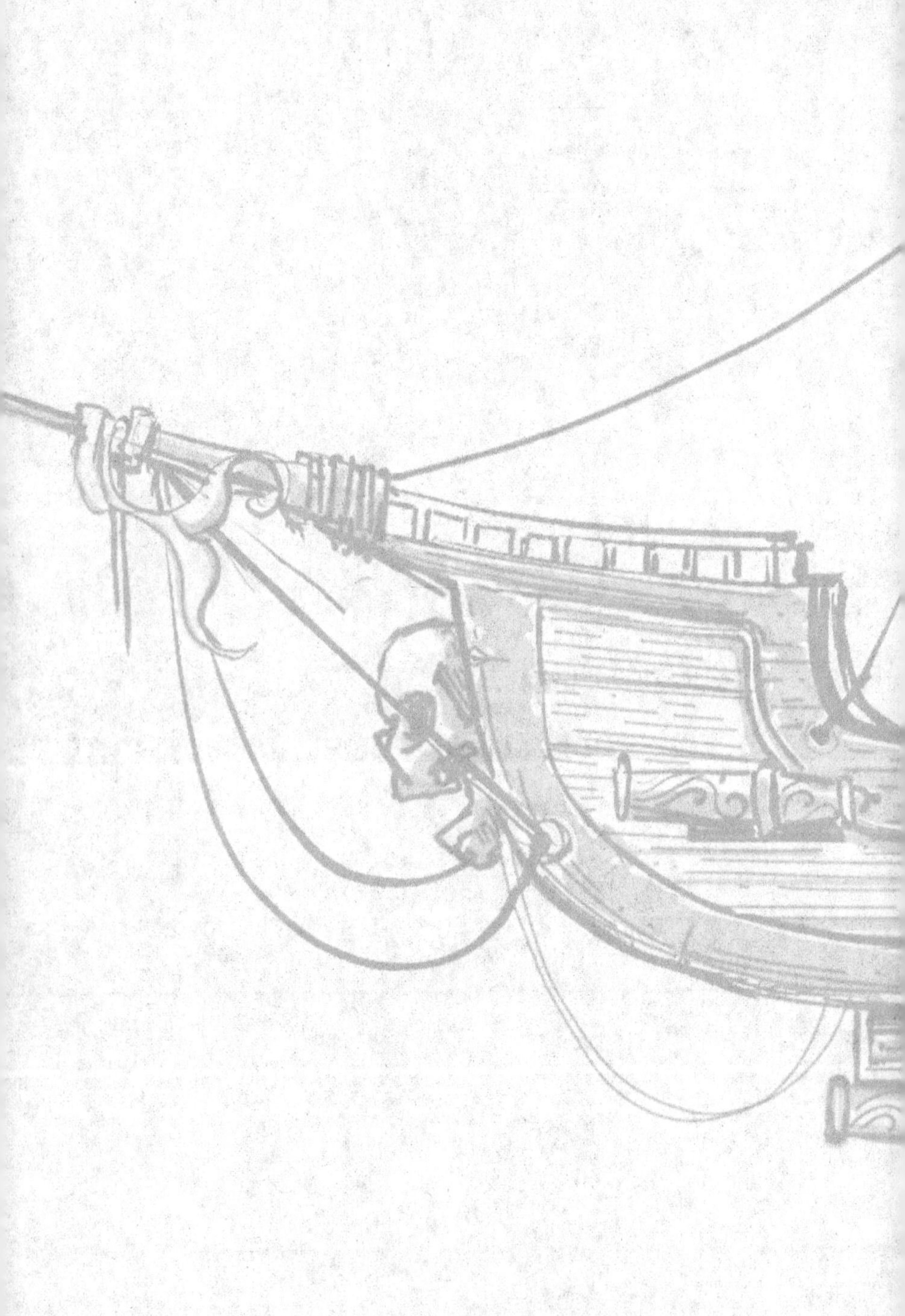

CHAPTER 23

Every step Jerry took was with confidence. She strolled through *Yarrow's* thin corridors, happy to find only slight modifications had been made to her since she'd been stolen. Jerry found her cabin, emptied it of the previous occupants shit, and dumped what she couldn't sell over the side of the ship. She didn't even watch it be eaten before she went belowdecks again.

Kneeling on the floor right next to the cot, Jerry slid her fingers along the wood until she found the single plank with a slight notch in it. Picking at it with her nail, she pulled it up using the tip of her knife. Underneath it was the gun she had purchased illegally, the one she was supposed to never carry according to the cards she had received after being freed from Joab.

Under it was a small cloth. Unwrapping it, she stared at the two locks of hair she'd kept there. Relief flooded her at the sight of them. It was far more than she had expected to ever find again. Running her fingers over them gently, she marveled at the texture. One chunk of hair was from her mother, and the other was from Arloa. She'd never thought she'd see this again. It was the only thing she had left of her mother, and she intended to keep it safe for as long as possible.

Jerry settled them back under the floorboard but kept her gun on her person. The crews were cleaning the ships as they all prepared to leave for the next part of the journey. Jerry slipped into the washroom, disgusted with how nasty it had become, and cleaned it before she took a shower.

As soon as she was ready to go, with her sword and gun on her, she left her cabin and went up to the wheelhouse. Vivian sat on the floor of the newly scrubbed wheelhouse, playing with two small devices in her hands as she focused on something.

"Care to share what you're working on?" Jerry asked as she took over the dash and brought up their coordinates.

Vivian gave her an excited look before jumping to her feet. Her hands moved about her wildly as she spoke. "You said we're going after *Calluna*, right?"

"Yes."

"I have an idea."

"Hit me with it." Jerry brushed her fingers over the brass bar at the edge of the dash, trying to decide what system she wanted to check first. She knew Vivian had already been through it all, but *Yarrow* was hers, and she wasn't about to skip double-checking it all herself.

Vivian chattered, and Jerry only half paid attention as she focused on her true love that was finally in her possession again.

"So I think we can do the same thing with *Calluna*, assuming you never told Ursula about the backups."

Jerry furrowed her brow and looked at Vivian. "Why would I tell her about those?"

"You told me."

"Because it was useful to me to do so. Trust me when I say I plan on changing them all as soon as this is done."

Vivian's eyes crinkled as she smiled. "I would expect nothing less. So is that the plan then?"

Jerry pressed her lips together and stared out the front window of *Yarrow*. Crews worked on both the other ships, and she could clearly see them still throwing shit into the ocean as they cleared out the stuff they didn't need or want. "Yes, but don't tell anyone else."

"Got it, Cap."

"I want to surround her. It shouldn't be too hard since *Calluna* wasn't in the greatest shape when we left her. I doubt Ursula has had time and credits to properly fix her engines and hull."

"Agreed." Vivian leaned against the brass bar, her thin fingers wrapping around the metal as she moved forward and looked out the same way Jerry had just been. "When are we leaving?"

"In an hour." Jerry walked out of the wheelhouse, the decision made, ready to tell the others.

The three ships moved directly toward *Calluna*. Jerry wasn't going to hold anything back. She knew where Ursula would go to hide, where she would try to find work and credits in order to feed the crew she was left with, assuming they didn't leave her the first time she made it to port. Jerry flew directly to the edge of Raegina's borders.

A small island on the edge of the borders was Ursula's preferred hideout. She had mentioned she'd evaded the authorities there several times. Jerry flew as fast as the medical vessel would allow her to go, since it was the one with the most weight and least power. She allowed them to keep pace mostly because she didn't want to lose sight of Yafe and Sacha. She wouldn't force them to be left behind without her protection.

"I see her," Vivian whispered as she stared down at the readouts on the dash.

"Where is she?"

"Not at the island, though, it looks as though that's where she's headed."

Jerry raised an eyebrow and glanced down. Ursula was either headed there or she was going back into harbor. Jerry had considered filing a complaint about *Calluna* being stolen but figured it wouldn't work to her advantage in the long run. Stealing *Calluna* back was a much better way to resolve the issue.

"I don't want to kill the crew this time," Jerry mumbled, not sure if she was talking to herself or to Vivian.

She didn't know if they'd been given a proper choice or not. They deserved the chance to tell Jerry whether they were with Ursula or against her, and whether they wanted to continue on a vessel Jerry now controlled. Rolling her shoulders, Jerry picked up her speed, impatience getting the best of her.

Astilbe pulled ahead with her, leaving the Kauket vessel behind. Yafe would figure out quickly enough what was happening. Jerry didn't want to get that close to the borders, especially if the authorities were already after her. She made a path straight for interception and prayed that Ursula wasn't paying attention—which, she had learned since talking to more of the crew, wouldn't be unlike her.

Before she knew it, she could see *Calluna* in the distance, moving at a slow pace as though she was stuttering over the waters. Jerry shivered at the image, running through all the scenarios as to what could have been the cause of it. She picked up her speed even more, now that she knew she would be easily seen. The sun was high in the sky when she arrived, handing the vessel over to Vivian as she went onto the deck with her chosen crew.

"Be prepared to board!" Jerry commanded as she gripped the rope she planned to swing in on.

Calluna's entire hull shuddered. The clinks and gurgling of the engines sounded awful. Jerry cringed at the noise as she took a board instead. Vivian settled *Yarrow* next to *Calluna*. It was far too simple. She shoved the board across, settling it on the railings so she could simply walk across them. Others followed her lead and soon enough there were four connecting boards and her crew on the deck. *Astilbe* arrived within another minute, doing the same on the opposite side of the ship.

Jerry held her hand up to command both crews to stay put. If anyone was going to run into this ambush, it was going to be her. This was her battle to fight and her revenge to seek. She was going to get even.

"Ursula!" Jerry called.

It would be much easier if Ursula came out willingly, but Jerry had a feeling she was going to have to track her down. Something about the ship felt off. It was too quiet, minus the engines. The booms were loud, far too loud to be a ship that was running within capacity. She'd get Azar on that in an instant.

Jerry took a tentative step forward, keeping her hand down and fist closed to indicate to her crew that they should stay put.

"Ursula!" Jerry shouted, this time an edge of annoyance in her tone.

She should control that better, but since the virus it was far more difficult to do. Even with the cirax in her bloodstream, she struggled to keep a tight rein on her emotions. The wheelhouse door was open. Jerry's heart thumped wildly. She glanced to Azar and pointed to the dash, telling him without words what his task was.

Stepping inside, Jerry looked around. It was abandoned. No one was there, which would explain why the ship was barely moving. Blinking, Jerry went to the door to the ladder, where she dipped below the main deck. She hated going down feet first with no idea what was below her.

"Ursula!" She tried again, her voice reverberating through the wooden corridors. "Come out and deal with this like a true pirate."

As soon as her feet touched the deck boards, the lights flashed on, which meant Azar was in the wheelhouse taking control back. Jerry walked slowly, far more tentative than she had ever anticipated she would be when taking back *Calluna*. She thought this would be a battle to the end for both of them, not a horror show.

Kicking open the first door, Jerry was greeted with nothing. The next door resulted in the same. She went cabin by cabin on that deck, finding no one. The rooms were all unkempt, fabric and items strewn about as if there had been a brawl in each of them, but no sign of blood. Jerry would have smelled that as soon as she stepped inside.

"Ursula?" Jerry asked this time, hoping that would get some kind of response.

The galley was filled with food packets, both empty and full, all over it. Some were half-eaten, but there was still no sign of the crew. She was at a complete loss.

Down one more deck, with two of her crew following closely, Jerry went. She had to find out what was going on. By the time she got to this deck, she stopped calling out. Instead she walked silently through the corridors, finding no one there.

It wasn't until she reached the lower decks, the storerooms, that she saw Ursula. Her red hair was dull in the dim light. Jerry straightened her spine, Ursula's chin dipped down as she stood stock still at the far end of the corridor.

"I'm not surprised to see you here," Ursula said as a taunt. "You never could leave well enough alone, could you?"

"This is my ship. Did you think I would just leave her to you?" Jerry narrowed her gaze, trying to figure out what the game was, but she was at a complete loss. "You stole her from me."

"I took what was mine."

"*Calluna* isn't yours." Jerry stepped forward, judging to see what Ursula's reaction time was. But Ursula made no move, remaining as still as possible. "Where's the crew?"

"Inside," Ursula answered and nodded toward the storeroom behind her. "I couldn't very well let them roam around."

"Are they alive?" Jerry's stomach clenched at the thought of what she might find.

Ursula didn't answer her. Instead, she stepped forward, raising her chin and her gaze. Her eyes looked wild, dashing around Jerry's face and behind her as if Ursula couldn't find one single thing to focus on.

"What's going on?" Jerry asked this time, still inching her way forward in the thin corridor. If they were going to get into a fight there, it wouldn't be to either of their advantage. There wasn't space to move, and Jerry had a pretty good idea that they would both end up injured at the least, dead at the worst.

"Did you know I met Blaise three years ago?" Ursula pointed her finger at Jerry. "He's quite a gentleman."

"What do you mean you met him?" Jerry's mouth went dry.

"Oh, I met him. I was a whore on his ship while you were in Joab. Didn't last too long, though. He liked me too much."

Jerry was so tense. She could barely feel her muscles moving as she walked forward, ready to grip her sword at any moment. "So you fucked him. Then what?"

"He released me."

Snorting, Jerry shook her head. "Blaise doesn't strike me as someone who just releases slaves."

"You're right about that." Ursula's eyes glittered mischievously. "He doesn't."

"What did you give him in exchange for your freedom?" Jerry was only a few paces away from her, and she slowed her advance even more, not wanting to frighten Ursula into acting before she had all the information.

"Who said I was free?"

"So you sold us out to him?"

"I did."

"You bitch." Jerry dove forward, anger driving her into action.

Jerry wrapped her hands around Ursula's neck and pushed her into the wall. Ursula clawed at Jerry's wrists, trying to get her to break the grasp, but Jerry refused to let up. She had nearly killed them all, and now it made sense why she had been surprised when Jerry had shown back up.

"Did you tell him we survived, too?" Jerry leaned in closer, her lips nearly against Ursula's as she pushed in harder, cutting off more of Ursula's air supply.

She knew she wasn't going to get an answer, and when Ursula's body collapsed to the floor, Jerry held on until she knew Ursula was dead—well, as dead as she could be. Jerking her head in the direction of the storage area, she silently told her crew to break down the door. They kicked against the locked door until it snapped and then pushed open the door, instantly covering their mouths and stepping away.

Jerry didn't have to wait any longer to know what the scent was. She held her hand up to stop anyone else from entering. "Grab me a light."

Before she got a light, Jerry put herself into the doorway, a hand on either side, as she scanned the inside. There were bodies upon bodies strewn one on top of the other. The scent of old blood was overwhelming, and Jerry knew any of their crew who were more newly infected were going to struggle with being in the vicinity.

A light was passed to her, and Jerry flicked it to the highest setting before raising the square lantern above her head. Her stomach roiled at the thought of what had happened in there. Blood was everywhere. She walked through the storeroom, checking as many of the crew as she could. Not all of them were dead—that was the worst part. Though once infected, they were hard to kill permanently.

Jerry made it back to the door and sent Azar inside to deal with the living. He touched her shoulder lightly. "She's coming back around."

"Of course, she is." Jerry clenched her jaw tightly.

Ursula's fingers twitched first, then her hands and wrists moved as she wriggled around on the deck. As soon as her eyes popped open, Jerry grabbed Ursula and dragged her to her feet. She shoved her forward and to the main door to *Calluna*. She hit her hand against the sensor so the inner door opened, then the outer one.

Her crew followed her, choosing to witness her folly. Or perhaps it was because they knew what lay behind that door and this one was still a mystery. Jerry shoved Ursula out to the edge of the door as it hung over the waters. She reached to the holster on her hip and pulled out the gun she had saved from *Yarrow*.

"What did he promise you?"

"Life," Ursula answered. "A solution to this damnable virus."

"There is no solution. There is no cure!" Jerry shouted at her. "You fell for lies."

"He said there was a new drug."

"Yeah, one that works half as well. It's no savior. It's a stop gap." Jerry stepped closer. "And what about the crew? What did they do to you?"

Ursula shook her head, pushing her lips together hard. Jerry knew again that she wasn't going to get an answer. Shaking her head slowly, Jerry stepped even closer, cocking the pistol as she raised it up and put it directly in the center of Ursula's forehead.

"You know what? No answer is going to be satisfactory. We're done here."

Pulling the trigger, Jerry fired. The bullet shot straight through Ursula's head, forcing her body backward. She fell, the plop into the poisoned waters below exactly what Jerry had expected. Standing on the edge of the door, Jerry watched as Ursula's body slipped below the sea as the poison ate away at her skin, giving her the ultimate death that Jerry hadn't managed to. At least this way she wouldn't feel the pain, though Jerry hated how merciful she was being.

Jerry stayed there until Ursula was gone. As she stepped back into *Calluna*, she closed and locked the doors. The crew that had watched her stood astounded, with wide eyes and parted lips. They wouldn't know what to say or how to react. Not that she expected them to. By all accounts, she had gone off her rocker, pushing her limits beyond what she'd ever imagined possible.

"Go help Azar figure out how many are left alive. I want to save as many of them as possible."

"Yes, Cap," several crew members answered. Others still kept their silence, but they did as they were told.

Jerry climbed her way back to the wheelhouse, ready to put the last half year behind her. It was time to move on and start again. She had her ships, she had her crew, and now all she needed was Arloa.

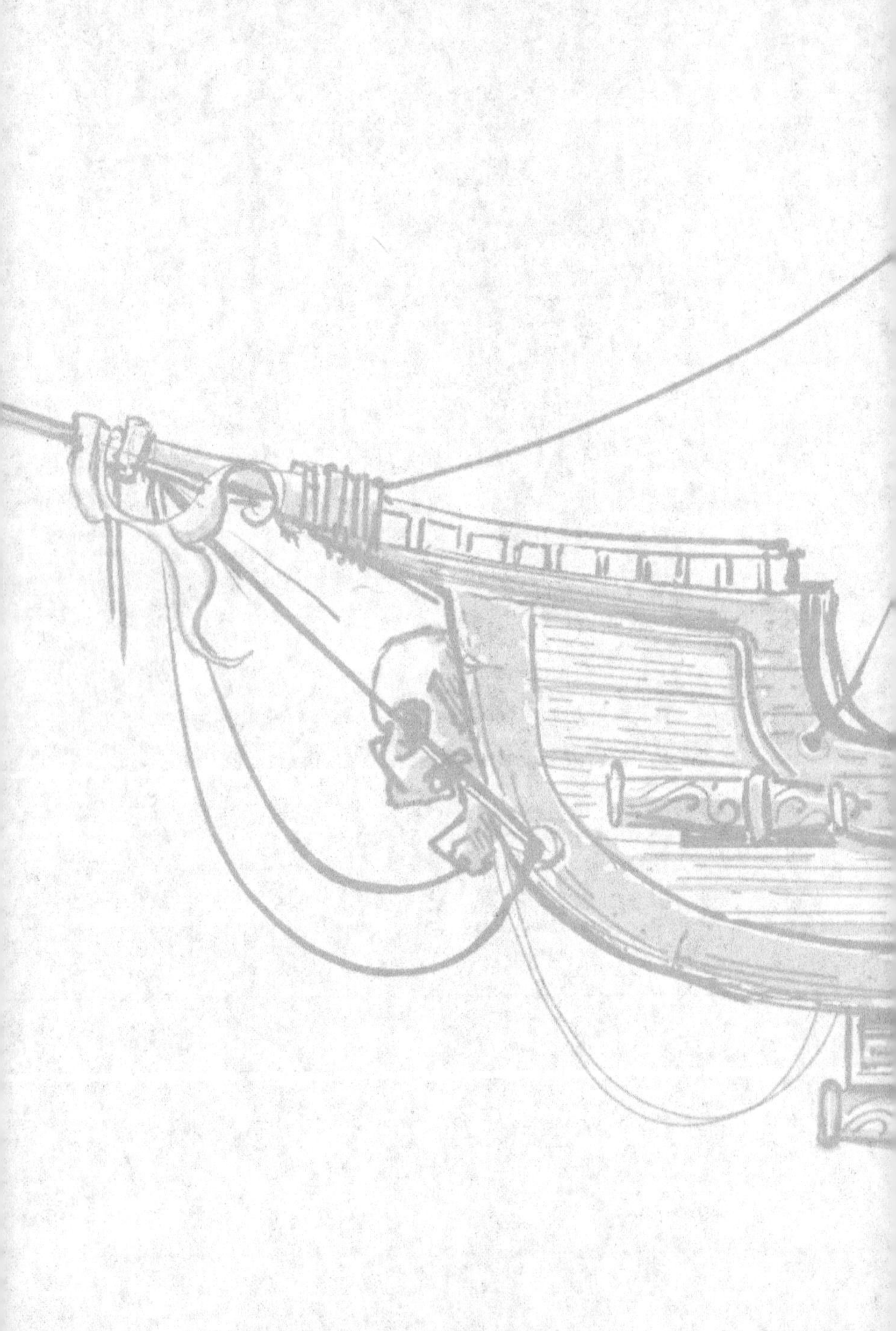

CHAPTER 24

"Why won't the engine kick on?" Jerry muttered as she leaned over the dash and glared at both Vivian and Azar who had their heads under it. She wanted to kick and scream at the stupidity of it all.

Once again, they were cleaning up a vessel. Jerry would be glad to never see another mop if she could manage it, at least not one that was filled with blood from the aftermath of a battle. Though for *Calluna* it looked far more like a slaughter than a battle.

The ship's systems were in bad shape, and Azar, Vivian, and she had spent the better part of the last day figuring out how to get her back to port. They'd had to stay put because *Calluna* wouldn't move more than a few kilometers an hour, although those extra brains they had were coming in handy when it came to what was left of *Calluna's* crew, all of whom said they would be loyal to Jerry and not Ursula.

"Be patient, Cap. There's a lot of damage here," Azar's confident voice echoed at her, slightly muffled from being under the dash but confident nonetheless.

Frowning, Jerry resisted the urge to push buttons on the dash to try and get her working the way she should.

"We knew she was going to need a new engine when you purchased her, and she's beyond overdue for it."

"Yeah, well…I don't have the credits for it at the moment."

Azar smartly said nothing, but Vivian popped her head out. "I mean I'm sure I can devise a way—"

Jerry shook her head sharply. "No, thank you. I won't be stealing funds from someone else or forging false credits to get by. That will put us on the radar of the authorities."

"Your choice, but let me know if you want me to look into it."

Jerry eyed Vivian's boots as she slid back under the dash. *Who is she?* She'd gone from an innocent woman who had caught the virus that they had cared for to a mastermind Jerry was more intrigued by every passing day. Ursula had wasted her talents and knowledge on *Calluna*, and not for the first time Jerry regretted not pulling Vivian over to *Yarrow*.

"Just tell me when we can fly."

"I'm not sure flying will be an option," Azar commented back. "More like limping."

"Great." Jerry hit the toe of her boot against the floorboards. "I'm taking a walk."

Spinning out of the wheelhouse and onto the deck, Jerry shielded her gaze from the sun. Yafe stood on the main deck, supervising a training she had going on. She was teaching a small contingent of the crew some hand-to-hand, and Jerry noted quite a few of them were from *Calluna*, likely also a way to teach them how to control their cravings.

Jerry silently observed everything for a few minutes before catching Yafe's attention. "Do we know how we're dividing them up?"

"Yes, Cap. The harder part is going to be how we'll sneak the medical vessel back into the harbor."

"Leave it to Vivian. She knows how we got her out and the codes we used. I imagine doing it in the middle of the night might be best. I'll send a message to Arloa as soon as she's back."

"You're going to clean her up?"

Yafe's raised eyebrow was exactly what Jerry had wanted to avoid every time Arloa's name came up. They shared a knowing glance before Jerry put her hands on her hips and broke eye contact. It was odd enough that she was returning a ship she had stolen, but yes, Yafe had been right to call her out on the fact she was going to leave the ship in the same condition she had found it—as best as she could anyway.

"Start dividing them up. I'm going to take *Calluna* and limp her home."

"Do you think it'll be noticed that Ursula is gone?"

"No." Jerry held completely still, the memory of firing the weapon, the weight of it in her hand, the heat as the bullet slid from the barrel, the noise it made as it left the gun all too near in her mind's eye. "No, I don't think she will be missed."

"That'll be to our advantage."

"Then again, it's common for souls to leave port and never return. I don't suspect anyone will be worried about her."

Yafe canted her head to the side. "But will you survive it? I know you two were friends."

"At one point we were. But this last year? I don't know anymore. She sold us out, Yafe. That's a betrayal I won't ever come back from."

Yafe's lips thinned as she nodded her agreement. "I hope you can come back from it. I'd hate to see you continue to spiral."

Damn the woman for knowing her so well. Sighing, Jerry brushed her palms over her pants and turned toward the wheel-house but stopped short. A bright light off in the distance caught her attention. A shiver ran straight up her spine as she stood stock still and narrowed her gaze, trying to see what it was, but it was gone.

"Captain?" Yafe inquired, as if she could see the hesitation and fear in Jerry's body.

"Get everyone where they need to go, now."

"Aye, Cap."

Yafe rapidly issued the orders. Jerry jumped from *Calluna* to *Yarrow*, running straight for the wheelhouse. She slid to a stop in front of the dash and stared down at the readout in front of her. Five fucking ships. They were sending a damn armada.

"Fuck," Jerry muttered. She hit her fist against the edge of the dash and ran back out. This changed everything.

Jerry ran as fast as she could back to *Calluna*. Yafe was quietly and efficiently moving crew into place, some already leaving *Calluna* and others staying. Jerry skidded to a halt. "Get everyone off this ship. Now. Speed it up!"

Yafe's eyes widened, but she didn't question the orders. Jerry jumped into *Calluna's* wheelhouse and kicked Azar's boots.

"Get out, old man."

He slid from under the dash, a confused look on his face.

"You, too, Vivian. Azar, get your ass to *Astilbe*. Vivian, I want you on the medical vessel with Yafe. Sacha is taking *Yarrow*."

"What's going on?" Azar pushed up to stand, leaving his tools on the ground in front of him.

Jerry immediately bent down and started throwing anything she could grab into the crate in front of her and cleaning up their mess. "You need to get your asses gone."

"Cap?" Vivian questioned.

"The authorities are coming. Five ships. Headed straight for us. I should have known better."

"Shit," Azar muttered.

Jerry couldn't agree more. She picked up the small crate and shoved it into Azar's hands. He grasped it. She held his hands slightly, making eye contact with him, exchanging knowledge without saying the words. She couldn't say the words. She couldn't admit was about to happen.

"You fucking get everyone home. You're in charge now."

"Cap—"

"Azar. I'm serious."

"Yes, Cap."

"What are you doing?" Vivian grabbed hold of Jerry's arm

with her free hand, clutching her devices to her chest with the other. "What are you planning?"

"I won't let you all suffer the same fate as me. Not again."

"Captain?"

"Get to the medical vessel. Get it back to harbor without getting caught. That is your one job. Azar, you make sure everyone makes it back safe, and you start up with Miriam. Got it? Take the credits she gives you and survive."

Jerry's heart raced as the realization of what was going to happen dawned on her. She could do this. She could survive this and not let her crew meet a similar fate, and she wouldn't let them be marooned to their death again. Azar was the last one off. Jerry took the boards they'd settled between the ships, unlatched them, and shoved them across to the other decks.

There was no one to tell her goodbye, no sweet nothings to say to each other. Her crew did what they were supposed to do. Vivian took off first since she was the slowest ship, flying farther out into the seas. Azar went in the opposite direction with *Astilbe*, his crew working hard on the deck as they continued to make that ship theirs. Yafe was the last to leave with *Yarrow*, and Jerry's heart damn near broke at the sight.

Once again, she was without her crews, without her vessels, and without her home. She was alone, stranded, and about to meet her death. Jerry went to the wheelhouse, hitting the engines so they would rumble to life, at least what life they could manage, and she flew straight toward Raegina's borders.

Reaching down, Jerry checked that her weapon was still on her hip, knowing that would seal her fate if she didn't get rid of it, but so would many other things on *Calluna*. At that point, she might as well sink her, but she didn't have the time. Grabbing her telescope, she looked out to see the authorities coming straight for her, two of the ships. The others veered off, no doubt to chase down Jerry's crew.

"Please don't get them," she whispered.

Dragging in a deep breath, Jerry pushed *Calluna* forward

before she raced belowdecks and found the single cannon that had been left intact. She loaded it with one of the five balls they had managed to transfer from *Astilbe* and pressed her hand to the sensor. This would get their attention. This would turn all their focus on her.

Using the scope and sensors, even though they weren't working fully, she aimed at the authority vessel closest to her. She fired. The cannon shot straight from *Calluna* toward the authorities, missing, but at least catching their attention. Jerry loaded a second shell and fired, this time hitting the ship.

Not needing to do more damage than that, she ran through the corridors and climbed the ladders to get topside again. She checked the sensors, which were absolutely useless. She'd forgotten they weren't working yet. Cursing under her breath, Jerry pulled up her telescope and tried to determine the old-fashioned way what was happening.

She was going to surrender, that much she knew, the question remained whether she would dive to her death before they could take her or not. She'd always sworn, since she'd left Joab the last time, that she wouldn't ever go back there. She would never subject herself to that again.

Calluna shuddered as a cannon volleyed back at her. It was overkill for them to do that, but they didn't know she was alone. They didn't know how many shells she had on board, and she'd already proven she had no issues firing on them. Jerry waited, drawing in slow deep breaths. All she had to do was wait.

Within minutes, she was surrounded.

Every muscle in Jerry's body told her to run for it, told her to end her ship by putting it into the sea and out of its misery, and to take herself down with it. Every nerve in her was ready to fight as she worked her tail off to keep it tamed.

Raising her hands up, Jerry stepped out of the wheelhouse. The flaps from her jacket blew in the breeze as she held her hands up by her head. Authorities swarmed their decks, holding weapons on her. This was a far different greeting than she had received when she'd been searching for Blaise. Ursula must have done something with *Calluna* to warrant this, must have used her in some heist Jerry was unaware of.

She blew out a breath and held still, her boots planting firmly on the deck boards. She could only hope that the others were able to escape, that she wasn't doing this for nothing. Dragging in breaths of the freshest air she would breathe for some time, Jerry stayed frozen in place. She still had her hands up as she looked from each authority to the next in front of her.

They were all dressed perfectly in their uniforms, declaring their position and their rank. They held their weapons as they had been trained. Jerry slowed her breathing, forcing herself to take a step forward. Boards screeched as they slid from the authority's vessels to *Calluna*. She didn't move. She didn't try to fight it because what could she do? *Calluna* was going to be lucky if she made it back to port.

She said nothing, listening as words were shouted at her to surrender, to give up, to stay still. She took another step. The world around her became silent as she focused on nothing other than making it to the edge of *Calluna* so she could launch herself over the side. She would end it. She would do a deep dive into the poisoned waters and never have to worry about Joab again. She would fucking go out the same way Ursula had.

"One," Jerry whispered to herself, counting her life down to the seconds she had left.

She thought of the clippings of hair she had stashed under the floorboards in her cabin on *Yarrow*. No one would ever find it. If Blaise hadn't, certainly Yafe wouldn't—although Yafe did know her better. She prayed Yafe was a good captain.

Glancing up, Jerry made eye contact with the one authority directly across from her on the vessel. They were so close. She wasn't going to be able to leap. She would have to dive. She'd never purposely tried to miss the railing of another ship before. There had been a few close calls here and there, but never anything that she felt truly put her in danger of falling into the ocean below.

"Stay still!" a male voice shouted across at her, his tone thick with authority she had never truly thought they had.

"Two," Jerry whispered.

She moved her hands to the back of her head, lacing her fingers together to keep them in place. Maybe if she did that, then she wouldn't fight herself as she launched herself over the railing. Her feet were sure as she walked slowly and surely, waiting for the opportunity to run but also trying to convince herself that this was the right decision. This was the direction she needed.

Jerry pulled her lip between her teeth, biting down hard to remind her of what life she had left. If she went to Joab, surely she would die there. She had nothing to live for because they wouldn't let her out. There was never escape from Joab. People talked about it—yes—but in all the time she had spent there, she had never seen one person successfully escape. They always ended up dead, hung up by their feet in the courtyard from the rest of them to see. *An example*, they would say.

She pressed up on her toes, testing her ability to move quickly and readying her body for the leap she wanted to make. She thought of Arloa—sweet, tenacious, audacious, confident Arloa. That woman was going places. Jerry had known that from the first moment she had seen her, when she'd walked into her favorite bar and seen her perched on the stool right next to Jerry's favorite one. They had each stared at each other like they had just found the world they were looking for, as if they had each discovered the key to life so unexpectedly.

"Stop moving!"

She sucked in a breath. Jerry pushed with her toes, her boots making sure contact with the deck.

"Three."

Jerry launched herself forward, nearly stumbling at the sudden burst of energy. Shouting ensued, but she didn't decipher any of it. She pushed her hands down to her sides and used them to give her more momentum. The shouting increased, pops reverberated in her ear as weapons fired. She winced as pain lanced through her leg, her arm, her chest. Still, Jerry rushed forward.

Stumbling, she reached the railing and grasped it tightly. She gasped as she leaned against the solid wood and slid onto her belly, pushing with her good leg to slide herself over the edge. The sense of weightlessness was far more than she expected. Clenching her eyes shut tight, Jerry dropped from *Calluna*, waiting for the poisoned waters to hit her skin, the searing pain she had always imagined she would experience as it consumed her body as a whole instead of only the small droplets she'd felt before.

Her skull cracked loudly as she hit something hard. Her ears rang. Her arm snapped under her body. Rolling to her side, Jerry clenched her eyes shut tightly as pain seared through her, overwhelming all of her senses. She drew in shuddering breaths, trying to catch herself, center herself. Hands grabbed her arms, her legs, dragging her. Her back scraped against a wooden deck, her shoulders burning as she was moved rapidly.

But she couldn't keep up. Her mind was a blur of pain and questions, and her gut was filled with failure and shame. Relaxing into the hurt, Jerry allowed the blackness that had been threatening to overtake her. In a moment, she was gone. Death was welcomed but absent.

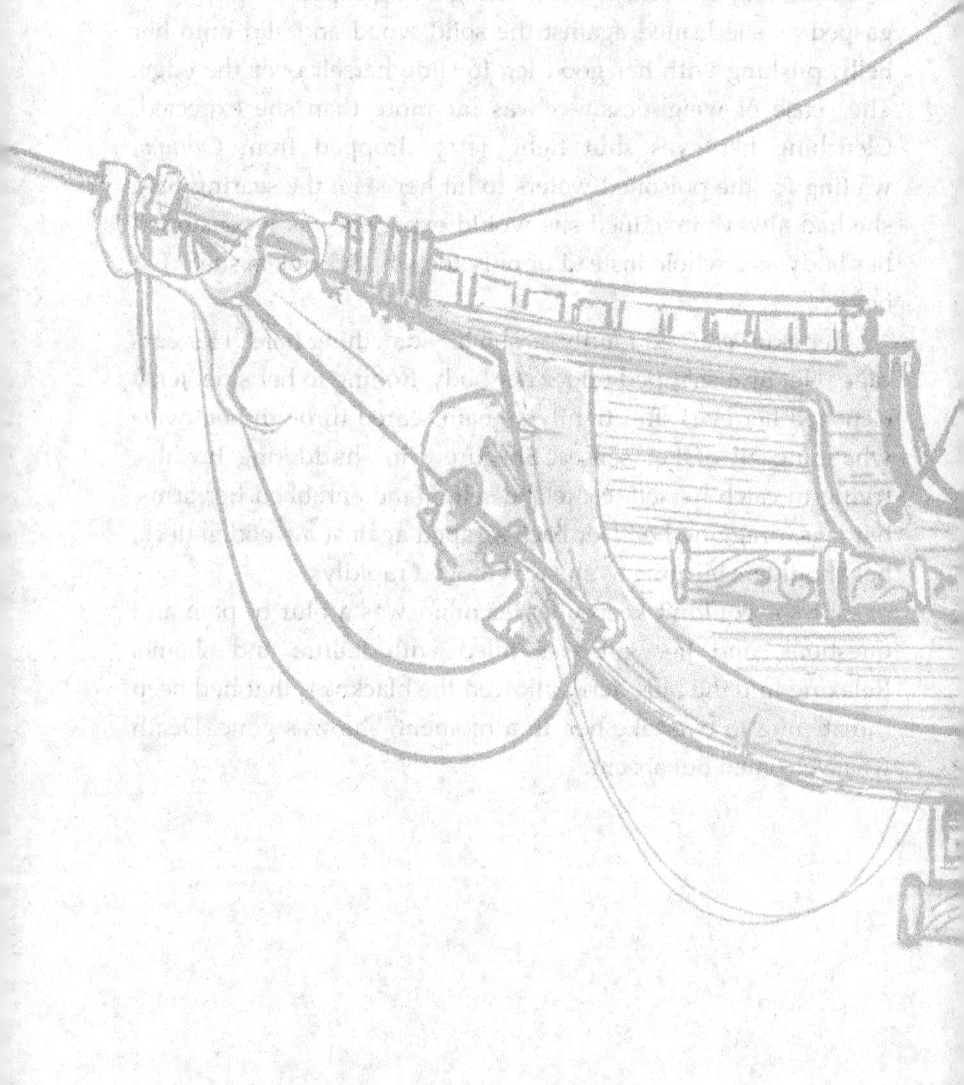

CHAPTER 25

MONTH ONE

Jerry gasped for breath. Her lungs hurt. The air burned them as it swirled in her chest. She coughed it up, not used to the pain. It had been so long since she'd been there. She swore she would never go back. She swore she'd never allow herself to be captured again.

What happened?

Her eyes were swollen shut, so she couldn't even open them to see what was happening or exactly where she was. Sputtering again, Jerry grimaced and groaned. She wanted to keep quiet and still. She didn't want to let on that she was awake. Not yet, at least. She wanted a few more moments of blissful quiet with only the burn in her lungs, the pain in her head, and the hurt surrounding her wrists and ankles.

Fuck.

That should have told her right where she was. Third floor, east wing, end of the corridor. If she moved around enough and could open her eyes, she'd be able to see the sky outside through a glass window in the ceiling. She'd been in this room too many times to count. She'd wished her own death in there, too, many times.

Pushing her tongue across her dry and split lips, Jerry coughed again, unable to hold it back. They would find her soon enough anyway. No doubt they'd put some sort of monitor on her like before, one that would tell them her bio-life exactly so she wouldn't die during whatever torture they decided on for that day. She would only feel like she was dying. And with the virus raging through her system now, they could very easily not kill her.

Jerry stayed perfectly still, slowing her breathing and making it as shallow as possible. It was the only way to survive the gas. She never figured out what was in the air when it was like this, but she knew enough to avoid it if she could.

Her head pounded, and she could only hope that the others had gotten away from the authorities in time, that they were able to outrun them and hide until it was safe to return to harbor. Jerry's heart raced as the thought occurred that harbor might not even be safe for them. She might have to move her entire operation out of Raegina or live permanently on the seas.

If she survived Joab again, which she realized was a stupid thought. She wouldn't survive. She was doomed to die here. Clenching and unclenching her fist against the straw on the cold cement, Jerry used the sensation against her skin, the cold seeping into her muscles and bones, to center herself. Maybe if she took deep breaths of whatever poison they had filtered into the air she would die. It'd be faster that way, wouldn't it?

With no other alternative and it being the only thing she had never tried the last time she was stuck there, Jerry drew in as deep a breath as she possibly could. *Fuck, it hurt*. It burned. There was no escaping it. Jerry wheezed as she dragged in another breath. Her eyes watered, and finally the right one popped open, but she couldn't see. Everything was dark, and it stung.

Gasping for another deep breath, Jerry forced her lungs to comply even though they didn't want to. She didn't want to be there any longer than necessary. She couldn't stay there. She would never survive this time.

Another breath.

Then another one.

It hurt so much. Her head spun, dizziness taking over her mind. She clenched her eyes shut, dug her nails into the pads of her palms, focused herself enough that she could manage one more breath. One more, that was all she needed. One more. Then the next one. If she could do this, surely it would kill her and she would end everything like she had wanted to. On her terms. In her way.

Hacking a cough, Jerry's throat scratched from the gas in the air and the phlegm coming up. She nearly wretched, but she managed to spit it out before she went back to her deep breathing. This time, she knew she was going to make it. Her head felt so light, and her body so weak. The dizziness increased to the point she couldn't tell which way was up and which was down. This was it. She was going to die this time.

MONTH TWO

Jerry's wrists and ankles were shackled to a giant X, her head hanging down with no place to rest it as the wood pressed into her hips and stomach. Deep breaths did nothing to alleviate the amount of pain that seared through her with each slice of the nine-tail whip against her back. She hissed when it landed, heat lighting through her as the small metal tips dragged across her already bloodied and split skin.

She refused to talk. They had asked her questions for weeks —at least she thought it was weeks—and each time she had refused to answer. But her resolve faltered. Not that she would tell them that. They stopped momentarily, and the scent of her own blood sent her into a tailspin. She wanted nothing more than to take a bite out of someone. She couldn't resist. The only thing that held her back how she was chained to the damn wooden X.

Her breathing was rapid, but at least the air was clear in here. She'd never known them to add the gas to this room, at least not in the month she had been there. This was a room she hadn't experienced before this visit to Joab, and it was certainly one she could have lived without.

They hit her again.

The blasted whip sliced into her skin, and Jerry cried out loudly, unable to contain it. Suddenly it stopped. She didn't dare raise her chin up, the thought of moving her spine was too much. The clicks of the shackles as they were unlocked surprised her. Someone threw a rough wool blanket over her back and then wrapped it around her before they dragged her off the X and onto the floor. They stood over her, towering and menacing.

Jerry didn't look up. They wanted to beat the defiance out of her, and she would let them think they had. But the next time she got a chance, she would kill herself. Just like the last time they had left her in the gas room too long, or with a meal packet that had sharp metal on it. She'd tried to slice her wrists, and they'd let her bleed until near death before sewing it up and preventing her from slipping into the underworld.

Just let me die.

She wanted to shout that every moment she got, but she knew without a doubt that if she did, they would most certainly keep her alive. They would drag out her life until she gave them what they wanted, and then they would keep her alive to make sure she didn't know anything else. She was one of the ones who disappeared at dawn, the weak, the ones who had something they wanted.

Roughly she was dragged to her feet, the slices they had

made to the soles stinging as she tried to walk on her heels or her toes. They shoved her shoulder roughly as they led her into the corridor and down the hall. They made her walk down to the first level, the brightest level in Joab. She glanced over her shoulder at the person who had been torturing her for the last hour at least. She didn't know how long it had been. Time was nothing in the walls of Joab.

The man was covered in leather, a deep brown leather that had splatters of her blood on it. He shoved her into a wooden seat and shackled her ankles to the ground. She wouldn't be able to move more than a few inches. She would hurt something awful when she was forced to stand up.

A woman stood at the front of the room, other *students* in the same position Jerry was in. She slapped a stick against the wall, the snap making Jerry's ears ring. Her face was covered in brown leather so when she spoke her voice was muffled, but her curly brown hair was pulled into a bun to keep it out of her face as best as possible.

"The lesson today is language."

Had Jerry been there for the first time, she would have groaned. They had tried to teach her the basics every time, starting her back on the beginning level as though she knew nothing and had learned nothing the last time she was there. It was torture enough to sit there and pretend.

MONTH THREE

Jerry was drowning. With her eyes clenched shut, she fought back as best as she could because she knew it would force them to keep her face in the bucket of ice-cold liquid longer. She had no idea what liquid it was, but she knew it wasn't water. Water was too precious a commodity for them to waste on this.

Swinging her head from side to side, Jerry stretched her fingers as the hand against the back of her head held her under. She would stay there as long as possible. She had tried, multiple times, to stay there longer than they thought necessary and every time when she was a moment from passing out, they would wrench her from the liquid and pull her back from death.

She hated it.

She just wanted to fucking die already.

This time she was determined to kill herself. She was determined to trick them into thinking she was alive until she was dead, but her head swam as it was impossible to keep the breath in her lungs any longer, and her movements slowed. It was hard to think. Hard to keep up with what she'd originally planned to happen.

They jerked her back by her hair, ripping out chunks at a time because she was so malnourished that her body had given up. Jerry gasped, unwillingly, as her body tried to kick itself into gear and keep her alive longer.

"Who do you work for?"

Jerry swallowed, the taste of the liquid hot on her tongue, but she didn't even have a moment to think about what the flavor was as they shoved her back into it. She gasped, the liquid hitting her throat unexpectedly. Jerry tried to focus, again, wanting to kill herself to at least end it for now, knowing she'd eventually awaken back into this hell.

There was no escaping it unless she could properly die. All she could do was postpone the inevitable. She could prevent herself from telling too much, from staying still for too long, from giving in to their demands. Jerry drew in another breath of the liquid, this time on purpose. Drowning seemed better than subjecting herself to this.

Again her head floated, and she gasped in more. It moved down her throat as she swallowed. She just wanted to die. No one could save her in Joab, no one could break her free. There was no hope of escape other than death or pretending to follow their rules enough to survive and be freed, but this was her fifth time back. She would be marked this time, and she would never be allowed into society with the rest of Penum.

This was her destiny.

She knew it had always been a long shot with her and Arloa. Something like this was going to happen, something that would separate them to the point that she'd never be able to return herself to Arloa's presence. Jerry gasped in more liquid, barely able to make her lips move to swallow it down. But she didn't want to swallow, she wanted to breathe it in, she wanted to stop up her lungs to the point she'd never be able to wake up—but that was a fruitless choice.

She was a zombie. The virus had taken over her and had given Joab the ultimate power to torture her without killing her in far too many ways. Relaxing her entire form, Jerry let them do whatever they wanted. She had no hope.

MONTH FOUR

Everywhere hurt. She'd lost all track of days and weeks and months. Even hours and minutes meant nothing anymore. She lay in the corner of her cell, the thin straw the only thing protecting her from the cold cement, but that was barely worth mentioning. She forgot how many times she had fake-died before being dragged back into the reality that was her current situation.

The cell door creaked open, the metal clanging as it was clipped to the wall. She didn't even bother to move. They would do whatever they wanted to her, how many times it took. Boots scuffled along the floor, the scraping loud to her ears. Jerry waited patiently for the tip of one to slam into her belly as she was kicked.

A heavy breathing greeted her. Confused, Jerry pried her eyes open to look up into the face of another leather clad authority. He bent down, gripped her chin hard, and dragged her toward him so their faces nearly touched.

"What's her name?"

Jerry shook her head, tears prickling the corners of her eyes. Even if she wanted to answer him, wanted to give in to what he demanded, she couldn't without more information as to who he was talking about.

"What's her name?"

Jerry bit the inside of her cheek to center herself. She wouldn't give in, not to that. Not to giving up any of her crew to this man. She lifted her shackled hands to his wrist and held on tightly, not harming him in any way, but holding herself steady in a way he wasn't.

"Who will rescue you?"

Jerry raised her gaze to his, locking her eyes on his dark ones. She couldn't even see what color they were in the lack of light in the room. She couldn't figure out what he wanted, but this line of questioning was so different from any of the others they had given her.

"What's her name?"

Jerry tensed. Something inside her compelled her to answer, and she gave the only name she could think of. "Kauket."

He dropped her and walked out of the cell, slamming the door shut. Jerry stayed shackled in place against the cold cement floor. She had no idea what happened, but she was glad for the break. Before she could calm herself, he came back. He knelt onto the ground in front of her and covered her head with a burlap bag. Jerry fought it, but she had no recourse to hope she'd be able to get out.

Crying out and screaming wasn't going to get her anywhere, so she stayed still and quiet, hoping that would feed her more answers than asking questions would. Her shackles were removed, something that hadn't happened since she'd been brought there. Instead of the heavy metal against her skin, she was tied up with scratchy rope.

She wanted desperately to ask what was happening but kept her silence again. Unable to see anything, Jerry was dragged from her cell and down the corridor. She didn't know where they were taking her. Left in the dark, she followed the orders of the hands against her body as she was shoved in different directions.

He pushed her down, making her crouch. Her toes spread in order to keep her balance, smearing in something wet and slimy. Jerry waited for the next silent command, and when the hand against her shoulder pushed her forward, she unexpectedly fell. Her skull slammed into a wall as she rolled and slid down a chute. A loud crash echoed before the top of her head rammed into something, causing her to bite her tongue. Blood filled her mouth.

When she stopped moving, she dragged in a deep breath. Hands on her arms and legs pulled her across the hard stones. Jerry tried to scream, but her voice left her as she was lifted up and flung like a bag of seed. She landed with a thud, pain shooting through her shoulder and hip where she landed. She kept quiet, still not sure what to say or do. Nothing of this had been what she experienced in Joab before.

Engines whirring told her she wasn't on the island any longer. Her heart fluttered with hope—something she had long thought had been extinguished. She was pushed into a room, her hands and feet still tied so tight that she couldn't move even if she wanted to. She was at everyone else's mercy.

Heels clicked against the deck as the ship lifted up. Did she dare to dream she was actually escaping Joab? No one had ever done that before. Or were they taking her to her final death? That would be so unlike them, though. If they were going to kill her, they would do it publicly, to scare the rest of the prisoners.

The door opened and snicked shut, a lock sliding into place. Every hair on Jerry's body was attuned to the sounds and smells around her. She was about to buck her way across the floor when the bag was lifted from her head. She squinted against the bright lights, so unused to seeing in this kind of illumination. She gasped as she looked into steel-blue eyes.

ABOUT THE AUTHOR

Adrian J. Smith has been publishing since 2013 but has been writing nearly her entire life. With a focus on women loving women fiction, AJ jumps genres from action-packed police procedurals to the seedier life of vampires and witches to sweet romances with a May-December twist. She loves writing and reading about women in the midst of the ordinariness of life.

AJ currently lives in Cheyenne, WY, although she moves often and has lived all over the United States. She loves to travel to different countries and places. She currently plays the roles of author, wife, and mother to two rambunctious youngsters, occasional handy-woman. Connect with her on Facebook, Twitter, or her blog.

BROKEN WOMEN FIGHT BACK

A prison break, a determined senator, and questions that need answers.

Escaped from Joab, Jeraldine Adelric is on the run. No longer a captain, she needs time to recover and plan her next move. As Arloa cares for her, she can't help but wonder how the virus that has culled the planet started.

With a new mission in hand, Jerry digs deep into the politics of Raegina while trying to rewrite her stars and make a new name of herself. But she can't stop longing for the seas. With Arloa's support and love, Jerry takes precise steps to secure her future.

Will she stay or will she go?

Releases May 2023